For Anthony

PASS - Fail

Thank you.

Bruce Ballister

Bruce Ballister

Copyright © 2023 By Ballister Books

Direct inquiries to www.ballisterbooks.com

Cover Credit: omega nebula, messier 17, National Aeronautics and Space Administration, European Space Agency, J. Hester (Arizona State University)

ISBN: 978-1733257183 Paperback

ISBN: 978-1733257190 E-Book

LCCN: 2022903891

Printed in the United States of America

1. Science Fiction—Fiction   2. Aliens—Fiction   3. Space—Fiction

4. Ethics—Fiction   5. Telepathy—Fiction

Other books by Bruce Ballister

Dreamland Diaries – Parts 1 and 2

https://tinyurl.com/h5bjxs

Orion's Light – Part 3

https://tinyurl.com/yaehvr4q

Room for Tomorrow

https://tinyurl.com/y9fnebtx

N. O. K.

https://tinyurl.com/eyz9dvhf

Welcome to the Zipper Club, (non-fiction)

https://tinyurl.com/uymp6ga

Reader Reviews:

This is an Advance Readers Copy

As an ARC reader, you can provide reviews. In fact, other than any feedback on critical stuff, that is why you have this not fully edited copy. I am hoping that after reading part 4, you will provide comments that will help me bring other readers into the fold. The Saga has gone full circle from the discovery of a small bit of space junk in the north Florida pinewoods, to a journey to the galactic center. If it was you, where would *you* like to go?

And don't forget to put your reviews on Amazon. The best marketing any author can hope for is word of mouth. Thanks for being an ARC reader!

As an ARC reader, I've provided this book at no cost so I can get some reader experiences, comments, reviews. Some will end up on the back cover, some may end up in the front pages of the book. Please provide any comments or advance review statements to:

bruce@ballister.com

Oh, and if you should find one of those persistent, hard-to-find, errors in spelling, a missing quote, etc. don't be shy about letting me know so I can fix the final copy. Thanks for being an ARC reader.

The Journey So Far

If you've found this book without having read the preceding three parts, the following may make it easier to comprehend. Brad and Connie Hitchens began this journey in 1976, when I began publishing his story over ten years ago. Some of you have been waiting a while to get here. My apologies; a few other books begged to be written first. Their story began in the north Florida woods with the discovery of a small bit of metal embedded in the base of a fallen cypress tree. The ancient tree was assumed to be over three centuries old, too old to have grown above the exotic metals found in the artifact.

Dreamland Diaries

Dreamland Diaries was not intended to have a sequel and included Parts 1 and 2. In Part 1, fifteen-year-old Bradley Hitchens begins the quest to prove the extraterrestrial origins of the small metallic rod, loses his home, and moves in with distant relatives. He loses his father as the long arm of the Air Force over-extends its authority while attempting to secure the mysterious artifact. Brad finds safe harbor in the small fishing community of Apalachicola. This is where Connie becomes a critical part of his new family circle, and where the artifact is lost when the family's shrimping trawler is lost in the Gulf. We also meet a mysterious entity in the woods that 'speaks' to them in psi, a subvocal telepathic medium that frightened Brad's mother into leaving home in fear for her sanity. Part 1 concludes with Brad's reunion with his mother in a small town near Las Vegas.

In Part 2, Brad and Connie take a break from their final semesters in college to dive the wreck of the trawler to retrieve the artifact. In the process, they once again come under the scrutiny of the long arm of the Air Force's Special Investigations unit, the B Team. Agent Martin Jenks gets to the wreck first but has to be saved by Brad and Connie. In return, Brad has been given a temporary reprieve from tight surveillance. Their freedom is temporary as they are both removed to the B-Team's HQ in Area 51. We will never know if the duct tape that permitted their escape was provided by Jenks in return for their saving his life. Part 2 provides the unchallenged scientific opinion that the artifact is "not from here." We also learn that the "voice in the woods" is in fact the AI controlling a crashed alien fighter named Jai. (Jī). After a few trial runs in the solar system, they decide to go interstellar.

Orion's Light

In Part 3, Brad and Connie make their first journey out of the solar system to Jai's homeworld. Their assumption, based on Jai's knowledge, is that the planet has been destroyed. Not totally, it turns out. The new rulers of the planet toss Brad and Connie into a local prison to see if they are contagious. They are befriended by a leader of the underground and after a harrowing escape, they become part of the resistance movement.

In *Orion's Light*, we also learn about the complex culture of the Elioi and the civil war between the space-faring branch that has occupied the system's asteroid belt and the homeworld's sister planet. The Elioi are a divided race: gravity-trained Dzurans from the homeworld and gravity-averse Dzurans of the sister planet.

The Erran revolt against the Dzuran overlords is victorious. Brad and Connie are provided a diplomatic shuttle for a return to Earth, but as Connie has become pregnant, she cannot make the trip. Brad will return to Earth with an ambassador for Erran culture and the Elioi. Connie will return when her Elioi friends deem it safe for an infant to make the several interstellar jumps necessary to reach Earth.

We also learn of a satellite placed in Sol's asteroid belt that has been stolen by an Erran prospector. The mysterious alien ovoid, assumed to be of Precursor manufacture, was shipped back to Dzuran orbit where it "cleansed" itself of the scientific team. Upon coupling with a drive unit, the ovoid departed for a destination nearer the galactic core.

Dedication

To the thousands on this planet who know and appreciate, or yearn for understanding of the finer angels advising the human spirit. However you seek truth, continue the search. For thousands of years, we humans have looked to the heavens for answers to our essential questions. Just imagine if the heavens actually answered.

PASS – Fail

Prologue

The Entity Arrives

The sphere-shaped ship entered the solar system along the line of least magnetic resistance, cruising comfortably along the central star's southern pole's flux lines. At a point three solar diameters from the star's surface, it began to cut across the buffeting bands of the central star's magnetic field. The ship approached on an asymptotic curve that would position it on the plane of the third satellite's orbit at a distance inside the orbit of its moon.

The entity aboard was pleased. The craft had bucked a little as it crossed the strong magnetic field bands. Under its subtle commands, the ship's guidance system maintained the appropriate headings. The sphere even got a little lift from a burst of plasma as it moved outward, matching the orbital plane of the target planet. The entity allowed itself another wave of pleasure as its craft slid on a mathematically perfect line, decelerating to meet the orbital period of the third satellite.

In all but the most recent maneuvers, the craft was essentially invisible. Its reflective surface was nearly undetectable by celestial observers as it moved through star fields, momentarily winking out pinpoints of starlight. Now, as it settled into its parking orbit

1

between the second and third planet, the sphere would only be visible as a tiny sunspot on the glaring brilliance of the central sun. That would change, the entity in command knew, based on the interactions with this system's dominant species and the directives of its mission. Analysis by the planet's intelligent species would later determine that the ship has settled into a stable orbital position labeled 'L1,' a stable position between the planet and it star.

The spheroid was an umbra ship; designed to cast a shadow. The entity controlling the ship had no illusions that the developing civilization on the planet would not discover the umbra ship. Its mission was to ensure that they *did* discover the ship, and its unique abilities as well as the companion monitoring vessel taking a position in the asteroid belt. The design of the entity's craft was to reflect and focus radiant energy in various wavelengths as needed for multiple uses. On this mission, it would have an entirely different function. The monitor would resume the long-term recording duties of its predecessor, stolen several years prior.

In time, all guidance and positioning indicators on the umbra ship signaled optimal solutions. The entity sent the appropriate report to the messenger for relay, then relaxed, assumed a form optimal for rest, flowed into its sleeping chamber, and entered a state similar to hibernation. It would maintain awareness of the critical communications systems and retake a form suitable for whatever a revised situation might demand. Over the next several months, as the locals counted time, its monitoring equipment gathered cultural data from the wash of electromagnetic emissions flowing out from the third planet.

One eye opened its slit, scanned the pilothouse, and closed. The entity could wait; time was fluid after all. It left sensor channels open and began to take in the growing myriad of life sign signals from the third planet.

The replacement monitor ship taking up position of the in the asteroid belt would be harder to spot as only a dark object in the field of other asteroids. The occasional blinking out of a background star would go unnoticed for much longer. That ship's small gravitational field would eventually attract enough smaller bits of asteroidal dust motes to camouflage itself. Its mission was to wait as long as need be. Discovery could wait on the cleverness of the system's emerging species.

1

They're Coming!

April 21, 2023, Wakulla County, Florida

Myahh Hitchens sat up suddenly, cocked her head, and said too softly for anyone in the house to hear. "Mom, they're coming." The import of the three words would change the worldview held by most human beings forever. She had already changed that worldview by simply arriving, by being the first human born on another planet. The secrets delivered into her subconscious would engage a shift in human behavior that set the stage for either its survival or its ultimate downfall.

Connie Hitchens overheard Myahh's message. She and her daughter had strong psi bonds. Connie looked out through the sliding glass door to the deck to see Myahh leaning back on her hands, staring into the clear blue sky of a warm spring afternoon, grinning, talking to herself or someone. She'd been doing that a lot lately.

~ ~ ~

The world had become used to the fact that humanity was not alone. It was no longer a question. Brad Hitchens had returned, seemingly from the dead, after an absence of twenty-eight years. The arrival of his wife and child nine months later had shocked the world. Their absence had permitted the Air Force to confuse reality and render the existence of a revived alien spaceship a lie. The two space travelers had brought back two aliens as ambassadors, putting to bed all efforts of the world governments to deny alien life. Although, conspiracy nets still disputed their reality as they continued to deny the Holocaust, the Apollo moon landings, and the 9-11 attacks.

Early on, few would believe the returning humans were the same young adults that had departed in the fall of 1986. Brad returned with the Elioi Ambassador, Shaand, in January 2014 with no notable signs of aging. His wife, Connie, their child, and the second ambassador arrived early that summer. Both were shocked to learn that almost twenty-eight

4

years had elapsed. It would take another five years for terrestrial science to understand the physics and meta-physics behind the grav-drive and the time shift required to push mass across millions of miles.

One of the first reactions of the U.S. government to the verified existence of an intelligent alien species in the neighborhood was the incorporation of NASA into Homeland Security. The European Union had argued over which country would send an ambassador to Dzura. China announced it would curtail its program to militarize its communications satellites. Russia had leaked the Chinese plan while denying that they had never had those intentions. Later, it was learned that the Russian armed satellites couldn't hit a moving target at anything over ten kilometers. Brad had already shown that he could eliminate the then-secret American military satellite defense shield. His ship, Jai, had been shot at as they cautiously approached the crowded orbital space they encountered when returning to Earth. Jai had reduced the feeble Space Shield weapons platform to a melted lump of exotic metals.

The flurry of hyperbole and outright BS over the new threat of REAL ALIENS published after the return of the planet's first interplanetary explorers and their young infant held a mixture of awe, curiosity, and fear. The media storm following the arrival of an actual ambassador from an alien planet had taken years to tamp down with carefully administered doses of truth and near truth. But xenophobes will be xenophobes.

The latest press release from NASA was the allowance of limited exposure to the Hitchens family. After all, the usually sequestered young beauty was approaching her eighth birthday. She was more important in global news feeds than the newest princess in England's royal family. Most of the articles in the checkout news rags had very little truth in any of them. Outright guessing and misinformation persisted.

Two media outlets had won the right to have first-person access to the Hitchens's household in rural North Florida. Aaron Aldridge, from CNN and Kimber Cunningham who represented a print conglomerate.

The Department of Homeland Security had foolishly hoped they would be able to reduce the presence of surveillance and protection at the deep woods residence by simply letting some slice-of-life information out to the media markets through both news and culture outlets. CNN had the received the first approval for an interview but was under DHS orders to not leak details until Cunningham's magazine conglomerate was ready for the press.

If the orchestrated news reporting effort was successful, perhaps they'd be able to get Brad Hitchens back on one of the late-night spots or one of the Sunday afternoon news feature segments. That supposed his current repair mission to the Webb deep space observatory succeeded.

Aaron Aldridge had written the only recent first-hand story to come out on the mysterious space-faring pair, Bradley and Connie Hitchens. His reporting, at the time, had been largely his investigation of their homestead and a chance fishing expedition with Brad's long-time friend, Sunny Rogers.

Sunny, a retired Wakulla County road supervisor, was now nearing his nineties and still worked as a part-time fishing guide. Sunny let a few crucial facts slip while showing a resourceful Aldridge the intricacies of throwing a cast net for bait, and Aaron had his scoop.

News that the young couple had a working spaceship was sensational. His blogged coverage of Brad and Connie's local story went viral. His social media page crashed from the traffic. Still, Aldridge had scooped the major media outlets, and his additional coverage of the NSA inquiries into their early flights around the planet had been the kick-starter for his career. This was big-time; he was going to go global! No longer a string reporter for a grocery checkout tabloid and a minor blogger, Aldridge had been picked up by CNN. He'd been equipped with a high-definition field reporter's camera with directional sound, a light kit, and one field engineer who would remain in the satellite truck.

While Aldridge checked his equipment, Mrs. Hitchens was down the hall, "fixing herself," her words. The Hitchens daughter was purported to still be on one of her hikes in the scrub but would be back soon. The backyard was a barely defined clearing with mostly grass nearest the homestead and low palmetto scrub blending into a mature pine forest farther away. He'd looked for the kid out the kitchen window but had not spotted the rarely photographed daughter. Due to the couple's increased new-found notoriety, one of the property owners farther down Wakulla Beach Road had swapped titles with the Hitchens. The entire household had moved to a location near the end of Wakulla Beach Rd, security had moved into what had been an enclave in the St. Marks National Wildlife Refuge. Homeland Security had used its leverage to acquire a compound deeper into the refuge to permit the construction of a new home for the reclusive couple, their young daughter. Beyond their new home, in a separate unit, the two ambassadors from Dzura had comfortable new home as well. Any visitor to the compound was now required to enter the fenced wildlife refuge property to find their small homestead and pass through a security screen.

While waiting, Aldridge absently scratched at an early season mosquito bite picked up while carting equipment from the truck to the house. He thought no one could survive a month in these critter-infested woods without a habitual coating of bug juice, but the locals seemed to be immune. *Hmm, maybe there's a story there somewhere.* Footsteps caused him to look up. Connie Hitchens had indeed fixed herself up. He found no words; he tried. The closer he got, the more intimidated he felt.

"How do I look?" She patted at her skirt, stopped, raised her arms slightly, and pirouetted. He stood, holding a lavaliere microphone, trying to stall, waiting for words to come. She was gorgeous. "Great, you look great." Her red hair, the bright red-hint-of-orange of a true redhead, had grown long and she'd worked to get most of the natural curl out. It cascaded across her bare shoulders in soft waves. Her figure hadn't been affected by either the years or her pregnancy, and he tried not to stare. Smiling with some embarrassment, he said. "The camera is going to love you." He approached with the lavaliere set up and raised the little clip-on mike. Her simple spaghetti strap top had a V-neck, inviting a hint of cleavage, and he hesitated. A sea of freckles spread from that forbidden area up toward her collar bones and the exquisite lines of her neck.

He wasn't usually this thumb-fisted near woman. He had somehow expected the beautiful, freckled country girl he'd remembered from the first coverage years before, not the full-grown, self-confident, and stunning redhead standing so close. At thirty-two, she was a jaw-dropping knockout.

"Here, I can do that." She took the small clip microphone in a simple gesture and clipped it to the edge of the V-neck, just below her collar bone.

Hmm, she's done this before. "Great." *Stop saying that; get your composure on.* He sat back into one of the two chairs that faced each other over a coffee table staged with a bowl of fruit and a fan of magazines. She sat across from him and took a sip of water.

The two stationary cameras were synchronized. He spoke into his mic, "You ready in the trailer?" He got an affirmative, looked up at Connie Hitchens, and smiled as he pressed a remote that started both cameras recording.

"OK, timestamp, May 21st, 2022, 4:30 pm. Location: Hitchens' residence, Wakulla County, Florida." His mouth seemed to stop working.

He punted. "We can start now." Aldridge looked down at his notes again. "Mrs. Hitchens, thank you for letting us into your home today. I understand and respect your need for privacy after the media attention

7

surrounding your and your husband's return." He thought of the barrage two weeks earlier when she and Lenka had been caught out on the bay, trying to fish in private. Lenka, or Leink-Naa, was the female ambassador from Dzura and her appearance in fishing garb had created a stir in the legitimate press and wild speculations in the tabloids. He tried to apologize for the press in general. "If I may, on behalf of our network and most reputable news sources, please accept our apologies for what must have felt like an attack." She simply smiled and nodded.

He needed her to start speaking. "Your husband's return, and especially the reality of his co-pilot Ambassador Shaand caused a huge shock. But that was about seven years ago, right?"

"Yes, I'm sure it did," she took another sip, "I was fortunate to miss all that hoopla."

"That may have been a good thing," he said. "The hoopla, as you call it, was the talk of the globe, all languages, all media, everywhere, for months. Let me start at when you returned, with your daughter and Ambassador Lenka. Can you explain again why Bradley Hitchens, er, why you didn't return with your husband?

"I really wanted to come back with Bradley. There was room in our ship, but the Elioi don't travel under grav-drive while gestating. While pregnant. By the time I was ready to travel, my friends in the creche had me fitted for a custom-fitted environment suit for me and an environment pod of sorts for Myahh."

"Yes, he said it was unsafe for you to travel while pregnant."

"My friends back on Dzura—" She looked off camera, off him, as if in memory of the far-off world, "—they warned against it. There was no recent medical data, but culturally, their females never did a grav-jump when they knew of a pregnancy. They just didn't do it. I made the decision. I had to talk Brad into leaving, into going home without me."

"That must have been tough." He let the thought hang, hoping she'd notice it.

She allowed a small lop-sided grin, recalling a memory. "Actually, I thought Brad agreed pretty quickly."

Her grin lit up the camera again, then she laughed, flashing a smile at him that would make the whole world fall in love with her. *Damn, she's something.* "Really? You had to talk him into going alone?"

"Yes, I know he was conflicted. But we heard there was probably an Erran prospector or two in the Sol system stealing billion-dollar satellites to be scrapped for their metals. That needed to be stopped as quickly as possible. We didn't know at the time about the time dilation problem of making a grav-jump of such large distances."

This was not a topic in his notes. He knew they'd edit out his awkward pause as he thought about the implications. "Right, you didn't have any reason to understand how much time you'd lost, just getting to Dzura."

"We were ignorant of everything except that our little spaceship knew more about how to get around than we did. We didn't know how or what to ask about the real physics of the jump. And the weird thing is, I was born in 1961." She paused, waited as Aldridge's jaw dropped. She thought he would have had that in his background.

"Um-hmm, that would make you—" Then his eyes furrowed.

She could see him working out the math. "I turned thirty-two in my time stream. Unfortunately, all my contemporaries are over twenty-seven years older than that." She shrugged, "Grav-drive time slip." His eyes squinted again. She added, "If the grav-drive jump is calculated correctly, there's a minimal percentage of the actual time lost in the journey. I didn't age more than a few hours on the jump, but thirteen years and about seven months elapsed getting to the Dzuran system. We didn't have any idea that in that short journey that we'd jumped over thirteen years into the future. But then, it's a long, long way to their star system."

"How far exactly is their solar system from ours?"

"I seem to remember someone said that it was over thirteen thousand light-years. I don't know how far that is." A sidelong glance betrayed her ignorance of astronomical geometry. "I really don't understand parsecs. It's a long ways from here and the jump was really several small jumps as we skipped from star system to star system. Jai, our ship's computer, said it was a path stored into system memory, when it first came online a few hundred years ago." She smiled, recalling a memory. "Jai said it was much safer to do it that way; helps to not fall into the grip of a black hole."

"Thirteen thousand light-years. Wow, so," he quickly did mental math, "light from their sun that's getting here now left that sun when we were in the dark ages."

"Yes, the eighth century. It wows me too. To think that the grav-drive can do that. Anyway, Brad left early with his friend Shaand as the proposed Ambassador. The need to deal with a supposed satellite pirate was both tactical and, I suppose, diplomatic."

9

"Diplomatic?"

"Sure. Brad was bringing to Earth a real live alien, Shaand. His full diplomatic uniform was calculated to impress. Brad wanted to put a stop to the theft of those multi-million-dollar comm satellites. Well, that was the hope. We didn't know that the thefts had stopped over fourteen years earlier or by the time he got back twenty-nine years earlier. Brad thought he would be welcomed back as a hero. He couldn't have guessed that it had been so long since those satellites went missing. And he hoped that Shaand would be accepted and given full diplomatic status. But that wasn't how it turned out."

"No, that wasn't quite the reception you'd hoped."

"Not at all. Who would have guessed there was a military satellite up there that could shoot at him?"

The interview was veering off track. The whole world knew that story. Brad had been blamed for the theft of the satellites stolen by a Dzuran prospector. After her husband's spacecraft had reduced Space-Shield 88 to molten bits, the American Space Force had been forced to admit it had developed and deployed anti-missile missiles on orbiting platforms. Old news by now. He wanted to get to her story. "Well, Mrs. Hitchens, the cold war's missile defense systems turned out to be not much of a danger, didn't it? So, I'd like to talk to you about your personal journey."

"Ok, fine." She flashed that smile again.

"You arrived eight months later, right?"

That's about right, closer to nine. I wanted to become more confident with little Myahh. I was a new mother, and there weren't any human mothers around to let me know what to do. I'd babysat for some pretty young kids in high school, but never a newborn. So nursing was, I guess, left up to nature."

"So the locals, the Dzurans, they weren't much help in that respect, I guess."

She chuckled this time. "No, they may have similar overall dimensions – two arms, two legs, two eyeballs in the front of their head. Not at all scary as you'd maybe expect from a space alien. But they carry their newborns on their backs. The newbies can grasp their mother's fur and suckle as the mother carries on with most of her normal duties."

"Wait, on their backs? They suckle on their mother's backs?"

"Yes, there are small nipple-like, well, nipples, in two rows of three along each side. The little guys hang on until they can sit up on their own. By then, they can grasp and hold things. They are often bottle-fed…pretty much like human babies, except they can hold onto the bottles themselves." She screwed her mouth sideways. "I hate to make this comparison, but imagine so many of our mammals that have young that can feed on their own immediately; some even cling on to their mothers as they do so."

"Fascinating." He noted the red elapsed time counter on camera one. Looking into the camera, he said, "We're talking today with Mrs. Connie Hitchens, the first woman to bear a child off-planet. We'll be right back after this break. And we're expecting to be joined by Maya Hitchens presently, so stay tuned." He tapped his remote that turned both cameras to stand-by mode. "Good start, how are you doing? Are the lights too bright?"

"No, not for me. I'm fine. How about you? Your forehead is getting a little shiny. Do you want me to turn down the AC?"

Great, now she's giving me staging advice. He blotted his forehead with a paper towel that had been in his chair out of sight. He took a sip from an off-camera tumbler and with a nod to her in warning, reactivated the cameras. "So, where is Maya? Sometimes she's called Maya-T? Did I get that right?

"Myahh, not Maya. It's a long ahh sound. Her full name, as you must know, is Myahh-Tra Louanne Hitchens. Myahh for her golden hair. Tra for the family name of the creche I was welcomed into when I needed a nursery. Louanne is for my mother and for dad's shrimp boat. Both are or were very important to me."

"How is Maya, excuse me, Myahh doing?" *Finally, get around to the main event.*

"She's fine, except for the isolation growing up. She's quite a talented young lady."

"So, there were no immediate side effects from traveling through space-time with an infant?"

"None that we can tell." She paused, fingered a small green-gold gemstone that hung from a simple silver necklace. "She claims she can remember it. I just tell her it's impossible; she was only a few months old after all. But she's always been a precocious girl." She stopped, screwed her mouth sideways. "I guess all moms claim their kids are special, don't they? We all have the smartest-kid syndrome."

"It's only natural, Mrs.—"

11

"Please, Mr. Aldridge, Aaron. Call me Connie. No need to be too formal now, is there?"

"Sure thing." He finally got down to what he wanted to talk about. "Connie, I know she's out playing right now, but we hoped that maybe we'd be able to talk with Myahh as well. Will she be back soon?"

"Any minute now."

Looking at her, Aldridge thought she looked distracted like she was listening to a soundtrack he could not hear. "Great, that will be great. I hope we get that chance." He flipped an interview card and started anew. "What would you say was your biggest surprise on returning to Earth?"

"Why, that's easy. Finding out that instead of being gone about eighteen months, that it was over twenty-seven years ago! That mom and dad thought I was long dead."

~ ~ ~

Myahh crept closer to the window. She didn't need to actually hear the conversation with her ears. She could listen to them just as easily by tuning her psi in on their communication. Except the reporter wasn't very good at masking his true thoughts when he spoke. The man kept looking at her mother's shirt and legs. *He is not a nice man.* She heard the man say, "Thank you, Connie. Is it true that when Maya was in Pre-K, she got a lot of other kids upset? Some of the parents who were contacted said there was something strange about her." But that was not what he was thinking.

Her mom said, "Myahh, not Maya; remember? The ahh is elongated just a tad, like the sound you might make easing into a bath. I think some of the parents were scared. I think they just thought Myahh had space cooties or something that was catching. No problem, I home-schooled her. She's really quite bright."

I'm bright? Myahh repeated the phrase to herself aloud, smiled. Then, transmitting to her mother in psi, *That man is a bad man, Mama. He's thinking about you with no clothes on. He is a S O B.*

Watch your language, little missy!

The thought command through her mother's psi channel was clear. *Yes Ma'am.* She obediently psi'd back. *But he's still bad. Watch his eyes.*

Sweetie, I know you will discover that being prettier than most has its challenges. There was a pause as her mother concentrated on her discussion with the man. *Then, are you going to come in? He wants to*

12

talk with you.

No ma'am, not if I don't have to; he's too creepy.

OK, maybe the next one. Go get yourself cleaned up. Dinner as soon as the reporters go away.

Myahh settled on her haunches between two azalea bushes at the edge of the house for a few minutes trying now not to hear, not to overhear on any channel. It wasn't working. Her psi talents were better than her parent's by far and the unbidden words flowed unfiltered. She got up and dusted off her knees, then slapped the dust and grime off her hands.

~ ~ ~

Aldridge tried another tack. "Mrs. Hitchens, Connie? When you first returned, you also were accompanied by one of the natives, uhmm, Dzurans. Can you tell us about her?"

"Please, Aaron. Not natives. Not in any sense except that they were *native* to their home planet. Their culture has been space-faring for almost a thousand years. They've been mining their asteroid belt for most of those centuries for rare metals not found in abundance on their planet or their sister planet Erra. Those metals allowed them to create the grav-drive that NASA and the U.S. Space Force have been so diligently trying to re-create in their labs."

He jotted notes in his digital pad while she waited for him to look up. She continued, "If you mean native in any way similar to the pre-industrial indigenous cultures that Europeans found in the Americas, or Australia, or Africa, you couldn't be farther off base. I hope you'll report that Elioi explorers had mapped us and declared the Sol system off-limits due to our primitive state. Only the most recent visits resulted in the piracy of those communications satellites."

Aldridge backed up. *Dammit.* "Sorry, I didn't mean anything derogatory by that." He was genuinely sorry. If he screwed this up, the other reporter from that glam rag would be the only story out. He was pretty sure no one held much interest in her Target clothing choices or her aunt's recipes. *Get back to it.* He turned his interview card over. "Connie, the friend you came back with, your companion Lenka."

"Good friend and trusted confidant, Leeink-knaa. We call her Lenka; it's easier. And she's much more than that, she is a full ambassador for cultural exchange."

He continued his line of questions. "Do you agree that reaction to Lenka was far different from the world's reaction to Shaand, the other Dzuran ambassador?"

"No doubt, Leeink-knaa," she modeled the correct pronunciation for him, "is a beautiful example of the female caste on Dzura." She paused, not wanting to inadvertently slander Shaand. "Shaand is a handsome example of a Dzuran male. He's nearing his prime age and has already risen to high clan status, become a diplomat, and learned passable English in a few months, for crying out loud. He has the strong, distinctive musculature of their male caste. He is a highly trained warrior, hardened by gravity and, well, hardship and deprivation, and necessity."

Aldridge thought, this is great; she's finally loosened up.

"Lenka worked in a laboratory, I'd love to tell you about some of the equipment I saw them working on, but I only got to use a very little of it practically. Anyway, yes, she's a wonderful person."

"Person? Isn't she—"

"Yes, alien. But why not. She's intelligent, has a personality distinct from her peers. They aren't, by any stretch, carbon copies of each other." She frowned at him, eyes hardened. "A lot of idiotic stuff has come out in the media and on your channel too. They are not a cross between a meerkat and a fox, and they are not clones, carbon copies. They are not different races. Males are tan to brown, females are white. Your peers in the press need to get a grip on their paranoid, xenophobic BS."

Aaron leaned back in his chair, holding both palms out in stop mode. "Absolutely, Mrs. Hitchens, Connie. I agree. One of the reasons for this visit is to get your views. After all, with the treaty signed at the United Nations being ratified throughout the world governments, the Dzurans are going to be allies of sorts."

"Not if our own Congress doesn't get off its collective butt." She was about to say more, stopped, hand over mouth. "Please, Aaron, you can cut that out, right?" She put her palms together in mock prayer. "Please tell me you won't let that out. We're gonna need Congress."

"Sure, I can edit that out. Don't worry." Privately, he thought, damn, that's going to be a hit. That'll go viral. I just have to have somebody 'steal' one of these cameras.

Connie said. "So please, Aaron. Take special care of these cameras and their hard drives. We don't want that out, do we? So, you be careful with those recordings, right? You're going to tell the crew in the trailer, right?"

"Yeah, no problem." She had read him like a book. He caved. He knew he wasn't going to betray the trust for a cheap shot at the do-little congress, as the last several sessions had been labeled. He would never know that she actually *could* read his thoughts like a

book. From his professional curiosity to his lecherous cravings, he was readable and bordered on disgusting.

2

Jhen-an Shay-Ka

From her favorite backyard sitting spot, the driver's seat of her dad's tractor, Myahh felt a strange tug near her listening place to the side of the base of her brain. She had been listening to the lying reporter inside, but this was new. It wasn't Jai. It wasn't mommy. And dad was a long way away. She could sense something new. Someone she remembered from far away was trying to talk to her.

Myahh shivered as an unseasonal chill rattled her spine, and goosebumps flashed down her arms and bare legs. Her brow wrinkled in concentration and worry. Her brain's psi tuner felt like she was playing with daddy's old radio, turning the dial and getting bits of words. But they weren't even in English. And it didn't sound like Spanish either; she knew that from Miss Carrera, the visiting lady from the library. *Down*, then again, *g'down*. Was that just a noise or the word down? It came again, more clearly. *Down, gd down.*

Not sure if she was feeling the correct intent, she got down off the ancient John Deere and stood next to the massive rear wheel when she understood the word. *Ged, Gĕd, Gudd*, and finally, *Good,*

Myahh stepped out from under the corrugated metal roof of the pole barn. Now, much more clearly. *Good. Smart girl.* She smiled. The psi channel was friendly and new. Who was this and where was she? Or maybe it's a him? Not as fun, maybe. Experimenting, she stood clear of any overhanging branches, spread her arms as if to fly, closed her eyes, and faced the sky.

She stood frozen in place for over twenty minutes, receiving messages she did not fully understand. The voice was friendly, like a wished-for sister, or her puppy before it was killed on the highway, or mommy when she was being playful, and it told her of things she could not understand. She was thrilled but a little afraid. Somewhere, in intense pulses of light and intuition, she understood the messages were coming from far away, beyond Earth. She found her hands pushing against the headache growing at the base of her skull and tried to ask the stream of information to slow down. Her retinas hurt even through closed eyelids.

16

This had happened before when she was trying to listen to conversations on the kitchen phone. The tinny sound the mouthpiece made was nothing compared to the imagery she could create if she knew who was talking with mom or dad.

The images and messages gradually slowed down, and became more simplified and understandable. She squinted against the bright sunlight on her eyelids. In rapt concentration, her lips puckered in a smile, the warm sunshine on her face filled her heart with joy.

The screen door on the front porch slammed. She heard her mother saying goodbye to the reporter. The voice had stopped. Her arms hurt from being held out so long. Myahh took a long breath, felt the world spin sideways, and fell to the ground. She thought she heard her mom scream. Then there were hands on her face, her neck, and under her shoulders, helping her to her feet. She felt the coolness of air conditioning and felt the familiar fabric of the couch. She was safe, all was good. She opened her eyes and smiled beatifically up into her mother's face.

"Mom, they're coming."

"Daddy, and Shaand? Are they coming home?"

"No, Mom, *they* are coming."

She tried to psi the word, but it would not come. She looked up at the ceiling and said simply, "Them," and let her exhausted mind rest in sleep.

~ ~ ~

Myahh had been asleep when the second reporter arrived, escorted as Aaron Aldridge had been, by a sheriff's deputy. Kimber Cunningham was from a magazine conglomerate. Depending on the sophistication expected, different parts of the interview might end up in *Vogue* or *People* or even *Le Monde*.

Connie had just completed the initial introductions when she heard a soft moan from Myahh's room. *Who's coming, honey?* She excused herself from the reporter's center of attention and, in a few graceful steps, slipped into her daughter's room and knelt beside her. Myahh was on the floor, eyes rolled back in an apparent feint. "Honey, are you OK?"

Myahh blinked, focused on the ceiling, then on her mother.

"Who is coming, My? Is it your Aunt Lucy?"

There was no response. "Myahh, hon? What is it? Who's coming." She was regretting scheduling the two reporters back-to-back. With only a half-hour between the two sessions, now her daughter had fallen or fainted. Aunt Lucy was on her way down from Tallahassee to help to maybe assure her that the girl was just exhausted. Myahh had opted not to be around if it wasn't absolutely necessary for the NSA-approved home interviews. Cunningham was doing her best to be patient, but the interview had been proposed as a mother-daughter setting.

"No, Mom." The girl turned to meet her mother's worried face. "Them. They're..." Her face scrunched as she searched her vocabulary. "I'm having trouble with the word."

At first, Connie thought Myahh said, "*Je ne sais quoi.*" Her own French was dusty from her first year at Chapel Hill. But even filtered through her daughter's tendency to speak in two or more languages at once, *je ne sais quoi* did not match the sound or feeling. Peering into Myahh's eyes, she saw the internal struggle. She reached down and stroked her child's hair, smiled. "Take your time, honey. It's ok." She searched closer in those psi undertones that Myahh was so adept with.

Myahh closed her eyes in thought. Her head turned again toward a wall lined with bookshelves and little else, cocked her head to the right. Her eyebrows furrowed slightly before her lips parted. Connie thought she leaned into the word as if pressing forward would help get it out.

"Jennen, Se-coo." Myahh enunciated the nonsense phrase, frowned, and tried again. "Jen-enne say-ee-coo." She smiled triumphantly. "Mom, I don't know how you spell that because I've never seen it before. But that's the sound." Her eyes widened, glistening in triumph. She seemed to vibrate, happy with the sound of it. "Jen-enn Say-ee-coo."

Connie, still kneeling on one knee, glanced back at the reporter. "Kimber, I'm terribly sorry, but I think we need to reschedule the interview. Today isn't going to work. Are you staying at the golf club's hotel? Or up in Tallahassee?"

Myahh said softly. "Miss Kimber's at the Hilton in Tallahassee." She looked up at the startled face of the reporter, narrowed her brow, and said, "She was going to stay at the Days Inn, but," she paused to understand slang she'd never heard. "She cashed in an eye owe you."

Cunningham's mouth dropped, followed by her pencil and pad. The little pad spewed an array of question cards. A mechanical pencil rolled under her chair. The young reporter, overly self-confident only moments before, proud of having landed this interview with one of the most famous people on the planet, fought the urge to wet herself or run, or both.

Connie had seen similar shocked reactions before. Myahh was

deceptively ordinary, At seven going on eight, she affected more mature behaviors she'd seen on TV and social media, but she didn't understand when not to say things she shouldn't know. Her mind-reading talents could be intrusive and her social skills were severely undeveloped. Her parent's repeated warnings not to read minds often went unheeded in moments of excitement. Connie stood, extending her hand in a formal request to end the interview. "Kimber, I'm truly sorry. That was...uncalled for, and I'm, well, I'm sorry. I'm sure you know, if you've done your background, that Myahh is special, ehm, that way. She has an advanced version of intuition. It's not mind-reading, she just tunes in, and, well..."

Cunningham knelt to retrieve her pencil, gathered the spray of cards and the pad, and stood. She struggled for composure. Something had picked at a part of her brain even as she was forming thoughts, and she heard this young girl saying them. She shook her head slowly from side to side. "No, that's just not right!" She stepped back, glanced over her shoulder, and took another backward step closer to the door. "That's not right."

"Kimber, please. I'll talk to Myahh about that if you want to continue tomorrow. I'm free after three." The reporter was about to take another backward step, one that would have crushed a plastic action figure of Myahh's dad dressed in an Elioi space suit, when the girl swooped in to retrieve it.

"Careful!" Myahh piped cheerily. "No need to be hasty. Please, you don't have to leave." She held the four-inch-tall figure cupped with care in her hands. She crossed the room to pick up a foot-long model of Jai, her dad's spaceship, opened the cockpit, and put the tiny jump-suited figure in the pilot's seat.

Kimber Cunningham looked behind her as if to get a fix on the doorknob, then turned back to face Connie Hitchens. She took a deep breath before starting, rebooting what she would have said. "Connie, look, I need to finish getting the story. A little more back story on your life. You and your husband have been so private, and I get it, but for all these years we've—" she waved a hand in the air in small circles, —"we've heard so little about your private lives, and really, there's this huge audience that wants to know how you got to know each other, all that. We'd be doing a special printing." She watched as Myahh inserted another figure into the cockpit's back seat in readiness for another sortie. The figure was a fair three-inch-tall replica of Connie Hitchens. Cunningham gave a subtle head jerk toward Myahh, "That—that's a whole 'nother story."

"Myahh, please honey. Can you give me a minute? I have to finish

19

talking with Ms. Cunningham." The girl eyed each of the adults in turn and started to turn toward the bedroom hallway. Connie called after her. "If you're up for it, I think she'd like to talk to you for a bit also. We talked about it, right?"

"Yes, Mom. I'll be good."

Connie moved slightly, placing herself in Kimber's line of sight to her daughter. "Yes, I'm sure, that's a whole other story. With some effort, she can turn that off. She's getting better at not tuning in. It's involuntary."

Cunningham nodded in assent. Connie continued. "This last year especially, something clicked. You know her early experiences early at school were scary for her and upsetting for almost everyone else. Even at the University School in Tallahassee, kids that had been pre-selected to be in a class with her weren't up to being tuned in on. Everyone knows that she is a budding talent, exceptionally smart, but..." She tried to connect with the reporter on a personal level. "And well, you just are going to have to be tolerant if she's critical of your questioning. Please." She reached out and took Cunningham's free right hand and clasped it between her palms. "Kimber, do you have children?"

The reporter nodded, thin-lipped. Showing nothing other than the acknowledgment.

"Then please let me protect Myahh. I know you want the story, need the story. Brad has finally relented, and to some extent, the Feds have finally relaxed." She squeezed Cunningham's hand firmly. "If you want that story, you have to help me protect Myahh. You don't know the Feds as I do, and," she closed her eyes briefly to allow a memory flash to pass, "I'm pulling the mother card here. I'll work with you, but you've got to let this one pass for some future issue. She's too young."

Kimber Cunningham slowly pulled her hand free. Resolve to carry through seemed to calm her initial flight urge. "Ok, Connie. That was just SO startling, I freaked. I'm sorry, I'm being unprofessional here. It's just so—"

"Not a problem, Kimber. What about tomorrow? Three-ish." She looked around as if searching for a clue to tomorrow's schedule. Nothing she could think of was in conflict. "So, I'll see you at three?" She felt her daughter in her head again. *Fine, so now she's leaving!* They both heard the back door creak open and slam shut.

With slightly more than perfunctory manners, the shaken reporter left. A thin orange cloud of clay dust followed her and the deputy's cars out to the Coastal Highway and she was gone. When Connie was sure the reporter's car had turned onto the blacktop, she called out. "*Myahh,* come in, honey. She's gone."

She cocked her head to the right, as her daughter had done moments before, listening. From near the pole barn at the back of the house, she heard-felt Myahh's answer. *Coming Mom.*

~ ~ ~

From a side room down the hall, Connie's closely-guarded guest had been listening and commented. "*Jhen-an Shay-ka.*" The message in psi was now unmistakable in its proper pronunciation. Leeink-Knaa opened her door. Connie saw her looking back, her forehead wrinkled in a smile.

Connie asked slowly, hoping she was wrong. "The Jhen-an Shay-Ka are the Precursors?"

Leeink-Knaa, her name Dzuran name simplified to a more human accessible Lenka, approached slowly. "Yes, the ones who came before. Precursors in your tongue. Sometimes in the past, they were thought to be gods. A few Elioi still do regard them as gods."

Connie closed the few steps and leaned slightly to embrace her friend. Her hand felt the white fur on Lenka's dorsal ridge rise slightly then soften and flatten. They drew apart to an arm's length. Connie said, "This is going to change everything isn't it?"

Lenka's left eye ridge rose, in a very human response, "Yes it does, and I not have idea how." She opened her palms in a Dzuran shrug. "No records exist on Dzura or the known systems. The Precursor clerics claim to have arcane knowledge, but factually, we only know of the sentinels."

"That's what was taken from Earth orbit to your world? A sentinel?"

Lenka's mouth relaxed in what Connie had learned long ago was a Dzuran frown and nodded. "Some of your media call it a messenger."

Connie could feel Myahh approaching. She turned to see Myahh standing half in and out of the sliding screen door. "Girl, get yourself in here."

Myahh entered the living room but turned and stared as if searching, out across the sea of salt grass that spread to the south for what seemed like miles. Connie and Lenka both felt the implicit and intertwined emotions boiling in the girl—loss and fear.

21

"Myahh, let's you, me, and Connie have a talk." Lenka's soft imposition on Myahh's reverie was as much an invitation as a caress.

3

Discovery

Mauna Kea Observatory

"Chuck, d'jou see that email from Culgoora? It's confirmed!" Pauline looked at the wall clock, then her cheater link to the Pacific cloud cover feed displayed on one of the several screens available at her workstation.

"Yeah." Chuck Pender didn't look away from the printout spewing from a printer. "It's legit. It's from their 30cm helioscope."

"Great, I need twenty minutes on the sun gun, then you can have the dome for your Io shot."

"I don't know, man." Chuck whined, "I've already got my shots set up for tonight."

Paulina Ybarra persisted, "Chuck, for a chocolate chip cookie I'll finish that setup. We're going to lose the sun in about forty-five minutes. There's weather moving in. I need to start pivoting the dome soon to avoid clouds." The observatory on Mauna Kea's upper shoulder was terrific for deep sky observations. Its remote location and altitude were ideal for optical astronomy, and the local ambiance at the bottom of the mountain had induced Ybarra to stay when her fellowship expired four years earlier. She was now certified on all of the systems the observatory could aim at the heavens. She also knew the cryptic email and coordinates sent from Australia's Culgoora solar observatory and a request to: "Look up, a new game is afoot under the sun" implied something more than a scrambled gumshoe reference.

"Make it a bag of chocolate cookies, Paulie, chocolate-chocolate chip." Pender reconsidered. "And half of next Friday's shift. I've got a date down the mountain Saturday and I need my rest."

"Date?" Pauline looked at Charles' bulk spreading the arms of his rolling chair and wondered, *to each his own, I guess*. "OK, tell you what, I'll take that whole shift. Bob's taking the kids into Hilo to watch that new Aquaman movie. I don't really give a damn about those things."

"Seriously? You don't like Aquaman, the Flash, or Superman, Batman, all those DC guys?" As he swiveled in his chair, its central spindle creaked under the strain. His three-hundred-plus pounds tested the strength of the chair's support. "Not even Wonder Woman?"

"Not even Spiderman, Ironman, or, ..." Paulina replied, she couldn't think of any other heroes. She was too busy calibrating the helioscope's aiming points. It wasn't hard, they were dead center on the sun.

"Those are Marvel, not DC."

"Like I said, I really don't care. But I do care that we're burning daylight and I need to get the gun in motion, and it'll take fifteen minutes to rotate the dome. If I don't start now, I'll have to wait until dawn, and three-quarters of the world's big eyes will have a shot at it before we will again."

"OK, Paulie, go for it." He pushed away from his station and headed for the refrigerator. "Homemade chocolate chips too, Paulina. Don't think you can buy me off with Famous Amos."

"Thanks man. You are super." *Super huge,* she thought as she slid her hundred-six-pound pixie self on her rolling chair into the big mirror's control station. *I probably shouldn't have used food as a bargaining chip.* Chuck was damn good at his job and had been her mentor, but he had added at least another ten pounds to his already bloated torso since she'd first come out of her graduate program at Cal Tech. She worried about him. She looked over her shoulder as he disappeared into the hallway that connected to the kitchenette.

She turned back to the control station and set the parameters for the helioscope to track the last few minutes of the sun before it slid behind the Pacific for the day. With filters in place, the familiar red-orange violence of the roiling surface was a vision of nuclear hell. Pauline had the same thought every time she viewed the sun's surface—Shiva, the fires of creation and destruction. The surface was not a solid thing, an edge, but the limit of human sensory ability to see into a maelstrom of nuclear fission and fusion wracked by unimaginable magnetic forces.

Then she saw it.

Near the middle of the angry disk, rendered in blues by the current filter. Just as the Culgoora team had said. Shifted maybe a half-degree or less from dead center, they thought, because of atmospheric diffraction near the horizon. Dr. Cook thought it would actually prove to be exactly centered along a line connecting the centers of mass of the earth and sun.

She would take her last readings as the sun kissed the horizon and strain herself to not jump to conclusions until she took a second set of position readings at dawn. But its presence in that location in the few hours since the California sighting already told her what she feared. It was holding position, an impossibility from an orbital mechanical perspective, unless the object was under power, expending energy to maintain that position. An immense amount of energy.

It was alien. And it was large. For it to even be visible against the brilliant disk of the sun, it was large. The Australian solar observer at Culgoora Station, Waru Cook, had only noticed it because he had been monkeying around with the focal length of his optical gun when it had popped into focus.

She looked at the clock. Sunset in Hawaii would be approaching solar zenith in eastern Australia. She got on the phone and after bouncing through the digital secretary's phone directory, got Cook online.

"Waru, I found it. Right where you said." She thought, *this thing is out there, announcements will be hitting the network of observatories soon.* But the distance calculation should be made first. The diameter of the Earth would give them an easy baseline to determine the object's true distance. Its position wasn't so much describable as height above the Earth's surface, but rather, its distance from it. For now, the Earth's radius would have to provide the first approximation. In their respective mornings, they could both repeat distance calculations with the longer baseline of the Earth's diameter and compare.

"I'm sending you my position readings, let's not make any waves out there until we've approximated its distance from the Earth." She paused, hoping for the right answer. Her scientific curiosity be damned, she wanted at least co-discover status. "Listen, have you made any announcements there?" She punched a few buttons just before the thickened horizon's atmospheric lens warped the sun's image and location. She sat back in her seat, exhaled a burst of pent-up anxiety, and sent the gun's attitude data to Cook.

"No, we've been waiting for you to verify." Cook's voice in her headset held a lilt of his back-country roots. He'd been named for the Milky Way in the tongue of his aboriginal ancestors. Waru Cook had taken, what seemed for him, an obvious career path when his math skills outpaced his rural school's ability to challenge him.

"Well, I've verified. It should be coming off your printer now." She thought quickly of the dozen other solar observatories scattered across the globe. "Waru, we are going to have to make a preliminary announcement.

If not, we'll be scooped. You get first sighting credits. We'll take confirmation calls. You're going to be very busy very soon."

Cook's response came with some hesitant breaks as if he were considering all that would transpire soon. "Yes, but Pauline, have you thought that maybe—maybe this is just another craft from Dzura? One we haven't seen before? The old empire had interstellar holiday cruisers. What if these things are the equivalent of a Calypso Cruise liner?"

Before she was really certain of her answer, Pauline Ybarra said, "Waru, if that thing is really aligned on a sun-earth axis, its diameter has to be huge, maybe a few kilometers or larger across. As far as we know, the Dzurans built very functional but fairly ugly craft. They had never spent much time on the beauty of their ships."

Cook started to interrupt. Pauline pushed on. "The only large craft the Dzurans ever built were destroyed during their civil war, as far as we know." She paused, searching for superlatives and failed. "This thing is big!"

Pauline didn't add the thought crying to be said, *and it's perfectly freaking spherical and perfectly reflective.* She mumbled to herself, off mic. "The Dzuran Navy didn't do that." Then a memory clicked, *that other thing, the egg thing in the asteroid belt was built like that.*

Cook brought her back to the present. "Pauline? OK. I'll make the announcement through official channels first as Culgoora Station, asking for secondary and tertiary verification, and make the call to the Morning Herald, BBC, the London Times, and probably the New York Times, so your Yanks don't get their panties in a twist. And—" the pause was longer this time, "—I suppose I'll be back pre-dawn to make my first observations. I'll send them over for you if you are cloudless tomorrow morning."

"Thank you, my friend. Before your email hit, I was hoping to get back to my exo-planet project but I think I'm going to get a nap before all hell breaks loose."

"You really think the media push is going to be bad?"

"Waru, get ready for prime-time evening news across the world. I had the chance to zoom in. Because the edges appeared to be glowing and the rest featureless, I went for maximum magnification. It is a perfectly reflective sphere. That would make it of similar origin, possibly, of the thing Chuck Pender found back when he was just out of grad school almost thirty years ago. That thing he photographed in the asteroid belt. That was a perfectly reflective ovoid. An ovoid with a perfect cube cut out of it." She swallowed and grimaced; bile had begun to rise along with mounting anxiety. "I think this sphere thing is from somewhere else entirely. From wherever the egg came from."

She turned to see Chuck Pender standing behind her looking at the last screen capture she'd taken as he scooped a handful of popcorn into his mouth. The scene was an extreme zoom on the edge of the object. The edge of the black arc flickered in the reflected light from the solar furnace beyond. But the clip was pixelated from extreme magnification. "Hey Chuck, I think you're going to want to see this."

He took two more steps to the back of her chair. He said, "Pull back so you can re-aim that shot at the center of the circle then zoom back in."

She tapped at the keyboard, "I'll put it back in the full natural spectrum." The ultraviolet view transitioned to the red-orange of the visible spectrum. As the view moved into the blackened center of the sphere, a light blue circle appeared. As the minute-long clip looped the pixels jumped a little. But plainly visible at the center of the blackness was a fish-eye reflection of Earth as reflected across one hundred and twenty thousand miles. The tiny dot, that's all it was, a dozen or so pixels in bright blue. Earth.

Chuck dropped his bag of white popcorn. "Jeezus, they're back!" Puffed kernels spilled out of the bag, trailing tiny tracks of white cheddar powder.

4

Briefing at NSA

Fort George G. Mead, Maryland

Colonel Maximilian Doherty swiveled in his chair to receive a last-minute briefing delivered in a sealed and taped manila envelope. Turning around completely to put the high leather chair between the folder and any eyes at the table, he slit the red top-secret tape closure and opened the folder. He flipped back the SF-704 secret document cover sheet to examine the folder's contents. The assembled brass, some top, others in their delegate and supporting roles heard the colonel mumbling and nothing more until the sharp mechanical buzz of a shredder sounded.

Doherty swiveled back around to face senior officers from the United States' Joint Chiefs, European Union, and UN Security forces. The Brazilian component of the European Space Agency had opted in when he'd heard of the meeting through less-than-secure back channels, and the Chinese delegation had been detained by a typhoon but established a secure Zoom channel and could be seen crowded around an executive airliners' conference table. Doherty could not wait for the weather. The results could be emailed after all. A pair of Russians from RosCosmos sat firmly back against their chairs sharing skeptical side glances.

The colonel scanned the eyes that were fixed on his, folded his hands with intertwined fingers, and cleared his throat. "One of my favorite modern philosophers, Carl Sagan, said something that I think goes, 'The universe is a pretty big place, if it's just us, seems like an awful waste of space.' When he said that, the search for extraterrestrials had just begun. We had only theories predicting the presence of other planets in the Cinderella Zone. And we had not yet met the delegates from Dzura. We have found that their civilization has grown and developed along a timeline that's roughly parallel with ours. Perhaps a little more than a hundred-fifty thousand years old, for the Dzurans, or rather the Elioi, as they call themselves, compared to about a hundred-eighty thousand years for us." The discovery of the Elioi defeats the Fermi paradox. He noticed a few blank stares. "Carl Sagan was paraphrasing what you may recall is the Fermi Paradox. Basically, if there is this massive potential for

28

hundreds of thousands of habitable planets in this galaxy alone, and the potential for thousands of civilizations that might rise to the level of interplanetary travel, where are they?"

"But Sagan eloquently considered that many civilizations may have flourished and died long before we began thinking about them. And that some may be alive and self-aware and looking for us across the vast emptiness of space and their radio signals will not reach our neck of the woods until long after we are gone. Neil DeGrasse-Tyson has more recently been saying basically the same thing." He was losing them; he could see their eyes drifting to their note pads. A few were fiddling with their pens. He gave up on the introduction he had planned to give.

"As its military liaison, I've been one of the lead SETI investigators for the U.S. for the past twenty-six years. The search for extra-terrestrial intelligence may no longer have an active mission. But while in its service, I've chronicled hundreds of bogus sightings and reports of abductions. The conspiracy literature on my agency's secret operations is not entirely false as you have all learned. Before our awareness of the Elioi, we were aware of two other races that have been visiting our planet for at least the last seventy years, but who seem to, to have—," he stopped, considering, "—who remain secretive and apparently unwilling to meet us as equals; to communicate with us as anything other than as specimens for their research." He coughed, paused for a sip of water. "There are some indications that others have visited in ages past. Whether they may or may not have had anything to do with pyramids is, well, hopeless conjecture until someone finds a tool or other artifact made of exotic alloys that were impossible two to four thousand years ago. But all that is unimportant for today's discussion."

He flexed his fingers and laid his palms flat on the table. "We know from the Hitchens interviews and Ambassador Shaand that there was an apparent other entity in our system for quite some time. And by other, I mean a civilization that is not the Elioi. Their existence is accepted by everyone but the usual flat Earthers. This other civilization's presence was confirmed by telescopes studying the asteroid belt." He looked down at his fingers and then up to the obligatory framed picture of the President on the wall. He nodded to a subordinate who tapped his laptop. An image taken of the monitor three decades ago appeared—an egg-shaped form with a perfect rectilinear shadowed opening. "There was this artifact, an object inconspicuously passing as an asteroid for perhaps centuries or longer. We do not believe it was an object of the Grays or the Whites, the two secretive varieties of visitors or the Elioi that we've recently met. That object was discovered by one of the space-faring Elioi and transported back to their system."

The two Russians gasped; the Brazilian was rapidly sketching. The Chinese, in their Zoom window, were practically nose-to-nose, but the translating machine was picking up their chatter anyway. Their Zoom window went dark for a few moments and reappeared with more heads in their view.

"At the time, the Erran element of the then divided Elioi was investigating the inner workings of that object. In their meticulous examination of the artifact's architecture, it was inadvertently triggered, er, that is, its control systems activated." Doherty paused, his right-hand fingers drummed slowly. He'd seen the video. "To the horror of those watching remotely, the object decontaminated itself, killing the investigating team as if it were an infestation. At some later time, another component of the object arrived, a near-perfect cube. The cubic component connected with the oval object, and the assembled structure left at physics-defying speeds into deep space in the direction of the galactic center." He shrugged, "There are a lot more stars closer in toward the galactic center."

"Excuse me." The Belgian delegate from the European Space Agency looked up from his notes. "The report we have from several astronomical sites is that the original object was an oval. What kind of object coupled with that oval?" He coughed into his fist. "I recognize that there are technologies at work here that we don't fully understand."

Doherty swallowed the laugh that tried to bubble up. *No shit we don't fully understand.* "That's correct, it was ovoid. Egg-like? No reason we know of beyond conjecture, other than its shape was optimal for hiding in an asteroid belt. The ovoid had a large square opening at one focus of the oval. We have reports from one of the scientists who witnessed the account from Erra's science complex that the object that arrived and linked up was a cube, also perfectly reflective. It inserted itself into the square opening. We are only guessing that the cube was some sort of propulsion and-or navigation system, or even a crewed command module used to relocate what we presume was a monitoring station."

"Excuse me," the Russian delegate this time, "you're presuming that—?"

Doherty raised a palm to signal stop. Though he had a career-long distrust of Russians, he worked at generating a calm presentation and tried to model equanimity toward all at the table. "Yes, I am afraid it is a case of having to make the presumption." He shrugged. "Anyone who was in the ovoid, either died immediately or wished they had because the calculated acceleration would have flattened anything living that we know of into a puddle of plasma. We have witness accounts who viewed some of the actions on vids from drones. Most of the witnesses from the nearby orbiting city-ship are now dead, casualties of the Elioi civil war. Having said all that, the estimated escape acceleration of the combined ships was above fifty G's."

Most around the table stared opened-mouthed, but the Belgian persisted. "How much of this, this need-to-know only meeting, is going to be based on presumption?"

Doherty screwed his lips sideways, debating how to answer. He decided to cut to the chase. "I had wanted to give you as much background as possible, to read you into the issue in as much detail as possible. But you are all intelligent and perceptive, so please feel free to examine your dossiers at your leisure." He put his hands flat on the table, one finger tapped the file he'd just read. "The essence of my planned presentation has just been confirmed. There is a new presence in the solar system." He paused scanning the faces around the table. "It is parked between the solar orbit of Venus and Earth in the ecliptic plane of the orbits of the regular planets, more precisely, in the plane of the Earth's orbit. We have been trying to determine its size, but it, like the previous emissaries, is a mirrored body and frankly, it's hard to find the edge."

The faces around the table reflected reactions from blank incomprehension, to wary regard, to awe. Viijay Nandu, the Indian representative selected because he had flown in the ISS, raised a hand slowly. "May I?"

Doherty nodded, still prepared to leave them to their dossiers. "Certainly Dr. Nandu."

"Wouldn't that mean it has an orbit that would shift by simple orbital parallax?" He paused, "wouldn't it shift out of position? There's no Lagrange point there."

"True, we thought so too, but after a few days of study, we find that it appears to be stationary." His shoulders relaxed, he settled back into his chair and leaned back. "Look, I agree, stationary is not the right word. It doesn't seem to be affected by the normal forces of orbital mechanics. It's not in any orbit that respects physics. The thing's just there holding a position on a line between the center of the sun and the center of the earth, defying Keplar's Law of orbital mechanics."

"I ... see." Nandu settled back into his chair, comprehending the impossible orbital mechanics that most of the rest had probably missed.

Doherty leaned forward again, elbows on the conference table. He knew very little more than he had told them and the information already in their information packets. Each was marked Top Secret and For Your Eyes Only. He wondered how many news cycles that would last. Or from which observatory someone sworn to secrecy would leak in the interest of humanity's right to know.

Doherty knew that the information would probably bring out the crazies, the rabble-rousers, the conspiracy nuts—and his favorites—the alienists who would debate in their own circles whether it was the Grays, the Whites, the Elioi, or some new species to blame. Each alien expert basing his opinion on a career's worth of fabrication and speculation, and in some part, real belief in the constructed outer world view shared and/or disputed by his peers. He shut his eyes for a moment and sighed. "Gentlemen, for the sake of your citizens, and the safety of your families, please. I implore you to respect your security clearance. Do not tell anyone until we know a little more. Until we can somehow make contact. Or hope *they* do."

At the far end of the table, a hand rose, tentatively.

"Yes, Madam Lewandowski."

The EU member looked down at her briefing material, then raised her eyes to meet Nandu's. She then made certain eyeball to eyeball contact with those on the opposite side of the table before meeting Doherty's stare. He was becoming impatient with the slow reveal. *What could this poser want?*

"Colonel Doherty," she pronounced the rank slowly in the three-syllable euro style, "I have heard through some channels, something that might be a rumor or may be factual, some additional information that is important for us here to share." Her hand was still slightly elevated, only her elbow had come down to rest on the burled hardwood table.

"Well then, Justine, please share. If you believe your source has some credibility, please."

"Colonel, on a secure line my ambassador mentioned that he understood this solar sentinel must be expending exorbitant levels of energy to maintain its position in orbit, and the sentinel in the Elioi system has to be expending far more due to the dual planetary configuration."

Doherty took the information in, considered the physics, and frowned. "My friend, do you remember that Dzura is a double planetary system. I don't see how a sentinel would maintain position between Dzura and its sun."

His pause allowed the Pole to continue. "That, Sir, is precisely why the report so worried my source. Maintaining a stationary orbit between Earth and Sun is, we agree, difficult. But for an object to do the same for a binary system is, well..." Her voice trailed off, not certain of her report's credibility anymore. She understood the complex motions of the two planets, Dzura and Erra, as they danced around their sun, Alal. "Perhaps, a simple inquiry, as if you were simply stamping out unfounded rumors?" Her voice rose at the end suggesting a question.

Doherty held Lewandowski's stare until the delegate's eyes dropped to her hands. "That *would* be a useful inquiry, thank you." The Pole's left eyelid twitched. Doherty now realized that the EU and the ESA knew more about the new visitors than he would have guessed. He also knew that a question-response cycle with the Elioi homeworld would take a few weeks on the only grav-wave transmitter on the planet.

Doherty examined his briefing papers and turned to the last page. Looking up and scanning the expectant faces around the table, he continued. "Ladies and gentlemen, I have another announcement to make. I have in hand a report from three observatories that there is, in fact, another visitor if you will; a new monitor in our asteroid belt. The placement of this alien craft in the Sol system coincides with reports from the Elioi ambassador's staff that a new monitor is confirmed in their asteroid belt as well."

He paused, staring at an unimportant speck on the opposite wall as he considered the mechanics. "It would appear that these two monitors in their respective solar orbits have been installed, or placed, almost coincidentally with the placement, or possibly replacement of additional monitors in or near the asteroid belts of both systems. I think we are talking within hours or at least less than a terrestrial day if the calculations are correct. I'm probably speculating here, but that almost assumes that we are watching and taking note and that the precision of the installation of those monitors is itself a message."

Doherty caught a few eyebrows raised in question. "That message being, that we are superior in so many ways to your two pathetic little species."

A hand raised at the far end of the table. "Colonel Doherty?" The Brazilian Space Agency's representative, Ramon Campos had his full attention. At sixty plus, he presented a trim, yet commanding, figure.

"Yes, Señor Campos?"

"Do you know of any effort from these new arrivals to communicate with either Humans or Elioi? Any transmissions in any wavelengths?"

"Excellent question. We began scanning in all possible frequencies as soon as we had confirmation of the Sol system sentinel, or monitor, or...whatever it is. For the time being, we are unofficially referring to them as monitors for lack of a better understanding of their function." He looked at his notes again then returned Campos' stare. "As soon as the news hit the astronomy world, scopes of all wavelengths were turned in that direction including the wide array of deep space radio telescopes, the various SETI arrays, and even our orbital eyes on the Chandra and James Webb platforms." He stopped the involuntary drumming of the fingers of his right hand. "In answer to your question, Ramon. Nothing. Absolutely nothing."

He thought, "I know there are going to be a thousand questions I'd like to ask."

Viijay Nandu raised a hand, as if in sympathy, with another question. "Colonel Doherty? One if you please, Sir."

"Certainly, Viijay. I'll try."

"What are our, your next steps?"

"You might as well know now. I think the announcement was going to be sent to the collected world press corps shortly anyway." He opened his dossier and scanned near the top of the pile. Finding the email transcript he needed, he paraphrased, looking up occasionally to make eye contact around the table. "And please, don't discuss this before the announcement is made. By then both ships will be airborne and free of threat of compromise."

"By 1800 hours Zulu tomorrow, Brad Hitchens, Shaand, and an officer not specified herein are to approach the object that's taken position just inside the asteroid belt. Their objective will be to draw near, seek communication in a full spectrum of frequencies used by both Human and Elioi cultures and use Elioi tech to determine if there is a life-sign aboard the craft. If it can be determined that it is an unmanned monitor, they will draw closer to see if they can draw any reaction short of their own destruction."

Amid the murmurs and side communications that sprang up spontaneously, three more hands shot up. He slapped his dossier closed. "And that, ladies and gentlemen, is all I have for today."

5

Duty Calls

A knock on the door interrupted Martin Jenks as he was tying his third trout fly of the evening. He closed his eyes, wishing that he had not actually heard it. Maybe it had been pinecones on the porch roof. It came again—a burst of five hard raps! He looked at the bright layer of yellow fuzz drying on the hook and grimaced. Another round of raps preceded a shouted hallo. Jenks pushed back from his workbench and went to the door to find a uniformed deputy with a fist raised for another round of knocks.

The deputy cleared his throat. "Sir? Sorry to bother you at this hour. Are you Martin Jenks?" That it was a quarter to midnight was a good enough reason for the apology, but not for the interruption. A look of hopeful anticipation on the young deputy's face was beginning to fade. He hadn't expected to see a black man whose well-salted burr head announced advancement beyond middle age. He'd expected to see a former Air Force master sergeant and was taken slightly aback. He looked down at his notes again. "Oh, uhm. Special Agent Martin Jenks?"

"Retired. That's retired Special Agent to you." Jenks said as he backed away from the doorway. He sighed in exasperation as he opened the door and gestured for the young man to enter. The late evening air had a pronounced chill. "Good evening officer, is there something I can do for you?" He had no real next of kin, so he knew this was not a notification of death in the family. Widowed for five years now, he was just past his seventy-first birthday and essentially alone in the world.

Jenks pointed to a knotty pine framed couch across a polished hand-built table from his chair and took a seat. The deputy, whose pin labeled him as McAllister, sat and cleared his throat again. "Agent Jenks, er, Mr. Jenks, I was sent to see if you were actually here. They said in town that you don't usually answer your phone or that it's disconnected. I got different versions."

Bruce Ballister

Jenks interrupted. "Couldn't this have waited for the morning? For daylight?" He pointedly glanced at the antique Seth Thomas gravity clock over the mantle. It was about to strike twelve.

Deputy McAllister responded, "Well sir, I don't really know." Fidgeting, "I'm a newbie on this squad, and I sometimes think they keep me in the dark on purpose."

"Um hmm, so you got the honor of a midnight drive up the mountain?"

"Well, actually. I just got night shift on the schedule and was in the squad room when the message came in." He reached into his jacket pocket. "I do have this for you." He pulled a folded envelope from his shirt pocket. Jenks immediately recognized the light blue envelope with its alternating blue and red diagonal piping around the edges. It was an official communication from somewhere in the Air Force bureaucracy. Tentatively, he held out his hand. The young officer handed the envelope over the table.

Holding it in his hand, Jenks saw that it was addressed to Special Agent Martin Jenks, with his current address in Grantsdale, Montana. He glanced again at the wall clock which, as he watched, clicked to midnight, and began to chime the Westminster bells. He had always loved the sound and often didn't even notice the chime. But now, with the deputy watching him, they sounded overly loud and foreboding. As he held it, the envelope seemed to gain mass. He wanted to set it down and open it over morning coffee.

He looked up from the envelope. "Were you supposed to wait for me to open this? Did you have instructions?"

"They told me to see if you wanted a ride in case you didn't want to leave your car at the airport."

Jenks opened the envelope and pulled out the single sheet of paper. He was stunned. They wanted him, again! The dated time stamp for travel was for the next day. He looked at the coordinates, nearly the same westerly coordinate and not that much further south. He looked back up at McAllister. "There's transportation at the airport?"

"Don't know sir, I was just told to give you that, to make the offer."

"You said you were on night shift, Deputy?"

"Yes Sir. Seven to seven." Jenks sighed in resignation, rose, and opened a drawer. He pushed its contents around, and found his aging flip phone. McAllister whistled softly. Jenks ignored him, went out on the porch punching numbers, and walked to the end of the railing. If he stood with the back of the phone facing down the valley, he could sometimes get a signal.

"Max? Martin here."

"We catch up to you at home?"

"I'm at home. That's not far enough away apparently."

A short laugh burst at the other end. "Martin, there's a jet on the pad in Hamilton." There was a pause as Col. Max Doherty checked his watch. "Least it will be by the time you get there."

Jenks felt bile building. His anger inexpressible toward the man on the other end. "How did you know I'd be here? I could have been up the mountain, back up in BC, out on the lake, anywhere."

"Lucky guess, Martin. Listen, this probably won't take long, but I really need you there." The voice on the other end sounded plaintiff even through the poor signal.

"First things first. I'm not on the payroll anymore. Where is there? And why should I be anywhere but here? I told you I was history after that trip to Factory Butte." He was frustrated and hanging on to residual exhaustion from the previous week's trip to Florida. "Last week was supposed to be it, over, finito."

Doherty's voice took on a supplicant's tone that verged on pleading. "That situation down south. Seems that there's been a flare up that needs your attention." A pause. "Have you heard the news about your friends down on the coast?"

"No, not a peep. Reception's not good up here and I like that." He knew exactly what was going on down there, but Jenks didn't want to admit to himself he was intrigued.

"Not on the phone. Remember? No phone is ever secure? Read the message."

"Right. Read it."

"You'll be back on your front porch in a few days. I promise."

"Max, really? You say that like you mean it. You do realize it's midnight here."

"Yes, and it's three a.m. in DC, and I need you there in the morning." Doherty waited for a response, but Jenks hadn't responded. "And Martin?"

"What?"

"Don't be so pissed off. You are reinstated with full pay and benefits." Col. Doherty's voice was a mixture of command, concern, and long comradeship.

"It's—" Jenks invoked an inner reserve, damping down his emotional response. "—my retirement benefits have been keeping in beans and bourbon just fine."

"I know Martin. When you leave a thing, you think you leave a thing. But sometimes the thing doesn't leave you." Martin had left Doherty listening to silence as he considered the fates. "Martin, you there?"

Jenks sighed; his breath, a thin blue cloud of mountain-chilled vapor, whisked away on the night air. "Let me get my travel bag together." He snapped the phone shut, thought briefly about throwing it to the trees, then pocketed it.

6

Pisser

Victor Paige slapped at a two-inch-long insect that dropped out of a scrub palmetto onto the side of his head. Both the human intruder and the resident insect moved to separate. Paige landed a slap on the side of his head shortly after the palmetto bug flew off into the early morning mist.

Paige cursed and elbowed another two feet closer to the frame house he hoped was the deep woods recluse of the Spacer Family. It was one of a few isolated private homes still inside the boundaries of the St. Marks National Wildlife Refuge on Florida's northern Gulf coast. Arching his back, he grabbed at the telephoto-equipped camera and aimed it toward the house that stood less than seventy yards away. At twelve feet above grade, the first floor provided parking and storage beneath the elevated floor required in the coastal hurricane surge zone. Two black nine-passenger SUVs were parked beneath the structure. A sheriff's green and white cruiser was parked a hundred yards up the driveway. *This has to be the Hitchens's house.* His initial view was almost in focus, but either the telephoto lens or the viewfinder had fogged in the damp air. "Dammit."

He dug into a front pocket of his photographer's vest for a lens wipe. As he polished the morning dew off his lens cover, a brilliant red dot, a little less than a quarter inch across danced across the back of his hand. "Shit! Laser scope!"

Fogged or not, he brought the camera up and snapped off a picture of the house. The digital camera's fake shutter sound was off so he snapped two more hoping the owner of the red laser wouldn't know he had the shots. The dirt and brambles two feet to his left erupted simultaneously with the subdued snap of a suppressed rifle. He felt his bowels loosen. He inadvertently let the camera drop to the dirt.

An amplified voice cut into the heavy haze. "Freeze! Do not move a muscle. Do not retrieve that camera. Do absolutely nothing." He heard the rustle of something approaching incredibly fast from under the house. A black Labrador retriever charged, braked badly in the loose soil, and stopped uncomfortably close to Paige's face. He didn't realize he'd lost

39

bladder control until he felt the warm liquid spreading in his crotch. Low and guttural, the dog whispered a threat from a satanic dream. Its breath smelled of recent kibble. Paige whimpered.

Black-clad boots approached next. "Good boy, Charlie. Good boy. Hold!" A gloved hand picked up his camera. "You on the ground, don't move until I say so."

Paige wasn't about to move. Aware of wet warmth spreading, he whimpered again; angry at himself for being caught so easily and angrier for wetting himself. He listened, immobilized in terror as the slide lock on the camera back clicked. Practiced fingers clicked open the tiny memory access port and popped out the memory chip. It fell, folded in half, in front of Paige's sweating face. The camera and lens followed— one, then the other.

The boot closest to him rotated slowly. Static pop. "Sir? Yessir. Got another one; third one in the last half hour. The perimeter detectors have two more coming in along what passes for a beach. And there's two more we know about out in the woods still. I think those are lost or just being clever." A quiet pause as the boots' owner received information. "Yes Sir."

Paige felt a hard, narrow object poke at his back near his spine. It could be a stick, could be the barrel of an automatic rifle.

"You. Get up."

He did so slowly and hoped he was non-threatening to both dog and man as he did. The Labrador issued another low growl as he stood erect. He took a half step back. He glanced at the dog. Its hackles bristled, reflecting shiny blue-black off the dew-moistened coat.

The commando-garbed figure faced him. His flat black automatic weapon slung casually across his chest. The guard's government issue garb made his own army-navy store purchases seem amateurish. Mirrored aviator sunglasses made eye contact impossible. "There were two others before me?"

"What did you expect? After last night's news flash, you'd be the only bright bulb who thought to come out here and snap off a few pics for the *Enquirer*?"

Victor did the math, three down, about nine more of his group were closing in. Reporters had gathered the night before in Tallahassee at a beer and pizza venue to plan strategies. Some would be arrested; some would get decent pics. They would share the results in their ad hoc reporter pool. Following gestures and minimal vocal instructions, Victor Paige walked toward the house he had been so furtively approaching just minutes ago. Coolness at his crotch and down his thigh presaged further humiliation to come. This was verified as they approached the black vehicle, and he noticed two other handcuffed shapes in the rear seat.

The guard's headset clicked again and something unintelligible spat in the man's ear. "Right." He looked up at Paige, "Sir, into the car with the other two." Then he noted the stink then the stain of urine spreading from Paige's crotch. The commando turned to him, cuffed a wrist to a car door handle, an winced in disgust. "Sir, let me get a towel from the house." As he walked off, Paige heard him mumble into his mic. "I'm going to the house to fetch a towel. Sum bitch pissed hisself." Another electric crackle, then, "Yessir."

Paige tried to stand proud, to ignore the dark stain spreading down his leg. It's cool wetness in a rising breeze branding him an idiot. Not soon enough, the guard returned with a towel. Gestures and nods were all Paige needed to hold out his wrists for the cuffs to be refastened behind him. The deputy doubled the towel and laid it out on the second row of seats. Paige caught his eyes and read the disapproval. The guard just said. "Stay!" before turning away. His tone was what he might have used on a dog.

"God," Paige said to himself as the door shut on the two previous captures. "I am so off this story." The two in the car's third row had air conditioning. The only upside to his situation was that he was no longer outside in the bug-infested humid hell of a hot Florida morning, he felt lower than dirt. *It's not even June yet for crying out loud. How can it be so hot?*

~ ~ ~

Martin Jenks rode down the narrow drive to the Hitchens' enclave wondering what further measures would be necessary to protect the site. Red and blue flashers at the entrance to Wakulla Beach Road would have warded off new interlopers, but the number of parked cars he'd already passed on the Coastal Highway indicated a number of groups had already come inside the perimeter from different directions. The palmetto scrub-lined drive to House One had been paved shortly after their relocation from their ancestral homestead at the top of the road. His car slowly approached the parked sheriff's cruiser. He lowered his side window, his eyes on the upper floors of the residence scanning for trouble. He absently flashed his ID badge at an approaching deputy.

Martin had argued at length with Brad and Connie for relocation to a much more secure location, but their determination to make do much farther down the road had been honored. House One lodged a full-time security detail, now badly overtaxed. House Two, constructed three years earlier three hundred yards deeper into the pervasive palmetto scrub, was deep into wildlife refuge property that was now clearly marked on all refuge visitor maps as: "Do Not Enter, Wildlife Sanctuary Area."

Locals with approved passes could still get access to the grassy beach but knew and respected the Hitchens family's need for privacy. Martin finished his scan of the house, mumbling, "thirty-two, thirty-three."

"Sir?" The deputy was handing the badge back to him. "You are free to continue on, Sir."

"Thirty-three damn cars that have no business being here." He remembered the count from his briefing file. "Up from the ten last week. I suppose it will get worse."

His blacked-out Escalade came to a stop behind two similarly detailed Chevy Suburbans parked beneath the elevated house. Jenks stepped out into a humidity level that challenged the senses. Trees dripped, eaves dripped, dampness immediately clung to any cool object and penetrated clothing. He remembered from his earlier work in the region that May was usually a dry period. This brought a dry huffing laugh that turned to a fist-covered cough.

He lifted his elbows in a futile attempt to air his pits. In one of the Suburbans parked on the concrete pad under House One, heads bobbed, probably trying to catch sight of him. He smiled grimly. "Ok," he addressed the driver across the hood, "let's see what we've caught so far."

He opened the back door of the occupied vehicle to the pungent smell of fear and sweat. Two heads swung his way and began to assail him with questions, or demands, or both.

"What are you going to do?"

"You can't keep us tied up here."

"That guy pissed all over the place. You can't put him in here with us!"

Jenks looked back at the handcuffed dejected captive standing next to a concrete house support. That one asked, "Are you going to bring charges or just keep us sweating out here?"

From the third row of the car, "I want a lawyer," and, "Arrest me or let-me-the-fuck-go."

Martin shook his head in amusement. He guided the standing, pee-stained captive onto the towel-draped seat in the second row and shut the door, amid a renewed round of complaints from the back seat. A black-clad member of the on-site security detail approached, bringing along another cuffed invader by the shoulder. "Special Agent Jenks, SO very glad you are here."

"Yeah." Jenks scanned the palmetto-lined perimeter of the yard. "Last week was just prequel, aye?"

"Yes Sir." A deputy in county green and gray took custody of the new arrival and parked the newest captive by cuffing him to an iron waterline that ran up into the house. The security guard continued, "Ten yesterday, but by then, probably half of these idiots were already in the woods. So far today we're up to nine." He glanced over his shoulder at the riot of green vegetation. "Sensors say there's more in the woods."

"I see four." Martin looked around. There were four accounted for right here, three in the car and one attached to the pipe. "Where are the rest?"

The guard gestured up with a jerk of his head. "Guest bedroom, running out of room up there. Sheriff's supposed to be sending his prisoner transport bus down. But it's only a nine-passenger van. He's going to have to make a couple of trips."

Martin nodded at the parked Suburban, calculating options. "Well, let's use one of these to help with that, OK?"

Chances were excellent that there were more out in the woods than they knew about. He glanced into the car's interior, then up at the supposed bedroom full of captures, then let his gaze again sweep the wall of green palmetto and high scrub that surrounded the grassed yard. "I'll call Langley and see if we can get a high-res IR scope on these woods. That'll help us locate any more that might be out there. Some are probably lost." He read the guard's name tag. "Pilcher, assume there's at least twenty more to be picked up from the woods. Another detail will be choppered in later this morning. Langley to Tyndall express." He looked out at the clearing to the south. He knew the half-mile buffer of salt grasses beyond cut off any clandestine approach from that direction. Farther out, a beautiful stretch of usually calm water extended a few miles before dropping off into the Gulf proper. He wished for a fishing rod and a different kind of day.

"I told you to stay!" The newest arrival was testing the grip of the handcuff against the size of his hand. The guard released the cuff and none to gently pressed the captive's shoulders up against a house support grayed with weather and speckled with algal green in areas where no sunshine ever touched.

"And fuck the horse you came in on, too." The new prisoner spat, narrowly missing Pilcher's boot.

Martin Jenks put a hand out to restrain the deputy, leaned toward the car full of captives, and addressed the closest captive to him, the only one not looking at him. "Hey, you."

Victor Paige turned; his embarrassment had morphed to rage. "WHAT? No one has said anything more than shut up and sit still. I want a lawyer, or charges, or a drink of water, or something to god-dammed-happen, or there will be hell to pay."

Martin smiled his best PR smile. "Sir, I respect that you may be uncomfortable, but we had a secure zone here. You all breached it, and in numbers that simply overstressed our holding capacity. I hear the Wakulla County Sheriff is coming for you and your—" He stopped. Thought about the captives upstairs. "Who are you all, anyway? He knew that he'd have a full day of interrogations, or more if they kept coming, but this might help. "Are you guys organized anti-somethings? What?"

A voice in the back seat spoke first. "Don't give him the time of day, guys."

"Oh well. OK, I've got all day." He moved to step aside and shut the car door. "But it smells pretty awful in there."

Paige's hostile glare softened to something that looked like supplication. "Please don't shut that door. Can we get out and stand until the sheriff's bus shows up?"

"Sure," Martin displayed only his public-friendly face. He'd dealt with hundreds of cases before, and could be commanding or beguiling as the case required. "But just one thing," and he switched into the local vernacular, "where y'all from?" As a black man raised on Montana's western slopes, his natural accent tended to a flat and untraceable broadcast English, but he had spent enough years in the south trailing the Hitchens that he could almost—almost pass for a local in polite society. He knew there was no way he could pass for a local in a black neighborhood, but it was good enough for these trespassers, whatever their intent was. Just now, all he cared about was containment.

No one had answered his first question. He lowered his sunglasses to the tip of his nose and peered into the Suburban, past Paige, and scanned the two in the back seat. "I said, where y'all from?" He just managed to step back fast enough to avoid a wad of spittle. He checked his shirt to see if he had really dodged the insult, shut the door, then glanced up to see how much longer before the sun's rays hit the black roof of the vehicle.

7

At the End of the Narrow Drive

At the end of the narrow two rut driveway leading to the new Hitchens home, one of the remaining commando-clad reporters crawled between two palmettos and eased out to look in both directions. Jackpot! *The* Hitchens homestead. Squads Three and Four were in custody. From the diminishing radio chatter, Squad Two was being intercepted. He keyed his handset and gave a click-pause-click-click signal for Squad One to advance.

Eyes left noted a gathering at target one, now known to be a blown target and in possession of the guard detail. They'd known there would be losses. Eyes right provided a good view of the quarter-acre clearing surrounding the main objective, the Hitchens homestead.

It was a new, but still a humble, home on concrete pilings sheathed in storm-resistant cement board siding. It was typical of thousands of Florida homes built above the hurricane surge zone. Two black-clad guards armed with radios, and two more in civvies stood under the Hitchens home near one of the parked vehicles. They were letting members of his group out of a black Chevy suburban and into a sheriff's prisoner transport van. The cluster under the elevated house seemed to be in an animated conversation.

Built to withstand hurricanes, the bottom floor was over twelve feet above grade. It was accessed by one of two stairways: one to the deck, another up into an enclosed stairway. The commando-clad reporter rolled sideways to relieve a cramp in his neck and maintain his view of the house and sent another click-pause-click-click message. He released the radio's call button as a piercing pain shot through the base of his brain. Behind him a cry of stifled pain. Across the roadway, a groan and a muffled, "What the hell?" Then his own head began to ache, no, to cry out in painful stabs that demanded he stop, wither into a ball, and cry softly for help.

He understood now that there would not be a successful assault on the house. There would be no story unless he pushed beyond the pain and made use of the pre-occupation of the guard unit. He got up and crept, keeping his profile lower than the four- to five-foot-tall palmetto scrub, then eased toward stairs leading up to a deck that had access to a double sliding door view into the house.

~ ~ ~

Connie sat with Myahh, soothing her with cooing and small strokes to the back of her head. Myahh, lay fetal curled in her arms, eyes scrunching in concentration. "Try not to worry about them, sweetie. The guards will protect us." At almost eight, the child sought solace from stress in her mother's arms, despite her determination to branch out, to see the world.

"But Mom, they don't like us!" She opened her eyes—black pools, irises thinned to mere green circles. She shut them in concentration. "Another one just found our house."

"Shhh, sweetie. The guards are taking care of them. There's nothing to worry about." In truth, Connie was very worried, and she hoped she was shielding her thoughts from Myahh. Brad was overdue. But as they'd learned. The long hops between star systems were fairly predictable and fast. It was the short jumps from polar entry to anything close to earth's orbit that could take a few days. Getting clearance from NASA to pass through the crowded techno-sphere of orbiting satellites also took time. Brad had said it was like crossing an interstate at night, except that the approaching trucks had their lights out and they were traveling at up to seventeen thousand miles per hour and could be approaching from almost any direction.

She looked at her auburn-haired beauty and tried to paint an unconcerned look on her face. "Honey, look at me. I'm right here, no one is going to bother us here." Myahh opened her eyes. Her irises were so dilated Connie doubted she could focus on anything nearby. The child turned her head toward Connie and the eyes did track her. "Honey? Are you feeling OK?"

A creak on the wooden stair to the south-facing deck indicated a weight at least as heavy as Brad's. Connie knew that her weight gave a particular squeak at the second step; her husband's step produced a multi-pitched complaint.

Myahh's head turned toward the noise, eyes closed again. She said, "There are six of them now. They are almost under the house. No, five. One is on the back porch. I told them not to come any closer." Myahh had always called the deck overlooking the needlegrass flats south of the

47

home a porch, a reference to the original Hitchens' cracker home that had front and back porches.

Connie could now feel the mental energy emanating from the intruder, she thought, very near the top of the stairs to that southern deck. She felt her pulse racing in her temples, knew that Myahh would pick up on her heightened anxiety, and wished to god that Brad was there. She didn't want to leave Myahh alone in the safe room. But she didn't want to engage the intruder alone. Where were the guards? Why hadn't they intercepted these guys? Six of them? Her mind raced through options.

She jumped, startled when the phone rang. She reached forward, holding Myahh close, and managed to grab her phone. The caller ID announced, "unknown caller."

"Hello?"

A shot rang out, somewhere close to the guard's house two-hundred yards to the east on Wakulla Beach Road.

"Hello?" Hiss and static. "Look, this isn't funny! There's a real situation going on here!" Hiss and static pops. "Is there anyone there?"

The hiss continued for half a beat before the line clicked and she heard over the poor connection, the familiar hum of the long-wave transceiver. "Hon? Can you hear me?"

"Brad! Yes, I'm so glad that's you." She felt as if the weight of the world had lifted. She took a deep breath and blew through pursed lips. "How far out are you?"

"Just finishing the last tests. So, just a short burn and translation through the atmosphere."

"How soon can you get here?"

"Is there a problem?"

She glanced toward the sliding doors to the bay-view deck. A shadow was lurking a few steps down from the top of the stairs. Its outline appeared to indicate a man talking on a field radio. She couldn't tell if it was an intruder or guard. Connie didn't want to cause Brad to make poor decisions in navigation, so she lied. "Yes, there's a report that some intruders are inside the perimeter. I think the guard detail has it under control." Myahh squirmed out of her grasp and stood stiffly facing the deck; a fierce, stiff figure leaning forward at full attention.

~ ~ ~

Martin Jenks saw a dark-clad figure sprint across the narrow driveway leading to the residence. He couldn't tell from a distance if it was one his or if he was a part of the circus they'd begun to collect as the intruders tripped various remote triggers. He scowled, suppressed a non-professional expletive, and keyed his mic. "Sutton? Graves? Pilcher? Anyone with ears on at the residence."

"Potts, here sir." A click and silence. Then, "Sir, there are multiple bogies coming in through the palmetto scrub from the east. They gotta be coming in through Refuge property."

Jenks hissed with barely suppressed anger, "Dammit, from here I can see one standing on the god-damned deck. Status?"

"Two apprehended, Sutton and Graves are going out on intercept."

"They've left their positions? Kee-rist," he muttered to himself, "heroes everywhere and no one wants to follow orders."

He keyed again, "Get that sucker off the deck, now, do ya hear me? And make sure you neutralize his dammed camera."

"Yes, Sir. Heading there now."

Jenks clicked again, "Where's Pilcher?"

"Not sure, Sir. She's been radio silent for about twenty minutes." A pause was highlighted by the threatening buzz of a yellow fly. Potts came back on the line, "She was on the refuge side of the perimeter. She may have been compromised. I hadn't had time to check her position."

Jenks wasn't sure when he'd started moving toward the Hitchens home, but the walk had turned to stride. He slid the radio into its holster as he broke into a Ranger's run. *I'm too old for this shit!* Only a few hundred yards, less than a minute he thought. He heard a scream from the house ahead. Not a female scream. "What the—?"

"Hold it right there." Martin had just run up to the base of the house, his sidearm unholstered. A man in an army surplus commando get-up was stumbling erratically down the stairs toward him. "I said hold it! Stop right there."

The ersatz commando stopped at the bottom of the stairs. His face a grimace of pain, he looked up at Jenks through watering eyes. Jenks holstered his service revolver. The man had stopped and leaned against the two-by-six railing, both hands to his ears. Martin took three steps toward the man and lifted his chin to force the man to look at him.

Hollowed eyes, black holes stared back. He recognized the look of bewildering pain. A migraine on steroids.

He shouted up at the house, loud enough to penetrate the double glass windows. "Myahh, calm yourself sweetheart. You're hurting the guy."

Gradually, the intruder's grimace softened from sheer agony to severe headache. "Sir, are you alright? Do you need medical assistance?" The man nodded as he yielded his camera to Jenks' gentle pull on its strap. "You realize I'm going to have to detain you but," he recognized the man's pain, "I think I can get you over to the medic. They'll give you a mild sedative." He pointed down the driveway. "That way. Let's go. Get you some separation and you'll feel better." He gave the man a light shove. He looked up at the deck, then the sliding glass door. Myahh was just inside smiling. He sent her an answering grin and a wave.

He picked up on a message; his psi skills were primitive compared to the varying levels of ability among the Hitchens. He picked up on the message that her dad would be home soon as he walked the moaning invader to the head of the drive and processing with the others. *Soon will not be soon enough.* He needed to get this family to a secure location.

Homecoming

Brad took a tentative sip at his steaming cup of coffee, then unabashedly slurped the too-hot liquid. The morning was cool for late Spring; a welcome relief to his neighbors along the North Florida coast who were acclimated from childhood to muggy mornings in the mid-eighties. Although cool, it was still muggy by any standard. Dawn's early light, filtered through the stand of mature pines behind the house, illuminated the moist air in slanted bands of light dusty yellow and darker blue-green. The season's last cold front from the poles had just made it across the Florida line. But, he knew, the afternoon had an excellent chance of temps in the low nineties. He sat on one of the several folding chairs arranged around the fire pit in the backyard of their new home. His first and only other home, the Hitchens family homestead, had many good memories, but too many hard ones; and it had been too close to the highway for privacy and more specifically, security.

The morning, animated by bird calls and the chirring of insects, was one of his favorite times of day. He thought back to the morning a few years back when on a similar dew-soaked morning, he had first become aware of the psi presence of Jai, his still-buried spaceship.

A short chuckle spasmed his chest muscles just enough for him to spill a few drops of coffee onto his T-shirt. He batted at the droplets, closed his eyes, and let the magical memory of Jai's emergence out of a muddy forest pool replay in his mind's eye. Barely hanging on in the howling winds of Hurricane Kate's landfall, he and Connie had stood transfixed. He with one arm around a pine, the other firmly grasping Connie's linked arm. The ship's iridescent force field glowed as sheets of cyclone-fed rain burst into steam on the ship's energy shield.

His eyebrows knitted at the ensuing memory of the dead pilot inside the ship and his initial confused understanding that the 'friend' they had been having telepathic conversations with for years was actually Jai, the ship's AI. Conversations with the artificial intelligence had driven his mother to the edge of madness but had drawn Connie into his world. He opened his eyelids and turned to his right. Barely visible, and only because of the heavy humidity and because he knew where to look, the spaceship Jai sat in cloaked mode. Brad thought he's probably listening to me think about him. I'm gonna have to see if he can develop a privacy mode that doesn't interfere with his security screening ops. The AI had always had a distinct masculine identity. But then, when he'd first encountered Jai's psi presence deep in the St. Marks National Wildlife Refuge's wild scrub woodlands, Brad had thought he'd been communicating with an grounded alien fighter pilot. He'd assumed a male. Now as he thought about it, that masculinity had only been an assumption. He'd have to ask Connie how he thought of Jai.

His revery was interrupted when he heard the familiar slide of the back door. He raised on an elbow to look up to their water-view deck. Connie was framed in the sliding door, she found where he was sitting and waved.

"Con? Is Shaand awake yet?"

In response, she stepped to the side as the sliding screen door slid full open. Shaand emerged holding two cups of coffee. He stood aside as Connie followed carrying three plates with the skill of a practiced waitress. Brad leaned over to reverse the cover of the fire pit, creating an impromptu breakfast table. Shaand silently sent out the simple psi greeting exchanged between friends that had no time stamp like the human "good morning." Both Connie and Brad returned it in their fashion that had become custom over their years as friends and confidants.

Settling in to the morning meal Brad turned to Connie. "Myahh still asleep?"

"Yes. She's a little worn out but she'll be ok."

Shaand spoke toward the tree line. "I am sorry the press broke through security lines." He scanned left and right around the backyard's lining of scrub palmetto as if more of the commando-garbed press corps might be hidden behind the wide palmetto fronds.

"Bastards." Connie mouthed a spitting motion to her side. "They somehow think they are entitled to know our bathing habits. There's a limit to what I can accept in honoring, 'the public's right to know.'" She snipped air quotes with a fork in one hand and a mug in the other. "The first amendment doesn't allow making stuff up and calling it news."

Brad said, "I'll talk to Colonel Doherty. He promised he was going to put an additional ring of motion sensors farther outside the line of sight of the house." He paused to take another spoonful of cheese grits. His thoughts ran to the Colonel's service as the new director of the B-Team. The former head of the re-authorized B-team, the disgraced Colonel Bud

Henderson, had been replaced. With his departure, the B-Team's former mission of blanking all serious reports of alien activity or UFOs with memory-erasing drugs and brainwashing was finally discontinued.

The Air Force's covert disinformation squad had made Brad Hitchens' life a cloak-and-dagger misery until the fact of an alien presence on Earth became impossible to hide. Henderson had stood before a court-martial for misappropriation of funds, undue harassment, and a slew of violations of the uniform code of military justice. In response, he had simply posted a series of memos, budget authorizations, and finally, emails outlining the members of the congressional oversight committee in charge. For good measure, he included minutes of several of the key meetings at which they had continued to authorize the B-Team's existence while denying its mission had ever been approved. Despite his efforts at blame avoidance, the actual evidence of an alien corpse and validated UFO radar coverage from multiple locations in Florida, Georgia, and Alabama had made the former mission of the B-Team moot. The cat was unbagged. Brad's alien ship had been observed too often in U.S. airspace.

There might have been more complications for the B-Team's former head, but the overriding news story during Brad's first year back had been the very real presence of Shaand. He was a living ambassador from another planetary system with limited, but usually adequate, English-speaking abilities. After being humiliated in a televised senate hearing, Colonel Henderson accepted the fact that his career was over and pushed for his aide to take over. Lt. Colonel Doherty took the promotion to full bird colonel and oversaw the transition of the agency from hyper-secretive to an information-parsing agency. I was still not a fully transparent agency; it *was* the Air Force after all. Doherty's chief responsibility was corralling the Hitchens family and the Elioi ambassadors to Earth while attempting to secure their safety on a human world. The job proved to be difficult considering Earth is populated by several billion paranoid xenophobes.

~ ~ ~

As Brad and Connie continued their conversation on their home's security, Shaand took in the complex flow of emotions passing between his Terran hosts. He had learned that the human concept of bonding love between couples, absent in his own culture, was of major importance in human family units. Born and raised in a creche, he'd become used to the fact that monogamy was a Terran cultural norm, even as Brad had informed him that it often did not work out. The additional fact that this particular couple had developed a psi bond as well marked a new

53

development for humans that might very well open a massive pharmaceutical market on Earth for the extract of the selli plant that opened and enhanced latent psi abilities. Before this could become a commercial option, the plant's extract had to be vetted through many countries' separate drug licensing agencies.

Human society was wrapped and bound in its multiple layers of ethnic and political separations. He knew that historically, his Elioi culture had separate countries, as the humans called them. There had been centuries-long sparring between the cultures from the northern and southern continents, and before recorded histories, even political separations between isolated groups. But with little intra-species differentiation, there was no record of ethnic contests. Essentially, there was one genetic variety of Elioi.

The working class was not allowed selli fruit, and in his understanding of recorded time, there had never been any sign of turmoil between the classes. The last major politically driven warfare had been between the planet-bound Dzurans and the space-faring asteroid farmers who had colonized Dzura's sister planet, Erra. The cataclysmic warfare drove eighty percent of the Dzurans from their homes and nearly destroyed the ecosystem of the planet. That war had been over four hundred years ago and now, after the revolt, the homeworld Dzurans held the upper hand.

Connie asked the two of them. "How was the trip? Can you finally tell me what it was about?"

Brad shrugged. "I have no idea why they wanted to keep it secret, from you or anyone. We simply went up to the ISS to test the new docking mechanism installed on the ambassador ship's airlock."

"Seriously?"

"Serious." Shaand answered. "Not know why for secrets. Seems like a good idea to me. If there is trouble on ISS, we can evacuate entire crew in twelve hours."

"Well," Brad countered, "we'd have to get to the secure hangar over at Tyndall first for your ambassador's shuttle."

"OK." Shaand corrected, "maybe twelve and a half hours."

Shaand's forehead wrinkled in a smile. He sensed Myahh's waking thoughts and could then hear her early calls of hello. Connie rose and went up to the house to tend to her. There was a lot to be said for the tenderness in a human family unit. He watched Brad's wife skip up the stairs to the back deck and turned to him, eyebrows raised.

He said, "Brad, I was just thinking about the structure of hooman families and comparing it to my creche class. I never felt neglected, but the intimacy of parent to child is missing. I can see that it is especially important to hoomans."

Brad sighed, "Yeah, human families have strong bonds. Very different from the creche loyalty, a little fiercer, I think." He paused reflecting on some families he'd known to be the exception. "I wish it was universal though. If it were, there would be a lot less suffering on this world."

Shaand's forehead now adopted the horizontal wrinkle, a frown. "Some creche not too strong too, on Dzura. Need more loyalties there too, I think."

They both looked up as Myahh flew down the steps and ran out into the yard. "Morning Uncle Shaand. Good morning, Daddy!" She bent over the back of his chair and hugged Brad's neck.

Shaand and Brad shared a look of understanding. They had been friends for years and much could be communicated in a look and a short psi burst. Myahh moved in front of her dad's chair, took her father's head in hers, and got nose-to-nose close. She liked to do that and cross her eyes, giving Brad a twinge of a headache. But this was no game.

She said, "Daddy, today is the day. They are here." She glanced over to her "uncle" Shaand and psi'd, *Today they are coming.*

I know sweetie. Then he vocalized. "I will have to leave soon to talk about the new visitors with some very important people. Will you promise to look out for your mother and Aunt Lenka?"

Myahh grinned and tilted her head coquettishly. "Of course, Dad." Then she straightened up, serious. "You do know I wasn't talking about those fake commandos, don't you? The 'they' is the Jhen-an Shay-Ka." She smiled now; head tilted. "The Jhen-an Shay-Ka came a long long way." Her pronunciation of the Precursor's chosen name was spot on Lenka's correction of her earlier attempts.

She blinked at a new thought. "Daddy?"

"Yes, sweetie. What"

"Can I go out to the garden today?"

Brad thought about it. He knew from Myahh's commentary that an entity in the solar 'anomaly' was talking to her. And that it was digesting decades of human history from terrestrial data sources. But whether it would arrive today, in their yard, or in some other world-shaking location, he couldn't pretend to guess. But, he thought, a short trip out into the woods to visit the garden might be a good idea. He could stretch his legs and maybe clear the path of any deadfall in case he wanted to go for a run later. Then a dark thought crossed his mind. What if any of the press commandos had happened on their garden as they sought unencumbered access to their backwoods property.

"Sure hon, let's go after breakfast."

He caught Shaand's eye. "Let's go check on the Selli Garden in a little while, OK?"

Moving On

Martin Jenks set his phone on the table, leaning it against a potted miniature rose that served as the coffee table's centerpiece. With some effort, he'd gotten his sat link connected to Creech AFB and Col. Doherty. He plugged the earpiece in for privacy, but he knew that Connie and Lenka would probably pick up on his conversation from downstairs if they chose to. Myahh, if she put her mind to it, could probably seek out and listen to the other side if she wanted to. A click in his ear signaled the line was finally open. "How's that signal now, Sir?"

The voice came in scratchy, but distinct. "It could be better. As much as this outfit spends on comm gear, you'd think we could do better. Don't ya think?"

"Yes Sir, I do." The noise in the background sounded more like lawn sprinklers than static. Martin wondered if the Colonel was on the golf course again, further compromising any signal. "Sir, we're running into what amounts to a major security problem."

"Yes!" Indistinct noise. "I read the morning sitrep on your breakdown in perimeter integrity. Seems pretty much non-existent. What are you proposing? Or should I ask, how much is it going to cost me?"

Martin had not had time to put together a plan, much less a budget. He could only wait a few seconds before Doherty would assume the line was dead and move on to the next golf shot. "Sir, the second house we've put them in worked great for almost six years now. But for the last two days we've had a concerted ambush of almost thirty commando-looking press corps trickling in through the woods. They'd send in decoys straight up the driveway taking out a number of our guys just to process the arrests. Others would be creeping through the palmettos, getting far too close. If any of them were shooting bullets instead of live-link video, we'd have our first inter-planetary situation. I don't think we'd do very well in that case."

"Um-hmm,"

Doherty's long pause made Martin Jenks worry that the line had actually gone dead. Then the background pulsing, tsk, tsk, tsk of sprinklers came in all too clear. *He must be walking the course.* Doherty's voice came back with a note of exertion. *Yeah, he's walking the course.*

"Jenks? It would take those fuzzy critters over thirteen years to find out, a few months more to mobilize, and another thirteen years to show up. I think we could take them."

Martin's incredulity did not escape his reply. The "Sir?" came out an octave higher than normal. He started over. "Sir. Colonel Doherty. You can't be serious." He thanked any God who would listen that Shaand was not due to arrive for a few more hours.

"No, no, no!" There was laughter on the other side of the line. "Just kidding, but you know? We got to the moon on a dare in nine years, think what we could do in twenty-seven."

"Sir!" The rising notes in Jenks's response mirrored his rising concern.

"No," more laughter, "it was just a reach. I mean, but maybe it's not so outlandish a thought that maybe we should be prepared. What do you think?"

"I think it's absurd, but don't quote me. And if you do, I'll deny it." Martin was glad he was pulling down a mid-range O-5 pay grade as a civilian advisor, instead of his E-7 retirement pay as a thirty-year retired Master Sergeant. He could mouth off to the Colonel when the man got in one of his moods. "Seriously, Sir? From what I've seen from the two I've gotten to know; they seem a peaceful lot. And besides, they just got through with a pretty disastrous civil war and I don't think they could retool. Their planet was blasted almost to their version of a stone age so they don't have anything like the manufacturing capability they'd need to be a threat. From the reports Ambassador Leeink-Knaa has been providing, they're still deep into rebuilding basic infrastructure."

"OK, just playing devil's advocate here. What about the losing side? They lost city ships and their ability to rule the homeworld, but their off-world capability to build space fleets is intact, right?"

"Well, I suppose so. I don't know." Martin hated to think of it now, but he'd had the same thoughts. He'd just never shared them out loud; not to anyone with rank. "But Sir, I have a more immediate problem I need the authorization to solve today. We can talk about those scenarios some other time."

"Go ahead, what do you need?"

"Colonel, I need to get the Hitchens and their guests off this property by tomorrow morning." He huffed in exasperation, turned to look toward the shallow saltwater bay where he'd rather be fishing. "And I really don't want to tell a whole lotta people where I'm taking them."

Silence, actually the rhythmic now-unmistakable sound of a lawn sprinkler filled his earpiece for a moment. "OK, yesterday was as bad as you—"

"Sir, any worse and there'd be bodies to dispose of."

"Then do what you've got to do. For transport, use assets at Tyndall or Moody. I'll send you authorization codes and just ask if you need something. Get it done, Martin. I trust you'll be inventive."

Martin Jenks felt his lungs go empty. The sigh of relief was so deep, he realized he'd been listening almost without breathing. "Thank you Sir. I'll keep you posted." He leaned back into his chair and ran his fingertips through the white burr surrounding his balding scalp. He thought, *I should get a haircut.*

1

Brussels

As they traveled the capitals of the world, Shaand was always duly impressed by the extent and complexity of the Terran global transportation system. His experience with the centuries-old train and transit systems on his native Dzura prepared him for the large public spaces of human transit terminals, but the various modes of travel amazed him. He'd left a war-ravaged planet with virtually no air transport capability. He knew from Grav-wave communications that much of its functionality had been restored, but the cities on the surface were still in major rebuilding mode.

His trip to the European Union's headquarters was multi-modal: arrival in Brussels via military charter jet, a direct flight from Tallahassee to Brussels. Then a short public train trip to the government building complex, and to Shaand's surprise, a brief auto ride through crowded public streets to the local offices of the European Space Agency. The variety of buses, trucks, private and for-hire automobiles, motorcycles and bicycles was overwhelming.

The rebuilding cities on Dzura were incorporating moving slidewalks in wide concourses designed for pedestrians. Almost nobody traveled in anything that wasn't a public multi-passenger vehicle. The comparisons were literally, worlds apart. He would never understand the human desire for the private transportation vehicles that crowded their cities.

The ESA's offices were expecting the visiting ambassador, but his appearance on public streets usually caused a stir. The trip might have been made in far less time in Jai, or Shaand's personal diplomatic shuttle, but the persistent human suspicion of Elioi presence tended to bring out the militantly xenophobic.

The High Representative of the European External Action Service had requested the briefing. Brad Hitchens considered it a courtesy call because NASA and the Joint Chiefs were in full support of the mission to check out the new monitor in the asteroid belt. They would be leaving for the distant ring of rugged asteroids almost immediately upon their return to Florida.

60

The destination today was a simple wood-paneled conference room. An elongated conference table was already populated with officials from the world's multiple space agencies. Many, Brad thought, were here just for the opportunity to meet the Elioi Ambassador.

Juan Alvarado of Spain, the current chair of the ESA's new projects sub-committee, left the podium and welcomed the two newcomers to the gathering. Brad shook his hand and stood back to allow Shaand a turn. Alvarado blanched, hesitated, then acquiesced to the required formality. He seemed to struggle through the handshake with the furry grip of the Elioi Ambassador. The four-knuckled, three-fingered grip with its symmetrically opposite thumb was unusual at first, and Shaand had learned to configure his hand to lessen the weirdness of his grip for human interactions.

Shaand was dressed in formal Terran business attire. Blue suit with a subdued pinstripe, light blue shirt, and gunmetal gray tie. But he knew that good tailoring never quite shook off the surprise of a first meeting. He put on the toothy grimace that mimicked a human smile.

"Thank you for meeting with us today. We are honored to meet with esteemed leaders of Earth's space initiatives. We come to you for information share." He looked over at Brad. In formal settings, he often felt insecure about his phrasing. Brad nodded, urging him on. "You now know that there are two—" he floundered for the word, "—objects in your star system. These are not Elioi. We not know from where, these objects originate, but we know of them from long before. If Earth vessels go to see these, take many years for mission design, then many months for travel. We have solution."

"So you understand. The Elioi have a primitive navy. Yes, we are in space for many hundred years. But long ago civil war was…devastating to our space capacity. Now, Elioi vessels have small weapons in use for protection." Several heads looked up from their briefing folios. The Elioi navy had not been commented on in their profiles of the ambassador. "I simple say, Elioi not have appropriate vessel for approach with hostile intent or show in force." Something in that last sentence didn't sound right, even to his own ears. English was a hard language, hardest were the fricatives. But there are so many different words and so many shades of meaning!

Brad offered, "Our discussion with NASA and the Space Force generals confirmed it best to investigate the alien vessel in a peaceful manner. We intend to use a ship with no offensive weapons."

One of the assembled diplomats raised a hand in question.

"No weapons? But this could be a very dangerous encounter."

Shaand agreed. "Yes, possible danger. I go, and too, Ambassador Hitchens. We go. Propose to take my ambassador's vessel. Only weapons are to shoot into vapor minor space debris. Hope to show no threat."

Brad stepped up beside Shaand, leaned into the microphone. "We have the sanction of the United States, as Ambassador Shaand has said. We seek your backing and approval also. It is our understanding that there are no initiatives at this time from the Russians or Chinese to attempt to reach these, uhm, visitors to our solar system." He looked around the table, his raised eyebrows an invitation to counter that statement. None came and he continued. "Through normal diplomatic channels at the UN, we are expressing our hope that no radio or laser signaling be made toward either of the two Sol system monitors prior to our visits."

The diplomat from France raised a hand. "Is there going to be a live feed? How will you keep us, or anyone, informed?"

Brad nodded yes, looked at Shaand, then answered. "I'm not going to promise a completely open channel. We know we can patch into Luxemburg's IntelSat communications array. Not a direct connection as the technologies don't mesh, but sort of a piggyback. The impact of something, well, anything that we find might need some buffering before it's released to the public."

Side discussions began in several corners of the table. Some of the diplomats and/or scientists around the table seemed to agree. The German facilities director from Darmstadt was overly loud in explaining to the Italian tech leader what had just been said. Not all of the diplomats looked happy about possibly provoking the alien craft. Some of the grumblings appeared to be growing more unreceptive to the idea of going there at all.

Brad waited a moment for the conversations to quiet down and raised his palms for attention. "Gentlemen, please. For the past seven years, Shaand and I have seen a wide variety of, eh, reactions to the Elioi Ambassador. They range from astonishment to suspicion to fear to simple xenophobic hatred." He waited for a beat, took a breath. "Even among the most liberal and welcoming gatherings, there is a noticeable visceral subtext of unreality, no, of non-acceptance of this new reality. People have said more than once that they feel like they are on a movie set." He looked at his friend, then meaningfully back at his small audience. "This is for real, there are others out there that neither of us understands."

Shaand interrupted. "We do not have idea what we find on our trip to the craft in the belt. We may find intelligent beings; a crew operating these monitoring vessels, or simple remote operated, survey, eh—"

"Surveillance equipment." Brad offered.

"Yes, surveillance machines." Shaand opened his palms wide in an Elioi shrug. "My friend Brad has same problem with some on my home planet. Is nature of most species, I think, to be afraid of what we do not know." He put a hand on Brad's shoulder. "I meet my friend Brad in prison. My old Dzuran enemy, catch him in space, toss him in prison with me and other prisoners to see if he had dangerous germ."

His smile, vertical wrinkles furrowing his brow, was lost on most of the gathering. "We not get sick. We become friends. We learn some speak to each other. We learn Brad is smart, we welcome Brad as trusted warrior. But this, only after time to meet, talk, eat together." No one caught his psi-expressed chuckle. "But first time I see Brad, I see ugly, hairless being. I scared. I think Brad get Dzuran prisoners sick with alien poison."

Brad took up the important dialogue. "Xenophobia is not only a human trait, a result of our tribal background. It may very well be universal. What we do not want to have is a camera feed live to the world media when we have no idea if we are going to find a benevolent humanoid dressed in shimmering gowns, or a scaled, seven-fingered amphibian with triple eye stalks. Whether angels or devils or machines, we need to be able to introduce whatever is found carefully or we will have the world in rapture or panic."

Shaand leaned into the mic. "The vessel found in your asteroids belt many years ago is from beings we call the Jhen-an Shay-ka, or the ones who come before. More simply in English, the Precursors. In our system, the Precursor monitor departed long time ago, before our civil war. Before Errans destroy Dzura twenty-seven years ago. The Sol system monitor leave too but taken by former enemy Elioi. In many years of survy ... surveillance, no contact from Precursors." He glanced over to his Terran friend. "Maybe we find nothing but cameras and radios. We may find nothing but machine. But maybe we find Precursor being, a watcher maybe. We simple ask, no leak news to public, we share what we find after briefing at UN security council first."

Brad felt that most of the salient points had been made and wanted to get on to their next step. "I trust you all realize how important it will be to avoid panic or even unwarranted stress in your respective populations. I know the people back in my rural country back home will go a little crazy if the other culture, the Precursors, ends up looking like insects or some other monster from their recollections of science fiction." He scanned the room, ensuring eye contact. "I trust that you all understand the delicacy of any information we might discover, and how important it is to agree on when and how to disclose it."

Several at the table seemed about to speak when a reluctant hand raised. "Just one question, then, *sil vous plait*." The chairman, a deep space researcher on the Webb telescope team asked, "When do you propose to leave, and how long will a voyage in your ambassador ship take?" He scanned the other faces at the table. "A few of us have been talking about this. Even if we had a launchable mission on a pad, and that's at least six months away, we would be another three and a half years at best in approaching an object in the asteroid belt. As it is, that object is not readily approachable for almost two years. The second object or vessel between Earth and the Sun would take almost two years if the mission did not have a return trajectory." He coughed. "That mission would be a suicide dive into the sun."

Brad cleared his throat. The veiled request for information on the technologies behind the Elioi shuttle's inter-system drive was the subject of ongoing speculation, its exhaust spectra had been analyzed and debated for years. "Mr. Chairman, Ambassador Shaand and I expect to be in an approach to the asteroid belt vessel's location within the week." Amid growing unrest in the small chamber, he raised his palms for quiet before continuing. "I know you would all like to have a glimpse of the technologies involved. I'm sorry. I will say that once clear of the Earth's magnetosphere, a matter of a day's travel using conventional physics, the jump to near the target is well, almost instantaneous. Then a normal hydrox propulsion-driven approach to the target, taking a day or more to ensure that the approach is not deemed threatening or, even worse, targeting." He smiled. "We certainly don't want to be mistaken for incoming ordinance. Do we?"

Nodding heads and smiles, and a few blank faces of incomprehension. Brad smiled and turned to Shaand. "How long do think it will take for us to get to the Solar monitor?"

Shaand said. "If distance calculations are close, perhaps a similar time frame. Still, such an approach cannot be thought to be a threat."

The committee chair's mouth hung open as if ready to pose a question. Brad asked, "Are there any concerns you all have that we haven't addressed?"

A hand raised slowly. "Yes?"

Brad invited the Italian astronaut who had been quiet.

"Do you need volunteers to assist?"

The offer was slow in coming in heavily accented English. But the intense black eyes of the young woman spoke of her sincerity. This was the first offer of help from outside the U.S. and Brad felt gratified. Maybe the effort to reach out to the world community was actually working.

"Ma'am, the first mission to the asteroid belt is manned by a former ISS mission commander, Colonel Leonid Kuznetskov of RosCosmos. He has been cross-trained and certified on the Elioi ambassador's ship for basic navigation." He saw the face fall and relax in disappointment. "But we will be more than happy to include you or someone from your space agency in the expanded training program. Please, do contact NASA."

11

Reverend Ehler

To say the church was huge would be an underestimate. The Good Reverend Ehler stood at his reserved parking space and scanned the new exterior modifications. It was a grand palace and a grand place to worship the word as he chose to deliver it. Only historical photographs of the building would reveal that the bones beneath its two-and-a-half-acre footprint were those of a former Walmart superstore. The chain had moved to a new superstore further out in the suburbs.

In the conversion from superstore to mega-church, half of the parking lot had been taken up and prepped as a multi-purpose athletic field. The shaded outdoor garden area had been retained, providing shaded outdoor play areas paved in rubber mulch for the younger age ranges of the student body. To his right, the auto shop was being renovated for a tech college. He knew the jobs of the future would be in the service industries and his young army of worker bees would be emissaries of his word as they repaired plumbing, electrical panel boxes, and refrigerators. To the left, a Pre-K through twelfth-grade school took up most of one and a half acres of floor space. In the center, under a forty-foot ceiling, was his tabernacle. His super-sized arena. It was all part of his plan, God's plan. There was no difference in his mind.

It all worked as long as he threaded the line between maintaining his credo's creationist roots and opting for just enough science in the curriculum to explain how all that tech stuff worked. He didn't really understand it himself.

Smiling with self-satisfaction, he shut his car door and walked to his private entrance thinking now of the day's telecast. He didn't need a crowd; a microphone would do just fine. The income from a televised appeal to the thousands on broadcast and blog was easily twenty and often forty times the take from the plate on a three-service weekend. Yes, business was good. Two weeks prior, the thirty-year mortgage had been paid off in its fourth year. Yes, business was good. Business was God. There was no difference in his mind.

The short private elevator up to his office suite was functionally the fastest route to work, but he often missed the walk through the grand entrance down the long, carpeted approach to the stage. He did not use a pulpit, all he needed was a clip-on microphone and room to walk around on the elevated stage while working the crowd into a frenzy. A well-rehearsed four-piece band and a genuine Wurlitzer helped set the tempo, the crescendo, and the climax. Boom, boom crash, payday.

This day was different. He had a new news story to bring to his flock. That little girl in Florida was said to be a human baby. But do we really know that? How did she get the skills that are being reported? Effortless mind reading, thought control, transmitted migraines? These were not human skills. The kid was a freak, and not a freak of nature. Not one of the messengers, prophets, disciples, or sages in the Bible had been able to conjure another's thoughts or project thoughts. And the military! That family was awfully close, perhaps too close, with the military. What kinds of abilities, tricks of mind control, and manipulation were being given to the American military? Does anyone really trust the government? Yes, there was a lot to talk about.

He sat down at his desk, shut down the email pop-ups, and got to work. Wednesday night's sermon was going to be great!

~ ~ ~

Martin Jenks adjusted his weight in Brad's chair, uncomfortable at his host's desk, uncomfortable in his bones, and uncomfortable with the incident assessment and the news he had to share with Connie. He reflected that he'd spent the lion's share of his career following, spying on, rescuing, and being rescued by the Hitchens. After the nearly three decades of their disappearance, he'd been tapped to be their personal concierge to the combined efforts of the U.S. government to protect the family from the overbearing and most recently overwhelming prying eyes of the free press. His hair had receded halfway back across his coffee-colored scalp, the remaining fringe was snow-white when it gained any thickness. His stomach was still flat from a grueling daily workout, but his knees seemed to be getting tired of the abuse.

CNN was on but muted. He had been watching the scroll underneath the talking heads. The news wasn't good. Images of the Hitchens house taken through a foreground of palmetto foliage clearly depicted members of his black-suited crew bringing a civilian in from the underbrush surrounding the Hitchens' house toward one of several black SUVs. The scroll read, "MEDIA AMBUSH ON SPACER HOUSE-

HOLD." The secondary line, a stationary overprint above the looping images read, "Hitchens household location leaked to press results in overload for local law enforcement." He didn't need the audio on, he'd been there after all.

Connie called out from the kitchen, "Martin, can I get you anything to go with that sandwich? Tea? Coke?"

"Tea please, sweet, no ice. Thanks." He looked through the picture windows across the expanse of needlegrass to the south. The view would be beautiful on any magazine cover to be sure, but it was hostile as hell for humans. Nearly impassible on foot, and populated by millions of biting insects, it was a better view than a reality. He knew the history of the area held remnants of salt vat installations used in the civil war to provide the southern army and economy with salt. He couldn't imagine the life they lived manning those installations. They were sheltered by copses of trees on small islands surrounded by the grasslands and distanced from offshore shelling by miles of ocean too shallow to bring in the gunships. Soldiers, civilians, slaves, and native Seminole Indians worked the shallows, boiling brine down to a brine slurry that was taken inland for air drying. *But the bugs! My God.*

"Oh my God!" Connie exclaimed coming into the room. "We've made national news again."

Jenks turned to face the television again. A panel of experts was ready to give their take on the few days' media storm in North Florida. He was happy to see that none of them were from the lunatic fringe. One was a retired Air Force general, another from Florida State University, a Dr. label preceding his name but expertise unknown, and another was labeled Rev. Drake Ehler.

Connie set a tray of diagonal-cut sandwiches and glasses of tea down on the coffee table. "So Martin, are they upset? What's the current problem?"

"I'm not sure, Connie. I haven't been listening." He shook his head in disgust. "They managed to get some video coverage out to the national press. We couldn't have gotten them all, just too damn many of them. Thicker than gnats."

Her face reflected her concern. "I'm sorry you had to cut into your retirement, Martin. It's been a while hasn't it."

"That's ok, if it weren't for having to get you and yours out of town tonight, I would have borrowed a to try out some new flies."

"What should I do? Brad's off..." She paused, in thought.

"What's his schedule?"

"Well, I'm not exactly sure where he is today. He and Shaand are in Europe somewhere bouncing around capital cities. They did the EU in Belgium yesterday, I think then they were off to Paris, Rome, Cairo, Tel Aviv, eventually, Brasilia, Tokyo, Beijing, and I think Mumbai. Somewhere in all of that, the two of them are supposed to check out that new thing in the asteroid belt. So, today, I really don't know where he is. Are we safe here?"

"You're good for today, tomorrow we'll be even safer. We have our guys patrolling and that innocent airstream camper up the road is actually a command and listening post. We've got motion sensors, IR cameras, and microphones set up on a perimeter a half-mile out. And patrols under and near the house at all times."

"Good, I feel better. And with all this extra protection, I feel better about Myahh and Lenka."

"How's Myahh?"

"Still asleep, last I checked." Jenks watched as she cocked her head, stared off into nothing then returned her sightline to him. "Yes, sleeping soundly. Well, either that or she's got her iPad under the covers again. But she's low on energy. She wore herself out listening to and harassing the press corps."

"Lenka? How did she take it?"

Connie beamed. "Lenka is a real trooper." She seemed to look off into space again. "Not only was Leeink-Knaa helpful in getting me situated after Myahh was born, but she had been on the team that helped engineer the downfall of the city-ships. She helped win the revolution, a real hero back home."

Jenks puckered and blew an almost silent whistle. "She's a companion to Shaand?"

Connie's head jerked back in reaction. "No, heck no." Her head began to vibrate a no, certainly a no message. "If anything, she's a companion to me." She smiled at a memory. "You know, she wasn't picked to come here because she was just handy at the creche nursery. She's a formidable force on her own."

Jenks thought about that. What did that really mean out of her element? What were her skill sets? "How about other help here, your family, er, you Aunt Lucy has an updated security pass. Do you still want access for your people over in Apalachicola?"

69

"Mom should still get access, and Aunt Lucy, yes, of course. She's great with Myahh and is even beginning to take some of our first harvest of Selli fruit to see if she can build up her psi ability. She was the first one to hear voices out there, years ago, before Brad, before me." She frowned in memory, "I think that was about 1975 or 6. Yeah, 1976 because I was about to become a senior that year. Lucy, by then had been gone for a few years, to Nevada." She looked up to meet Martin's eyes again. "And yeah, if you can still arrange it, I'd like to be able to have my own mother and my brother's family over if they can come." She thought about their impending move to Martin's mountain redoubt. "When we get back, that is. I think it's important for Myahh to stay in touch with her family and for Lenka to see how an interconnected human family gets along."

Martin just nodded, thin-lipped in distraction. "Sure, I'll get them all new gate passes. But those guys out there today are my people, not deputies. I'll have to get a list prepared." He sighed, one of true regret. "And Connie. I think I'm going to have to shut down access to Wakulla Beach."

"Oh Martin, no! Really?"

"As long as you're here, as long as Myahh and Lenka are here, there's a danger that somebody with bad intent gets through the screening, meets up with somebody out on the flats and brings in some serious weaponry, maybe only remote surveillance equipment. This place just isn't secure enough."

He watched Connie deflate. She'd had to give up the home she started with Brad in his family's homestead because it was too close to the Coastal Highway. The new house, much further from open public access, was still off a county road and only accessed by approved locals. "Dammit Connie, it's just not working out."

He felt a twinge of psi invading his thoughts. He was getting used to its utility but was still surprised by the unanticipated intrusions. He recognized that Lenka had been listening from her room. "Yes, Lenka, there is danger to you too." He said it aloud but addressed it toward the hallway. Momentarily, a door opened and the female Elioi ambassador came down the hall to join them.

She said, "Martin, I think you correct. Need more safe, secure location for Myahh." Lenka was almost five feet in height, her white fur complemented by a navy-blue one-piece uniform. Its only identifying emblem, the three-cornered logo signifying her home sun and its twin planets. A light blue braid around her left cuff signified her status in the diplomatic corps. Her critics said she looked like a cross between a meerkat and a fox. Martin thought she had a she-wolf's predatory stare unless her hairless forehead relaxed in the wrinkles that signaled a smile.

He followed her stare toward the still silent television. "Lenka, I'm sorry, but our media is blowing itself up again with too much idle spin."

"Is spinning?" He recognized her look of vocabulary confusion.

"The people they bring on to discuss what they think are facts are too often only concerned with their agenda. Their agenda, is more often than not, hostile to anything that could suggest humans might not be the highest form of life."

"That silly." Lenka glanced toward the ceiling and the infinity of stars beyond. "Too many possibilities out there we not know. How can humans think they highest form of life?"

Connie shook her head. "Seeing is believing. One of our old sayings. I think they will need some visual proof. Maybe if something like one of the old Erran city ships appeared in Earth orbit, they might get an idea, become just a little more humble."

"Humble?" The complexities of English still confused Lenka.

Connie tried some synonyms, "respectful, deferential? Uhm, maybe meek in recognition of greater status or attainment."

Lenka nodded. Lately, she had consciously taken up human mannerisms, nodding for understanding, shoulder shrugs instead of open-handed displays for uncertainty. She wasn't very good yet, as Shaand had learned to grimace, mimicking a human smile. She said to Jenks, "Human media need some government control?"

Martin shook his head. "No, I'm afraid that will not happen. We can try to affect what goes on our televisions by providing content, but we can't tell them what they can't show or talk about. At least, not in the free world." He saw a flicker of doubt, then understanding as she found meaning in her many studies of Terran politics.

As worrisome as the national press was, he was more concerned with the state of local security. A flicker on the television screen distracted him. The scene had closed in on the face of the Reverend Ehler, which if anything, appeared to be in a state of rage not usually seen on the normally sedate CNN. He reached for the TV remote. "May I?"

Connie turned to the screen, eyes widening. The banner below read, "Evangelist claims Errans to be ambassadors to the Devil."

As the sound came up, they listened; "... cannot be tolerated. We have repeatedly warned that the government should immediately quarantine not only the young Hitchens and his common-law wife, but now especially their devil child Mia who is proving to be too dangerous to be around real humans. Survivors of last week's events in Florida demonstrated her abilities. She has no doubt been endowed with these talents by Satan himself or his able cohorts on Dzura."

He was cut off by one of the engineers in the control room as Wolf Blitzer tried to regain control of the conversation. "Reverend Ehler, the Hitchens have, in effect, been in quarantine in their remote homestead."

Ehler countered. "That may be so in theory, but they meet with the outside world, they buy groceries, they come in contact with people, reporters last week, and others. Young Brad Hitchens and his alien friend are in Europe right now spreading no telling what kind of germplasm and any other kind of alien influence that we can't even begin to imagine. And they're meeting with planet Earth's heads of state one-on-one and these are REAL LIVE ALIENS we're talking about. It amounts to germ warfare, and NOBODY SEEMS TO UNDERSTAND!"

Blitzer artfully interrupted again as Ehler sat back to draw breath. "Reverend, as I read it, the Hitchens household was minding its business and was assaulted by the Renegade Press, as they like to be called. They are comprised of reporters for your radio channel, the *Enquirer*, the *CheckOut News*, and other, well, more spurious news sources. Their household was essentially under attack."

"And rightly so! I tell you—" the reverend shifted his gaze to the camera with red light on, "—AND I TELL YOU ALL—" his voice had spiked but the softened into a conspiratorial tone, "what those men endured as they approached that house was sheer mental agony. What kind of seven-year-old is that? They might tell you it was some sort of high-frequency jamming gear. I've heard that report, but I heard the Cunningham story too. That child of Satan is the source of that, that, mental torture. I tell you—"

Blitzer's smiling face took center screen again as Ehler's sound feed was cut, he pivoted to his left. "Dr. Pankovich, what—"

In the background, the voice of the guest from the university was loudly trying to object. Either Blitzer or someone in the control room had a mute button handy for the reverend's collar mic and allowed the voice of Blitzer to interrupt. Blitzer's head appeared. "I'm sure neither the NSA nor NASA would have allowed them out of their decontamination chambers if they had not been thoroughly examined." He turned to the other panelist. He said over the withering comments of the reverend. "Dr. Pankovich, can you fill us in on their mental, er, abilities?"

"Yes, thank you, Wolf. I'm sure the probes of the daughter Myahh would have been disturbing, but she is an untrained child. Her parents' telepathic abilities that were honed while incarcerated on Erra are not out of line with abilities that have been achieved by others here on our own world without any alien intervention. It is a matter of tuning out a lot of the oral language skills humans have developed over the years and tuning up an innate mammalian ability to judge intent, emotion, fear, and other more basic instincts that we share with other higher vertebrates, especially mammals."

"So, Dr. Pankovitch, you think we all have this ability? That any human being, with training, could develop these skills?"

"It's an abomination, I say, an abomination, a travesty that we—." Ehler's microphone may have been turned off, but his rantings were being picked up by the professor's nearby audio pickup.

Dr. Pankovich shot a nervous side glance at the ranting minister to his left, then returned his glance to the camera he'd been instructed to address. "Absolutely, psychic abilities of the human mind go far beyond what most of us use day-to-day. And the Hitchens' claim that they were first contacted by the artificial intelligence controlling their spacecraft is substantiated by workers who have been probed while servicing that vessel. Its inanimate intelligent operating system is capable of tapping into the abilities of Errans and Humans to communicate." He turned his body slightly away from the reverend to distance himself from the angry but now quiet populist minister. "From a technology point of view, it's just a matter of dialing up the right frequencies, then developing the transmitter/receiver. I've got to hand it to the Elioi, it's a damn fine interface for a fighting machine and its crew."

"As for Humans, it may be," Pankovtich continued, "that eating certain dietary ingredients while on that other planet could have accelerated, or enhanced their ability to communicate through psi, as they call it. We may think of it as ESP or mind-reading. They simply enhance speech with psi-nuanced communication. We know of some psychotropic or mood modifying drugs that stimulate areas of the brain that we are just beginning to investigate. We see these developments as a positive step forward in human evolution."

Blitzer's head appeared without the other guest. Martin pointed the remote at the TV ready to turn the sound off. "Well, the talking heads will continue to talk, won't they?"

"And these aliens, these monsters, still practice slavery!" Pankovitch was seen wiping a spot of spittle from his cheek as the minister ranted on, unaware that his mic was off, his camera feed off. The professor grimaced and raised an eyebrow in question to Blitzer. He clearly wanted to be somewhere else.

Wolf Blitzer's headshot reappeared. He was nodding to Professor Pankovitch that he could leave the stage. "Thank you, Reverend Ehler and Professor Pankovitch for joining us today." He seemed to be forcing his eyes to focus on the scrolling script front and center, but his body language was clearly tense, as if ready to leave the set. "I'm sure we will be interested in following up on some of those points."

Martin tapped the power button and became aware of a presence behind him, startled and turned to see Lenka standing behind them, her brow furrowed in the horizontal ridges he'd learned indicated concern.

"It is not slavery!" Even to Martin, the five-foot-tall alien seemed agitated. "Their life is what they know. I do not know if they can be more."

Connie had gotten to her feet and enclosed her friend in her arms. This simple human act would have been a horrid transgression on Lenka's home planet, but Lenka had become used to human emotional physicality and did not appear to mind being hugged. Connie stepped back a pace and said, "Lenka, my dear, on this planet, and the way many human cultures now believe, if the menial working class on your world is of the same species, then they should be given the same opportunities."

"But, from birth, their creche, everything is different."

"I know, hon. It will be very hard for you to understand. And not too many years ago, most cultures on this planet considered some other humans, less able, less capable, and from birth, were sorted by class and on the class of the parents and would be forever assigned menial work."

Martin stood now. "Lenka, you see that I am different from Connie, correct."

Even as they faced each other, he felt her probing, looking inward as she and Connie could do, felt a tug at the back of his head and a few simple phrases formed. *Dark not light, eyes black not blue.*

"Yes, Lenka. Those are superficial," he rephrased. "The outward appearance of the different races of Humans. But we are not different where it matters."

"Where it matters?" From Lenka, it was a question, not a statement.

"Yes, what makes us humans different is in our—" he looked at Connie, "—our hearts, our minds, what we think of as our souls." Connie finished for him.

Martin chewed at the inside of his lip. He'd known of the basic structure of Erran society and been uncomfortable with the comparison to his own ancestors' slavery. He began, "Lenka, only two generations ago, I would not have been able to go to a school with Connie or Brad because of my skin color. Four generations ago, I might have been killed for being alone with Connie in her house. For simply holding her hand. Humans have changed much in a very few years."

He turned, gestured toward the TV, now a black rectangle. "That man is wrong in so many ways about the Elioi. You are not evil; you are not from the devil. Every idea in his head is based on old earth mythology and his own need for attention. The Elioi, Errans and Dzurans, are not creatures that should be feared simply because you are different. But there are many things that will have to happen before we humans are as open and friendly as your friends Brad and Connie." He looked down, thinking about humanity and its internal evils. "Lenka, humans have been killing each other off for hundreds of thousands of years, simply because a group of others would be considered as not the same as us," he tapped his chest with both fists. "We saw outsiders, or strangers as a threat to our supply of food, or our resources, or our group's sense of security."

He felt another tug at the base of his skull. This time he could tell it wasn't from Lenka. He turned to see Myahh approaching from the hall. She was a dominant psi force and he allowed her to question and probe. He sat, allowing her to sit on his knee. He got a sense of reassurance from her. "Myahh, did you understand everything I was trying to tell Aunt Lenka?"

She simply looked up at him and smiled, nodded. She said, "Yes Mr. Martin." She looked up at Lenka, who had moved closer a few steps when Myahh jumped into his lap. "And she does too. But in her heart, she is crying."

12

To the Asteroid Belt

"Brad, move around to the other side of monitor ship. I think what we look for is on other side." Shaand's voice had a peculiar tone over the Ambassador cutter's speakers.

But Brad considered the syntax his Elioi friend had used and thought how far they had both come in interspecies communication. The modified diplomatic skiff they were using for this preliminary investigation of the messenger, or the 'egg', as it had been called, had advantages that Jai didn't. First, it had an airlock, which would permit EVAs without depressurizing the entire craft. Second, it was not ostensibly an armed platform. It had been fitted with shielding capability but carried no offensive projectile or energy weapons. It could vaporize small rocks or debris as a defensive measure. Offensively, the most it could do would be to damage an opponent's communications array or fry a hostile party with its thruster's ionized wash as it exited. Being an unarmed vehicle, it presented no threat to an intelligent observer and hopefully to the artifact left by an advanced intelligence.

Brad fingered the shuttle's controls gently, taking it closer but on a path that would allow observation of the far side of the smooth reflective ovoid as they passed beyond it. Pivoting the craft as it passed across the object's orbit, the anticipated square depression delineated in shadow became clearly visible. "Shaand. I guess that is where the thruster module goes."

"Yes Brad, according to the reports from the Dzuran logbooks. The original monitor had an empty square opening just as this appears." He waved his hand at the dark pit in an acquired human expression. "When it activated, it summoned a square module and left. We don't know if it was a habitat for a crew that also contained propulsion systems, or other…we do not know. The miner that stole the monitor and took it to Dzura didn't have the foresight to record a vid of his first sighting. He was an opportunist, not an explorer."

"Too bad." Brad wondered about their approach into the interior. Would he be hailed, threatened, or shot at? "Did the logbooks indicate what happened in that hole when the first monitor activated?"

From the back row of the eighteen-passenger shuttle a voice answered in a mashup accent that hailed from Russia's heartland and years aboard the ISS.

"Ambassador, review of the video taken during those tragic moments show the rock debris, structural materials, the Erran research craft, and any support cabling were ejected."

Colonel Leonid Kuznetskov had demonstrated a high aptitude for learning how to maneuver the Elioi's ambassador shuttle.

Brad called back. "Leonid, was there any indication of whether it was blown out, or mechanically ejected?"

"It's hard to know from this video. It's a little grainy, but it's clear the ejecta was simply blown out of that cube-shaped cavity." The Elioi record of the 'cleaning' of the first messenger probe had to be copied by screen capture from the original due to incompatible digital formats. The space engineering section that was monitoring the EVA crew inside the monitor vessel switched to exterior cameras when the interior feed blinked out. He paused the playback when it shifted to the interior shot. That video record was a horrific four-minute depiction of the monitor 'cleansing' itself of debris, the research team, and their equipment. The screams and squeals of agony made most observers watch it with the audio off as the strange yellow sterilizing beam traversed the interior of the vessel.

The Colonel added. "There was, in one of the reports I reviewed, an analysis of that debris field. The ejecta all seemed to have the same velocities away from the monitor, regardless of mass or density. The analyst's conclusion was that there was a mass-rejection force field energized at the base of the square depression that could clean it prior to the docking with the navigation/propulsion unit that arrived later."

"Thank you, Leonid." Brad considered the options. Originally, he and Shaand were to explore the new monitor, determine if the access holes at the base of the square depression on the first monitor existed on this replacement. Those holes, actually narrow tunnels, provided access to the interior 'control room' as it had been named. The enclosure was open to space and an artificial habitat had been installed by the first explorer, a prospector who discovered the anomalous satellite in the Sol system's asteroid belt. No one examining the video transmitted from the Elioi study of the interior had discovered anything that looked like controls for pressure doors that could seal off the room.

The shuttle, designed for a crew of three and eighteen passengers, held just the three now. Ambassador Brad Hitchens of Earth, Ambassador Shaand of Dzura, and RosCosmos' Colonel Leonid Kuznetskov. All wore matching vacuum-worthy suits of Elioi manufacture. Kuznetskov's presence as a backup pilot also served as a witness to events should the messenger vehicle prove hostile to the planned EVA of the other two crew members.

The three occupants were intent on the growing image on the forward screen. The reflective surface made size determination difficult. This object appeared more like a hole in space than a physical object in it. Their own reflection was little more than a small bright smear. It had only been discovered in the Sol system a few weeks ago. Its recent arrival was attested to as it had not yet begun to attract dust and small debris. A nickel-iron asteroid of similar size and apparent mass would be covered in rubble if it had spent centuries on-station as the previous monitor had.

Checking instruments again, Brad did the mental conversion of the readout for distance to object and shook his head. No, it just didn't seem correct. "Leonid, can you repeat that?"

"Commander Hitchens, our distance to the objective is four hundred, thirty-two point oh-nine meters. Fourteen-hundred seventeen point six two feet and closing slightly." There was a brief pause. Enough for Brad to reconsider his estimate of its size. Early measurements taken when they had stilled acceleration to nominal zero relative to the movement of the object had been a little over three hundred and fifty-seven meters long. As he thought it, Kuznetskov reported the update. "Based on assumed geometry of the curved endpoints, the object is three hundred fifty-four meters in length, at the widest point near the opening. The circumference is one hundred seventy-two meters. Opening for access is eight-nine point oh three meters on a side and approximately half that depth depending on the cube's intersection with the curved outer surface. That dimension has not been verified."

"Thank you Leonid." Brad turned his head slightly to his left. Shaand was studying the same video feed, looking for anomalies. At a little over a hundred yards square, their shuttle could easily park inside that opening. But was that at all a good idea?

"Shaand, what do you think? Similar to the one taken to Erran space?"

He said, "I agree. Either the same model or same ship."

"You think it might be the same one? Cleaned and recycled?"

"Shaand hope not the same ship. Bhoang-srol ship if so." He sought his memory for the words in English. "Graveyard boat. Many Erran scientists died on a ship, same as this."

Brad sat back in the command chair. It was a little small for his frame, but he fit. He hadn't considered the idea that the 'messenger ship' sent out of Erran space almost thirty years ago might have been fitted out and sent back. It was as possible an explanation as it being from the same assembly area that fitted out the second ship of similar dimensions, now floating gently in the Elioi's asteroid belt. Probably doing the same thing, whatever that was.

Brad asked, "Leonid, how about getting us closer?"

"That is the mission objective, yes?" Leonid's Georgian-inflected Russian accent offered the yes with no change in pitch.

"Affirmative. You have the com. Match rotational period of access portal and approach to twenty-five meters." Their objective, the monitor satellite, grew in their screen. Through some piloting magic, the square opening grew in their view and the starfield behind the messenger craft rotated slowly behind it.

Kuznetskov fingered controls and its apparent size shrank. "There. Now screen same as window. Now expand view." The image of the silvered oblong grew steadily, taking on form as the halo of pinprick starlight outlined its smooth mirrored exterior. It stopped growing when the shade-darkened square opening nearly filled the screen. The slow rotation of the messenger ship brought sunlight into the base of the square, revealing some accumulated dust and small rock, but on a background whose reflecting patina suggested the same mirror-like skin as the ship's exterior.

Shaand expressed in psi, *Good to know. That shell coating must be for eliminating or reflecting deep wave radiation.*

Brad simply psi'd back, *yes.* He knew that in his friend's vernacular, deep wave radiation meant gamma rays. Their shuttle craft's protection from gamma-ray bursts required the energy expenditure of the shield and a few micro-seconds warning. He turned his attention back to looking for any visible detail inside the square opening. The view ahead was dizzying. They had locked on to the slow revolutionary period of the object, directly opposite the opening. That opening was the only deviation from the mathematically pure curves of the object's exterior. Long-range optics included ultraviolet, visible, and long-wave band thermography.

Scans for waste gases had revealed no other discoverable openings. His obvious question, and the object of much discussion by panels and pundits on earth, was if there were no openings or structures on the thing, how did it do its supposed surveillance function? Where were its antennae, cameras, or other sensory equipment? Was it a monitor at all? If not, what was its function? Was the base of the square opening actually the sensor array? Was there a sensor array behind that mirrored exterior?

Was the messenger ship itself, simply a trigger? Was it a test for the presence of a space-going species similar to the monolith in Kubrick's *2001 A Space Odyssey*? The discussions pre-occupied far too much airtime for the data that could be provided. This was the best reason Brad could think of to propose the trip in an Elioi craft.

Shaand toggled the camera zoom to fill the view screen with the base of the opening and turned on the forward landing lights. As expected, near the opening's base on the side nearest the center of the thing, three circular openings were visible. The smaller openings could be the connection ports for communication devices or anchor points for the cubes that seemed to be necessary for the monitor ships to alter their orbits. "Look there." Shaand pointed to pairs of small indentations located near the corners of the cube, two at each corner. Dark oval openings with the same mirrored surface. "Anchor points?"

Brad noted the geometry and realized that a pair of circular rods extending from the cubical drive ships could be extended into those openings to lock them into position at strong points built into the hull of the ovoid monitors. "I think you're right, Shaand. At least it's a good guess." He pointed to the three circular openings. "So those must be where crew and supplies gain access?"

Colonel Kuznetskov said, "Tapes from Erran research team show that yes, those openings were access points. I can replay that portion of the video record if you like."

Brad and Shaand both agreed yes, they wanted to see the video.

The forward screen shifted to a view that showed a similar square opening in oblique view. A small Erran craft was visible resting on accumulated asteroidal gravel. Two of the openings had been cleared of debris and dangled communication cabling. The round port covers had been swiveled a hundred and eighty degrees to provide access. The third was not open and showed that the rock debris had accumulated to a depth of about twenty-five percent of the diameter of the round access tunnels. As they watched two scientists exited the Erran craft and floated toward

80

the center opening. The tunnel to the right carried a tangle of cables into the interior.

The two space-suited figures floating near the square opening's access ports provided scale. Brad estimated the openings to be at least six feet in diameter. He wondered if was that an indication of the size of the other alien species? Kuznetskov fast-forwarded the record to a point when four suited figures exited the central tunnel in an apparent hurry, a fifth squeezed out of the cabled port. Two stayed behind to help pull a sixth figure free when the field of view filled with rapidly pulsing brilliant yellow light.

As they watched, six suited Errans, their ship, and tons of asteroidal debris began to drift spaceward from the bottom of the hole. The Errans flailed for purchase, two had jetted drives in their cuffs and each grabbed onto one of their fellow scientists. Two unfortunates sped off alone into the darkness beyond the screen's view, the others in pairs, all to the same fate. They were being jettisoned from the opening by some form of repulsion field. In the next minutes streams of material, inorganic and organic in smaller parts, began to stream from an opening that had appeared closer to the center of the oblong.

Analysts had derived earlier that this opening was located immediately over the interior chamber that had been the object of the survey team's research. The opening had simply opened like a camera's iris where no opening or mechanism had been visible. Stop action study of the ejecta had shown that the stream of material included body parts, equipment, and cut-up pieces of cabling. Everything that seemed to be of Elioi origin was cleaned from the ship. The unoccupied machine or craft had been purging itself of foreign objects.

The pulsing light became momentarily brighter as the last of the ejecta cleared the opening. The view was then eclipsed by the form of a cubic component that closed with the monitor ship then eased into the square opening with delicate precision. This view shrank in size and had to be manually zoomed in to retain any useful clarity. The Erran ship maintaining the exterior view was rapidly leaving the vicinity. Leonid switched to another channel as the diminishing image of the paired monitor ship and the new drive unit shrank in the first channel's view. An alternate camera, possibly from another ship stationed farther out, had recorded the cleansing of the square opening of all foreign materials, the venting of the inner chamber, and the subsequent re-orienting of the combined monitor/drive ship's attitude and its abrupt departure from Erran Space.

Brad sensed strong psi contact. He looked up to meet Shaand's intense gaze. In communication that was becoming much easier for Brad, he and Shaand had a private psi conversation that debated the mission ahead. What might have taken human speech minutes was resolved by psi bond in seconds. They would go in together and leave, if it came to that, Colonel Kuznetskov alone as a witness.

13

Inside the Messenger

The approach to the ovoid messenger ship that had become labeled 'The Egg' as uneventful as it was cautious. Brad thought its perfectly reflective surface was useful for two reasons. In the blackness of space, that sort of surface would be extremely hard to see and would also have an extremely small reflective signature for radar or other position fixing technology. Thinking about it further, if it was as reflective of other spectra as it was for visible light, it might also be a great shield of gamma radiation. Space was a deadly place to hang out without radiation protection.

To no one's surprise and everyone's relief, there had been no noticeable reaction to their approach. The craft simply continued to rotate on its long axis at about one revolution per three and a half minutes. Kuznetskov finished locking the shuttle into an approach that would allow them to be gently acquired by the messenger ship by setting down on the face of the square opening and locking into any equipment found. He would withdraw as soon as the two EVA crew were safely through the airlock.

Docking proved uneventful, Brad and Shaand used suit jets to fly to the bottom corner of the docking port closest to the three tunnels that, assuming it was identical to the first messenger ship, would lead to the craft's inner chambers. They tied their safety tethers off to one of the anchor structures at the bottom of the craft's docking bay. Looking out through the opening, Brad expected a sea of gravel, rocks, and boulders; his imagined understanding of the asteroid belt. He could see almost nothing in the immediate neighborhood. For the original messenger to have been covered in gravel sized debris, as had been reported by the its discoverer, it would have had to be in place for centuries.

Now, floating near one of the access ports, and looking out into the black emptiness of space, the shuttle was no larger than his fist. This was his first indication of the scale of the Messenger. The docking port's length and width were about one-sixth of the length of the craft. *This boat is big!* As he watched, two puffs of vapor noted the departure of the

83

shuttle to a save remove. It shrank with distance and rotated slowly out of view.

The reality of the apparent emptiness of the asteroid belt weighed on him as he looked out at the space formerly occupied by the shuttle. On the next rotation, the small shuttle's image dwindled to one of the lesser visible stars. The decision to move the ship to a remote viewing station seemed prudent after reviewing the 'cleaning' of the Erran research ship and the debris field of ejecta that spewed into vacuum. The small craft became invisible in the background starfield a little too soon for his liking. *If* there were other asteroids around, they were too small or too distant and invisible. He hadn't realized how much empty space there was in the belt.

He turned to the business at hand. "Shaand, are you close to finishing with those measurements?" Shaand was measuring the half-meter round openings at the corners of the base in case they might be useful in the future to anchor research ships.

"Yes," Shaand replied, "and I think this one has been used before. Scrape marks on the openings look like heavy equipment attached here."

"OK, take pictures and we can talk about that later. I am ready to enter the large chamber but want you close by to help if needed." Brad pulled himself a few feet into the largest of the three openings at the base of the square docking station and waited. Rising humidity levels began to fog his faceplate. In less than a minute, Brad felt a tap on his shoe pad and Shaand psi'd his readiness to help.

Brad pulled further in, aware now of his claustrophobic sweat response. The suit and its environmental support pack just cleared the limited access tunnel's walls. He hadn't developed a reaction to small spaces until he'd been trapped in the murky depths of a sunken shrimp boat several years prior. That was in the warm waters of the Gulf of Mexico. This time he was in the cold, and equally deadly vacuum of space. In either environment, loss of air meant death.

Looking ahead the tunnel made a slight curve to the left but appeared, in his helmet light, to exit into the large 'control chamber' similar to the one recorded by the Erran research team. Cautious hands reached for the inner edge of the access tunnel. Pulling slowly, he advanced until just his helmet was exposed. If the chamber could be said to have a floor, the tunnel entered just a foot above that floor. The amorphous chamber defied most geometrical descriptions beyond rough oval. In contrast to the mathematical precision of the ovoid and rectilinear descriptions of the exterior, the interior was organic, seeming to have been grown in place.

He felt another tap on his foot. Shaand had pulled himself into the tunnel behind him. "OK, I'm going to go all the way in."

"Be full of care."

Brad smiled at the misused 'careful,' but reminded himself of how poor his own use of Elioi idiom was. Shaand had once advised a young cadet recruit at Annapolis to have an erection when he was trying to tell him to stand straight. The entire cadre had trouble hiding their grins at that one. But there were more serious issues at hand. Would this vessel try to rid itself of impurities that would include these two new intruders?

He pulled himself forward and floated to the end of his tether. It was a fast way out if needed. He had used tethers when diving in murky waters and figured this would be useful if a rapid exit became necessary. The interior was entirely foreign to his eyes. Scanning the space, he found no clue as to form or function. Even grossly inelegant Erran ships exhibited structural elements dictated by physics and the similar symmetrical bipedal form of their bodies. True, the ships had tubes rather than hallways, but control centers looked similar. Form followed function. He could even fit in the command chair of his Elioi spaceship with little discomfort. But this room was a chamber of indescribable wonders. He glanced over at the helmet comm array to ensure that his helmet cam was on.

Brad felt a tug on the tether line and looked back to see Shaand entering the 'control room.' "Shaand, this looks exactly like the chamber in the Dzuran video." His voice, distorted by his headset speaker, registered awe.

"Yes, it does." Shaand pointed across the chamber to a flattened area that tilted about thirty degrees toward them. "That is about where the Dzuran miner's habitat was set up." Shaand released the spool on his tether and with a small puff from his ankle jets, launched himself toward the shelf. He called back to Brad, "The explorer set up shelter here and stayed for days with safety."

"Do we know how long he was here?"

"No. He was an asteroid miner who was exploring the original messenger ship and got tangled in cables back in the tunnel. The record does not tell how long before rescued."

"Cables?" Brad looked back toward the entrance tunnel; there were no cables.

Shaand explained. "He was trying to set up a gravity field and atmosphere in here to help in exploring."

85

Brad scanned the room again. He turned on the multi-spectral beam in his left arm cuff and shone it on the walls. He pushed it toward the infra-red with little effect and then tried ultraviolet. Immediately, portions of the walls and ceiling began to fluoresce in a brilliant display of bright bands in red and white. Blue ovals appeared on sections of wall that had no background texture. "Look at that!" In one of the blue ovals, rows of symbols appeared in the ultraviolet. If he moved the beam away, it reverted to the dull gunmetal gray of every other surface. Shining the beam around the room, numerous other sections of the wall exhibited the same effect, although some of the areas were rectangular, circular, or other recognizable geometries. He turned to illuminate the wall behind. It was covered in areas that seemed to have lines of text.

"Well, that's informative. These others, the makers of this vessel, have vision in the ultraviolet spectrum." He turned to see Shaand shining his cuff lights on areas of the wall on his side of the chamber. In the ultraviolet wash, some of the previously random structural elements took prominence, standing out as dominant among the swirls and other undefinable shapes. Brad's estimate of the size of the 'control room' was far less than what he thought of as the volume contained in the remaining volume of the ovoid. What else was there to this craft? Unknown propulsion systems? Unknowable technologies?

Brad remembered the helmet cams. "Leonid, are you picking up anything more than dull gray on the camera feed?"

The audio signal was poor, nearly indistinct, but he heard the response. "No, I'm just seeing gray walls with strange shapes. The signal may be affected by that reflective surface."

"Can you hear me clearly? Your transmission is weak. See if you can boost your signal or tighten the beam." He considered the reflective surface of the ship's exterior. "Try aiming directly into the square opening."

"Yes, Sir. The ship has rotated relative to my position."

"Right, I'll move closer so the time that I can send/receive into the opening will be longer per rotation."

"Can you establish a lock on the access opening?"

"Yes, Sir. I'll move closer but maintain a position off-center of the opening. I'll try to lock onto the rotation of the monitor ship."

Shaand said, "Colonel, be sure to stay clear of that opening."

"Absolute."

That last was much improved. Better clarity and signal strength. "Shaand," Brad said, "how does this ship act as a monitor of activity in our system if its reflective surface bounces off most signals? What is the point?"

"That is a good question," and after a pause, "maybe we have misunderstood the purpose of this ship. Maybe it is not for listening, but for finding?"

"You mean, it's like a trigger?"

"Yes, Brad. Not meant for listening for signs of civilization, but for being found. If it is physically triggered it reports back to home. Its home."

Brad thought about that. The first messenger ship found had been physically moved from the Sol system to the Elioi's home planet. Its makers had summarily cleaned it and sent it home. Now replacements were stationed in both systems. "I don't know Shaand, this messenger station was put back here to replace the one removed by the Dzuran miners. They know there is an intelligent species here." He continued pulling at strands of the puzzle. "And, if it is a trigger, and not a messenger or monitor, why would they send one back here and to your system?"

"I not know, my friend. They know an intelligent species stole one and moved it." Shaand reconsidered; it had been over an hour since they approached the alien spacecraft in the shuttle and ran a full frequency scan on it. "If any of this equipment is on, they know there is someone here now." As they searched and recorded the physical aspects of what they considered the control room, Shand added. "Perhaps there is another purpose for this ship now."

A colored splash of light began reflecting on the inner lining of his helmet. He turned around to find that one of the 'text' panels near the access tunnel was flashing in a multi-colored display. Its rectangular border flashed through the rainbow spectrum from deep reds, through orange, then yellow, green, and on through the visible spectrum to deep blue. Inside the rectangular border, circles began to form, giving the impression of depth, as a tunnel's receding curves would define it's tubular form. After a pause, it repeated the display. Shaand came to a stop beside him, putting out an arm to grasp Brad's suit grip.

"This is not in the record of the Dzuran examination." Shaand's voice had a different uncertain quality. Was this caution? Fear? Shaand had been beside him in a prison break, close-quarters combat, and cabinet

87

and board meetings across the scale of importance. Brad had never heard or felt his friend exhibit fear before.

"Shaand, where did the first messenger's cleaner start?"

His partner turned and pointed to a small circular rise in what they had considered the floor. "There." A small yellow cylinder rose, pulsing softly.

"We should leave, Shaand. That is the cleaner, right?" As he said it, he was actuating his suit's maneuvering jets. He aimed for the tunnel opening and felt the first push from his boot jets. He forgot about the safety tether. Its loose coils snagged on Shaand's environment pack, diverting his course. He felt the line jerking as if Shaand was trying to untangle the connection. But he couldn't correct the altered course of his trajectory. Physics again. He would keep on the new track unless something changed it. He actuated the palm jets to slow, but they didn't change his direction. He was rapidly approaching the wall panel with the pulsing rectangle of light. He twisted around catlike as he drifted and shifted the aim of his palm jets but too late. He felt a minor bump, then—

He'd heard Shaand's warning shout, then nothing.

He saw, felt, heard, nothing.

He might as well have fallen into a blacked-out sensory deprivation tank. He could sense nothing but the interior of his suit.

~ ~ ~

Still in the messenger ship's "control room," Shaand tapped the com button on his wrist panel repeatedly. "Brad! Brad, do you hear me? What happen?" In his mind, he knew that Brad had just careened into a screen that pulsated in a repeating pattern from deep reds through the spectrum to the Elioi limit of vision in the far ultraviolet and into black. He had been formulating a theory that the display began below his visual receptive ability, dialed through his spectral sensitivity, and continued beyond before repeating. Could it be testing his visual reception?

Brad's disappearance into the spectrum-flashing panel stopped that chain of thought. The remaining loose filament of Brad's severed tether recoiled into a loose floating tendril extending toward the chamber's entrance tunnel. His friend Brad was gone. Could he have gone through the panel? Into the panel? To where? The panel appeared to be a part of the wall separating his chamber from the square opening in the ovoid shell, not some portion of the messenger ship that had room for another void, another chamber.

Cautiously, with his more delicate palm jets, Shaand moved toward the pulsing display. The prismatic display stopped, the rectangle lost color, resolved to the neutral gray-brown of the surrounding walls. The only differentiation was that it was an even planar surface while all other surfaces were a riot of unfamiliar decoration, shape upon convoluted shape, without known purpose.

He reached out to the panel tentatively; it was solid to his touch. He turned to get his bearings; turned back. This was the panel that was so alive with color moments before Brad slipped disappeared. It was now inert, colorless. A chamber entrance? A teleportation portal? Somehow their activity had, what? Shaand considered the short access tunnel to the docking chamber behind the panel. It wasn't thick enough to enclose a very large space. He tapped his com sleeve again.

"Brad, Brad!" He tapped his wrist panel's controls, invoking a multi-frequency output. "Brad, if you can hear any of this, please respond." As he waited, the only sound breaking the utter silence of the place was his too rapid breathing. An experienced spacer, Shaand realized with increasing distress that this was the first time he had been alone in space. He was in his EVA suit, in an alien artifact's ante-chamber, or control room, or specimen collection room; the options kept morphing, or, remembering the fate of the Dzuran scientific team, a decontamination chamber.

"Brad! Communications check, Brad. Do you hear me?"

Nothing. Only his breathing.

"Colonel Kuznetskov?" Click, pause. "Leonid, are you on station?"

"Kuznetskov, here. I'm on station. Do you need assistance?"

Shaand turned to the small rise that had been the source of the 'purification' beam. A yellow crystal had risen from its center and began to pulse. Time to leave.

"Leonid, SitRep to follow for transmission to JPL but make cautious approach for extraction. I'm coming out. The messenger has become hostile. Repeat, the messenger is hostile."

14

Inside the Umbra Ship

Ever so slowly, deep shades of gray took form in the void. Brad turned his head slowly from left to right, attempting to get a fix on the unfamiliar dark shapes; to see if they were moving or he was. Weightlessness was not new to him. But finding a frame of reference, where was down, was a first priority. In a ship, down is the deck. In space, down is the ship. Even if there was a planet nearby, home was the ship, home and safety. Here, six, or were there more, nearly black planar surfaces enclosed an undefinable void. Nothing presented itself as a clue to "down-ness."

He stretched out in all directions and tried to reach any handhold or surface. If he hadn't had a suit helmet he would have tried blowing to see if the simple force of jetted breath could change his position relative to the dark shapes. He was unsure of the atmosphere inside the chamber and decided against suit jets. He looked again. Edges began to form, surfaces to shape, were they brightening? Yes, the background ebony was brightening to deep shades of gray; forms were becoming more distinct. He recognized an irregular rectangular octahedron, but his point of view was near its center. He sensed movement, but not his own. Angles shifted, wall surfaces softened, morphed into new shapes, blended, and solidified. When the motion stopped, his point of view was inside a slowly rotating rectangular solid. One of the walls grew a central rectangle. Soundlessly, a perceptibly lighter shade of not black emerged from the wall. Was it square? He contorted, catlike, to rotate to face the change. The rectangular surface continued to emerge from the wall and stopped as its depth from the wall was about equal to the object's width. He subconsciously began to think of that wall's side as down.

The protrusion that he'd thought at first was going to be some kind of viewing screen, took on solidity, at least one surface did. The sides that were perpendicular to the wall thinned to transparency then disappeared. His view of the shape shifted, he felt movement, undefined by acceleration. Was he moving? Or was the floating rectangle moving. He thought, *is that a floor?*

Bump. His helmet hit a barrier. His view of the oblong had shifted now. Narrow sticks or protrusions at the corners lined up with his field of view. He felt for the barrier and found himself being drawn to it ever more strongly. *Resist!*

He struggled against the irresistible force pushing him against the barrier until, when he was pushing against it with knees and elbows, he realized what had been a weightless chamber was now dialing up gravity. There was a new down. He pulled a knee under himself and stood erect. As the first light pressure of gravity increased, making standing easy, he turned to look at the rectangular object.

It had resolved in this new spatial orientation to be an ordinary table. As he watched, again turning his head from side to side to scan for any other detail, he noted that it had taken on color. The table was brown with streaks. He moved cautiously toward it and saw a pattern that appeared to be wood grain, but a gross approximation of woodgrain. No real grain, but the gradations of brown he might have expected of wood. Peering closer at it, the image of faux wood was pixelated in tiny overlapping ovals. As he watched the ovals shrank and divided, providing greater detail in the faux woodgrain.

Looking around him now, there was a down, so there were sides. He noted the 'room', formerly an irregular octahedron was now a rectangular enclosure. Not quite rectangular, but a close approximation. Light levels continued to come up. The walls were still gray, but there were definitely edges where the newly resolved floor met walls and ceiling.

Aah, the ceiling. It was lighter still and brightening with every glance. He tested his weight by lifting up onto his toes and found the enclosure was approaching Dzuran normal, about eighty percent of Earth's normal gravitation. He walked with ease, but with caution to the nearest wall, feeling its smooth texture under his gloves. It was soft but unyielding. A padded cell? When he pressed again, a slight impression of his handprint remained momentarily and morphed again to the original flat surface.

Pounding in his ears prompted a glance at the readout on his wrist pad. His pulse was a tic above one-forty. He told himself to calm down. He took a deep breath and closed his eyes, concentrating on long, slow, deep breaths. Checking the monitor again, his pulse had dropped below one-fifteen. Good.

Turning to the room again, a table was clearly defined now. Sharp edges and corners. A small chair was now visible on the other side. Was it there before, unnoticed in the original gloom? Its back was just below the height of the table. He walked over to it, pushed, found it movable. He pressed slightly against the table. Unmovable. OK. Am I supposed to sit?

He wondered; *Did I ask that question? Was it presented to me as a suggestion?* Yes, I am supposed to sit. He suppressed a laugh. The entire discovery process he'd just gone through had been one of suggestion, feedback, suggestion, feedback. Feedback from what? Something was trying to make him feel comfortable without knowing what frame of reference would make him comfortable. Maybe the chair hadn't been there at first, but his impression that a chair wasn't there had caused it to form, had given it form, even if it was a little small.

He turned to examine it more closely. It was a simple dark gray chair with four thin legs that at first appeared to be too insubstantial to support his mass, even at eighty percent. At second glance, they were thicker, they'd become more capable, or, in his new estimation of what was going on, more visually appropriate to the scale and the purpose of holding up his weight.

He sat. *Was this by suggestion?* He wasn't tired. Excited if anything. The illumination was now brighter too. An even light that seemed to emanate from the walls and ceiling themselves had increased to a level that he could probably read small print. If he'd been asked, he'd have estimated the enclosure to be about ten feet by sixteen or maybe a little longer. The table would be, he guessed, about three by five feet and close to three feet high. He was seated in the chair along the long side of the table. He thought, *What now?*

Yes, what now?

Startled, he jumped up, knocking the chair back. It slid noiselessly to the wall and rebounded as if off rubber and stopped just short of his legs. He had a chilling memory of being interviewed by Jai years earlier. Turning he found the source of the voice. It was solidifying into a shape that was almost human.

15

Meeting the Visitor

Myahh struggled against the flood of information coming her way. The voice of the Visitor was loudest, most compelling. Both soothing and demanding, the voice readied her for an unknown it knew would be disturbing. Also demanding some diminishing fraction of her attention was her Uncle Martin. He was up on the deck, keeping watch and worried beyond her own comprehension about her family's safety. She stole a listen to his thoughts. Her gentle prodding developed scenes from his memories that hinted at a place of refuge with grand horizons, dramatically different landscapes. Perhaps that would come to pass if the Visitor did not act first.

Then there was the intruder. He was in the palmettos, barely visible, far enough away, that he did not seem threatening. But she could not spare the mental energy to inquire, to look into his mind. And besides, Mom and Lenka had both been begging her to try to stay out of the minds of strangers. The intruder was trying to listen to Uncle Martin with a machine. Stupid. She could show him how to do that with his mind.

Then the Visitor called out to her again.

She gave her mind's energies back to the Visitor. The vision of her dad's office came into sharper focus. The visions came again, but of a peculiar gray room reminiscent of their home, and more words that almost made sense, and now a image of daddy in an empty room. Just daddy and a table. And a shape like a person, but not a person. And the other being was strange too, but not like Aunt Lenka. Trying to focus on it was like looking through water. Myahh opened her eyes and looked up at the low clouds scudding in over the grass flats beyond their coastal home. That helped, but the words came again as she let the clouds drift past. Mostly the words told her not to be afraid of the journey. *Did they know about tomorrow's trip to Martin's mountains?*

The first flash came as a surprise, enhanced by her wonder at her sudden loss of weight. She sensed her body rising from the ground. Instead of flailing to reach for something, anything solid, she did as the voice commanded. She tucked her arms around her folded legs and tucked her chin down onto her knees. The second flash took her breath away. The

Visitor's voice continued to caress her fears, calm her being. She accepted without fear that she was no longer lying in the dirt of her sandy clay front yard. Thoughts of her mother worrying about her were met with gentle persuasion that they would be able to talk later.

Myahh became aware of movement. She wanted to uncurl, to look ahead, down the colorless tunnel, but the soothing voice of the Visitor discouraged that impulse as soon as she looked 'down.' It did seem as if the motion was down, but not like falling. She relaxed, allowing her body to uncurl slightly from its tight fetal ball. Her sense of motion sped up and a slight sensation of nausea eased. As she let all her muscles relax, no push, no pull, the motion sensation increased. That was the key. Don't resist. She followed a suggestion that she shut her eyes to ignore the tunnel. She hadn't been tempted to reach out to touch the walls but as her eyelids closed, she felt her speed increase.

Odd, no breeze. But speed! To where? The question was answered with an image of dad's office, only there were changes. She hadn't noticed that her motion had stopped and that she was now in a strange copy of her dad's office. The walls were out of focus, his desk was about the right size, but the objects on it were indistinct. It seemed like a memory of the room, a dream of the room without the detail. Her attention was drawn to his picture wall. As she looked closer, she recognized his diplomas from Arizona and Florida State. Pictures of her dad and Uncle Martin and the old man she knew only as Uncle Sonny, smiling, holding up fish down at Wakulla Beach. A photo of her with her parents standing in front of the United Nations last year? She turned from the wall when she heard her name called.

"Myahh?"

She turned a saw her dad, kneeling with outstretched arms. "Daddy!"

He was wearing an Elioi spacesuit. She allowed her muscles to relax, to uncurl. As her legs extended, her orientation shifted. She accepted the new down, rotated into that plane, and felt gravity push against her feet. He was moving toward her, his mouth moving unheard inside his helmet.

She heard his psi call out. *Myahh, are you here? Are you real?*

Yes, I think I'm here. The Visitor brought me here.

There was a strange moment, child and father, facing off. One in dirty jeans, blouse, and high tops; the other in full deep-space EVA suit.

He cracked the seal on his helmet, took it off, and knelt down to take her into his arms.

Brad said, "We've been talking about you. They are very interested in you as a spokesperson."

She spoke softly into his ear. "That's what my Visitor has been saying. I'm not sure I can do that."

I am glad you are both here.

They both turned to see a form that though bipedally hominid, was neither Human nor Elioi. Its facial features were indistinct but morphing rapidly into a human face. As the features came into sharper delineation, it smiled and nodded, a most human gesture. *Welcome, both of you.*

"Myahh, this I think, is your Visitor. I've come to think of him as the Messenger."

Yes, the smile returned, *I certainly am a messenger and a traveler.* His gaze appraised them both. Is it common for humans to appear so differently in their form within a close genetic grouping?

They looked at each other, then back to the Messenger. Brad spoke before Myahh could. "She looks much more like her mother than me. She is also a female human; they are generally smaller and tend to have softer curves and features. Though there is a lot of variation."

Myahh added, "I have my mother's face, and his skinny body and his stringy hair." She peered at the visage that was solidifying its form. Its features became more distinct as she watched. "You can change your shape?"

The Visitor spoke aloud now, in easy non-colloquial English. "I can take almost any form, depending on the local physics." It shared a wordless internal thought with her psi channel reassuring her that it was the same entity as the Visitor she had been talking with earlier. It added, "I wanted to make you both feel comfortable. The atmosphere of my homeworld is not healthy for humans. I did not want to have this interview through a containment barrier."

Brad gestured at the solidifying form of his office as additional furniture and details began to take on more accurate shapes. "Are these shapes real? I mean, are they hard real-world physical objects, or are you painting an illusion for that same comfort level?"

"Real, or illusion, there's an interesting conceptual and existential argument in itself. But I don't want to get into the philosophy of metaphysics on this first visit." The entity gestured behind him to an

95

image of Brad's slouch couch that had taken shape along with the other furniture in his home office. "Please, feel free to get comfortable." The entity sat in a side chair and waved a very human hand toward the couch.

Brad and Myahh moved toward the couch, a worn, saggy pillow-top piece in familiar forest green. Both felt its firmness, testing to see if it would support their conception of weight.

"Go ahead, it will work fine. I assure you." The Visitor's voice was a neutral broadcast English with no detectable regional traits.

They sat, feeling the texture. Myahh ran her hand along the arm testing its resistance against her memories of using it as an afternoon napping location.

Bradley, Myahh. I'm sure that by now you are wondering if you are dreaming; if this is some trick of a hallucinogen that I have somehow infected you with. I assure you, that is not the case. You are actually here with me on my craft.

Myahh asked, "Where is here?"

Brad added, "And how did you get us both here?"

"One at a time, I think is your proper response here. You are on my craft as I said. It is between your star and your home planet. The Sun and the Earth as you call them. Our distance from your Sun is approximately seven-eighths of your planet's diameters from Earth." After a short pause, it offered in psi, *about six point one million kilometers.*

Brad realized that the Messenger had been alternating between psi and audible speech. He tried a test. *Can you hear this?* He psi'd.

"Of course."

"Then, can you speak audibly? For our ears?"

"Yes, too much psi talk can give us Humans headaches, and I'm pretty good at it." Myahh said aloud.

"How about this?" The entity spoke slowly, but clearly.

Brad said. "That's very good. How long have you been studying—" he started to say 'us,' then opted for "—Earth?"

"In round numbers, a few thousand of your years. I returned recently due to a notable change in...conditions."

"What about the Elioi?" Myahh asked.

"A little more. I could check records." It appeared to smile, or at least to Brad, it expressed humor. It continued, "not me all the time of course, but another similar to me."

Myahh tilted her head to left, appraising the Visitor's appearance. Its transition into a human form seemed to have completed. A soft white gown draped across its shoulders covered most of its physical body. Long dark hair with a slight curl surrounded a face that was hard to place as male or female. Myahh asked, "Are you a man or a woman?"

It smiled. "Neither. But I understand that your race is normally binary, that is, one or the other with a few exceptions. Do you have a preference of which you would like to see me as?"

She thought about if for a second. "I've always thought of you as a guy. I don't know why."

"Ok, how's this?" As the watched, subtle facial features around the jaw line and brow became more pronounced. Its skin darkened, hair shortened, a soft dark beard and mustache appeared. It would have been considered well-trimmed by any measure. The white gown transformed into a light beige business suit. As the transformation concluded, the Visitor's appearance would not have been out of place in any Mediterranean marketplace, except perhaps for the bare feet.

Myahh laughed. "Wow! I wish I could do that."

The Visitor smiled. "Perhaps in another incarnation."

"Inca nation? Huh?"

He smiled at her, provided her some simple explanations through psi.

She sat back into the armrest of the old green couch. "Ohh! Neat!"

He gained a better understanding of the teachability of young humans and knew that teaching older humans was going to be much more difficult. He looked up to see Brad Hitchens smiling at him.

Brad said, "You are really very good at communicating, at speech. How…" He didn't know how to phrase the question.

"It's my job. As an emissary I must learn the local languages and keep up with the current usages because languages change so fast. My title, in fact, would most closely translate as Emissary, or Shǐzhěhě, or Afgezant, or Emisariusz." Again, there was a hint of humor embedded in the next, "there are so many human languages."

Both Brad and Myahh began to speak and their different questions overlapped. Myahh persisted. "How many languages do you speak?"

"From Earth? I suppose you mean from Earth."

"Yes."

"About eight with some fluidity, two or three more with no nuance. That gets most of the media streams I've been monitoring. There are many, many more that have an insignificant media presence. I know of them, but it's harder for me to study them because of their weaker broadcast signals."

Brad got his question out. "How long have you been here? Sharing an orbit with Earth?"

"Not that long, but it's not my first visit by any means."

Myahh asked, "Why us?

"Ah, well. There's the thing. There is the rub, as you say."

The being looked at Myahh. "It's more about you. I've scanned, surveyed, and conversed with quite a few on this planet. And I've chosen you."

Brad, concern in his voice, said. "Chosen for what?"

It said, "For my emissary. The Emissary's emissary." It shifted a cold appraising gaze to Brad. "And you."

Myahh was struck mute, her mouth hung apart slightly. Her lips moved, but she could not utter a word. Words would not come but thought did. *I am supposed to be an emissary?*

He addressed them both, personally, shifting his focus from one to the other as he spoke. Letting both of them understand their importance. "Your world has found itself on the doorstep of interplanetary travel. Due to your actions Bradley, humanity has the opportunity to visit another world, another entire culture. It's my observation that your leaders are working on treaties, understanding, and an unusual outpouring of global goodwill as noted in your recent media. But, I also note a fair amount of hostility, bred from fear of me I suppose. My presence here now has added to the questions many of you have about what other beings, what other species are out in that vast chasm between the suns. A messenger is needed to present that to your world and it needs to come from the newest generation."

The entity leaned forward, elbows on knees, still shifting his gaze between the two. Brad thought this was a gesture of confidence-building, of intimacy. This emissary had clearly been studying human interaction for a long time and with attention to detail, intent, and nuance.

He continued. "I cannot be the one. A being from the great emptiness out there. This has happened in the past with other travelers, other species, and they have been mistaken for gods. I am not here to start a religion." He watched them, waiting patiently.

Brad finally found a response. "You are going to have a hard time with the religions already here." After a short pause he added, "Most I can think of have a history of demanding its followers commit mayhem and murder to the point of killing off all unbelievers because the connection between the religious order and political order is so strong."

The Emissary straightened and smiled. "You are both very perceptive." He looked at Myahh, drew her consciousness in. "That is why you and I have been having such long conversations. I need to be sure."

Brad reached over and took Myahh's hand. They exchanged a glance that asked if each other was ok. Brad turned back to the Emissary. "What exactly, is your mission here?"

~ ~ ~

In the underbrush lining the Hitchens' yard area, the intruder tried to make sense of what he knew must be reported. But how do you believably describe a small child reaching out her hands to the sky and fading to nothingness? She had been there, a moment ago, curled into a ball, talking to herself. Then she stood, looked up at the few overhead clouds and … nothing! She simply vanished. Maybe the preacher was right. This girl *was* in league with the devil.

16

Montana

Victor Paige arrived at Missoula's diminutive airport tired, disheveled, and excited. His network of anti-alienists had introduced him to Bob O'Lary, a ham radio operator nearby in rural Idaho, who had gathered a few supporters to meet him for the early briefing. One of those was a member of a casual biker group, Satan's Spear. Several were dentists, lawyers, or other professionals. Most were more hardcore; mechanics, welders, a tattoo artist, and a mid-level crack and opioid distributor. Just enough beards and bare-armed muscle in the group to provide visual menace. They waited for their cue to follow just outside the airport entrance.

Victor and his ham operator friend idled in the small private aviation lounge talking to the one late-night custodian about an overdue chopper. It was their excuse for being there and anxiously scanning the runway for arrivals. The lounge consisted of one aging leather-covered couch, two matching aging leather chairs, a small glass-topped dinette table, and soda and chip machines. In normal hours of operations, the small lounge also offered coffee, cheeseburgers, and nachos.

No, Victor had said, there was no registered flight plan, just a simple up-the-mountain flight to a remote cabin. Victor thought his cover was clever. He was going to a cabin, Martin Jenks' cabin. He just didn't know where that was yet. He had a phone in his pocket that Satan's Spears' lawyer member could track and follow from about a mile back to avoid suspicion until they would arrive at this 'secure' cabin he'd heard about.

~ ~ ~

Martin Jenks and his charges, Connie and Lenka, arrived via small jet at close to 2:30 a.m. All emerged from the cramped but comfortable Lear jet, tired and hungry. They did not head for the private aviation lounge. Martin explained that there were no creature comforts available after midnight and that the immediate need for a pit stop could be made while still in the hangar. The waiting van would soon get them up to his mountain retreat. Besides, the flight west had gained them some extra nighttime hours and they might get a nap before dawn. At just under 40,000 feet, they'd made the trip from Tallahassee to Missoula in a little over four hours and had gas to spare. Even though the night might have two extra hours, Connie didn't envision getting any nap time in. She'd gotten a cryptic psi message from Myahh that she was with the Visitor and would talk to her later. She'd had no choice when Martin had insisted that they leave, for her and Lenka's safety. She was worried as any mother would be but was consoled by the knowledge that Myahh was with the being controlling the two new alien ships.

The black Ford Transit was comfortable and much roomier than the Lear jet. Jenks had ensured that the van would be from the NSA's vehicle pool and was equipped with advanced radio, bulletproof glass and side panels, and blow-out proof tires. It rode with the heavy feel of a Brinks truck. He was glad to be back in Montana and looked forward to coffee on his porch when the night was finally over.

~ ~ ~

Victor's companion, Bob O'Lary, wore a black technical onesie with a gear belt under a plaid overshirt. Due to the loose folds of the shirt, Victor couldn't tell what most of the gear was, but there was clearly a holstered pistol resting under his left armpit. Bob had been standing at the window wall that looked out over the Missoula Airport's private aviation flight line. In front of Minuteman Aviation, a few small Cessnas, an old Piper hi-wing, and a V-tail Beechcraft were tied down less than fifty yards away. As O'Lary scanned the planes' lines, bright landing lights approached along the long runway from the southeast, it used less than half the runway a commercial flight might have taken and peeled away from the passenger terminal and headed toward a set of private hangars to his right.

O'Lary interrupted his examination of the new arrival. "Hey, Victor!"

"Yeah?" He'd gotten his second cup of barely palatable coffee from a dispenser behind the food counter and looked up, a little guilty for being where he shouldn't have been. "See one of those things you want to buy?"

"As a matter of fact, yes. There's a Cessna one-seventy-two out there that I'd break my bank for if it wasn't for my wife. But more to the point, I think your friend just landed." He buttoned up his plaid overshirt in preparation for venturing back out into the cool night air.

"What! Where?" Victor hurried over to join his friend at the window.

101

O'Lary pointed to his left. "A plane just came in from over there, and taxied over to that hangar over there," he pointed right, "not to the passenger terminal, or to here, where most private flights would have come to check in, make a pit stop, etc."

"You think that's them?"

"This place is pretty small potatoes, Victor. I'd be thinking that not a lot of flights come in here at O-2:30 hours and peel off to a private hanger. The fuel tanks are over yonder," he pointed left, "not there," he pointed right. "Ain't nothin' over there but private hangars."

They both began running for the door. In Bob's car, Paige asked. "Where are you headed?"

"To the driveway on Hwy 10 that has the closest access to that hangar."

"Great but hang back. I don't want them to know we're following." He glanced over to see Bob shaking his head, annoyed? He thought, "Dammit, could I be more obvious?"

O'Lary pulled into a parking lot that served the regional smoke jumper facility, left a get-ready message for his posse, and waited. Two miles up the road a contingent of Satan's Spears waited, smoked a few, drank a few, and waited some more. In a few minutes, a black-on-black Ford passenger van emerged from a nearby hangar and headed south.

"Follow him." Paige's urging was unnecessary. Bob had already engaged the clutch and was moving, lights out, toward the driveway.

"Call Harry," O'Lary said through an unlit cigarette bobbing from his lip.

"Right." Paige fumbled in his pocket for the biker lawyer's phone, dropped it to the floorboard, retrieved it, and hit the start button. He pushed the combination for access and dialed the biker's phone. "Harry, turn on your tracker. They're here and on the move."

He heard a very country inflected voice come back. "Tracker's been on, like Bob said. Where the heck a ya'll been?"

Paige didn't want to get into it with the biker. He looked back at Bob's unlit cigarette. "You trying to quit?"

"Man, I've been trying to quit for twenty years." He flashed a grin back at Paige. "Besides, it's easy to quit. I've done it four or five times already." He laughed unconvincingly at his own small joke.

Paige's excitement grew. They were here. His quarry was here. A gang with muscle and an appropriate mindset was following up behind. They were finally going to get an up-close and very personal look at Connie's alien friend and that little girl freak. Then he thought back to the episode in the yard. She had disappeared, but certainly, not disappeared - disappeared. Just gone, poof, out of his sight. He had been concentrating on the guy on the porch. Surely, she was just up ahead.

The drive was uneventful. Red taillights a few hundred yards up the road. The bright glow of a dozen bikes following about a mile to his rear. After O'Lary turned onto Hwy 93 southbound, he turned anxiously to see that the bikes followed. They did. *A great thing, GPS tech*, he thought. His spirits jumped into a higher gear as they motored through a sleeping community. The intermittent motorcade was traveling south illuminated by a bright moon lit the landscape in shades of grey. Good omen?

Just beyond the slightly larger community of Corvallis, the van ahead pulled off to the west. The cross street had an intersection light but appeared to head off into darkness. No business district here. O'Lary drove through the intersection, turned into a gas station, and returned to the side street with lights off. "Good move, Bob. You've done this kind of thing before?"

O'Lary turned to stare at him below bunched eyebrows. His eyes reflected pinpoints of the blue-green glow of the dashboard lights. After a considering pause, he said. "Just say, that, ehh…" choosing his response carefully. "I've had my share of midnight adventures along the Canadian border."

Victor took this in. Good. He was in the company of practiced counter-culture pros with skill sets he needed and wanted to learn more from. He felt with his foot in the footwell and found the reassuring presence of his camera bag. This was going to be a major fucking deal!

Looking downslope behind them in the side mirror, could see the glow of the bikers lights following at some distance. Shafts of light occasionally hit treetops below them on one of the lower switchbacks of the serpentine road. He heard the crunch of gravel and, looking forward, noted that the road had gone from pavement to gravel. A cloud of dust indicated the recent passage of their target. The road climbed, turned into a side canyon and began to follow the convoluted folds of the canyon wall to their left.

The white cloud of gravel dust abruptly ended. As their vehicle came to a stop, they could spot a soft cloud of dust drifting lightly over a

Bruce Ballister

cut-back driveway that headed farther up the mountain wall at a steep incline.

O'Lary said, "Call Harry and tell them to proceed at a low idle, running lights

only."

"What? Why? We've got them cornered."

"Shit man, those bikes are going to make an unholy racket in this canyon. We may have already blown surprise and we don't know what that Fed has up there. Think like a cop if you want to take down a cop."

Victor did as he was told. He looked up to assess night visibility and was disappointed to see no sign of a moon, no stars. Outside of the dim glow of the car's dash lights and running lights, it was seriously dark. Despite his fears, he soon heard the low growl of motorcycles approaching from down-canyon. Then, one by one, bikes approached using their yellow running lights to stay on the two-rut gravel track.

A thousand yards up the mountain, Connie touched the back of her head. A sense that she was a psi receptor took hold but she found it hard to concentrate. "Martin, can you slow down or maybe stop a minute?" The van came to a stop, its headlights illuminating a rocky cut bank and dry scrub. She stepped out of the van and walked to the back, trying to concentrate. She thought she heard the rumble of a waterfall down the mountain.

Then, clearly in Myahh's psi, *Momma?*

Yes, Honey? Are you OK?

I'm fine, I'm here with daddy. I'm sorry I didn't tell you I was going. It was all kind of a sudden.

Where are you? We've been worried, sweetie. Why did you run off? Wait, you said you are with dad?

We are both here with the Visitor. He's a real nice person.

Where is here, baby?

I think it's his spaceship. He says we are between the Sun and the Earth.

Connie blew out a hard breath, in a mixture of elation that Myahh was OK, and awe that she was somehow a million miles distant in an alien spaceship. But she had learned to accept that sometimes, the impossible could be possible. A flash of lights on foliage on the driveway below them lit up trees on the other side of the canyon. She realized that she hadn't been listening to a waterfall; motorcycles were heading toward her.

Honey, I've got to go right now, I'm safe with Uncle Martin. I'm happy you are with daddy. We can talk about it later. She looked up to see Martin's impatient face illuminated by the van's taillights. She didn't need to hear his urgent plea to get back in her seat. She was already moving. As the van started back up the sinuous driveway, she asked. "Martin, can you put in a call to Houston Control? Brad is safe. He's not with Shaand, but he's safe. He and Colonel Kuznetskov can come back." She could read Martin Jenks' quizzical expression in the back glow of headlights on granite. "Martin, we're going to be safe now. Shand and Brad are OK, and we're OK."

His face was set in the hard determination of performing his mission. He'd seen the glow of headlights below them, heard the low growl of a dozen or more motorcycles reverberating through the canyon walls. "I wouldn't be too sure of that, Miss Connie. Let's just get you two up to the cabin."

17

Reverend Ehler Has a Bad Dream

The good Reverend Drake Ehler was pleased with himself as he prepared for bed. If he could have whistled while he brushed his teeth, he would have. The sermon he'd just finished for Wednesday night's call-in was a dandy. As he opened the lines to listeners on either the television cable feed or the online feed, they were still paying rapt attention to his opening remarks. So, expand and expound, and ramp up the call-in credits or debit lines that were open during and for twelve hours after each show. Yes, Wednesdays were hot, but tomorrow was going to be a bigger one. Pillow plumped, wife kissed, he rolled onto his back, assumed his favorite get-to-sleep pose, and drifted off.

His mood the following morning was as far from the previous night's mood as possible. Sleep, typically easy when he'd finished a milestone, refused to come. At one o'clock, he roused for the first of his nightly trips to relieve himself. He decided a snack might settle him, let the stomach juices demand enough energy that he might fall over that elusive edge into darkness. He found crackers and peanut butter, and with a glass of milk, he settled into his easy chair. Late-night comedians were having a field day with reports of the media ambush on the Hitchens' Florida homestead. The intruders had been dubbed camera commandos or deep-cover commandos by some of the networks. One actually had done due diligence and knew they called themselves the Renegade Press Corps. His own confidant in the RPC, Victor Paige, was to call in the morning with a report according to a text he'd largely ignored when finishing off the sermon.

Before he finished the crackers, he'd fallen asleep. His first dream-state images were of black-clad commandos slipping through heavy foliage. He'd never met Victor, but his dream-state mind put him alongside the reporter.

He stepped into a clearing in front of his imagined construct of the Florida Hitchens house surrounded by exotic bushes. As he approached a set of weathered wooden stairs to the house's deck, he was approached by a girl helping an elderly man.

"Reverend Ehler?" The young girl seemed to know him. Not unusual, he was famous after all. A household name.

"Why yes, I am."

The girl gestured to her stoop-shouldered companion. His wizened face had the look of a hard life and a gentle spirit shone from his eyes. The old man stood still, appraising him. The aged face did not look pleased.

The old man addressed him in a thin. cracking voice but it had a peculiar sense of command. Perhaps he'd risen to some height of industry or politics before age had reduced him. "Drake Ehler?"

"Yes, I said that." He was on the edge of being annoyed.

"Come," the old man said, "come sit with us. We'd like to talk." He indicated a small patio furniture set that Ehler hadn't noticed earlier. They sat with the old man opposite Ehler, and the girl sat at a third side of the four-sided table.

Ehler took a closer look. "Who exactly are you?" He noted a shimmer, or maybe it was an imagined translucency, about the pair. Dreams only approximated reality anyway.

The girl spoke for the pair. "I'm the girl you've been ranting about for the last week or so. I think your book tells you 'He that is without sin among you, let him first cast a stone at her?' Did I get that right?"

"Yes, that's from the King James Version," he allowed, "but it's a little dated."

"Dated or not, don't all translations have the same message?" Her look was of genuine interest.

"Well, yes but—"

The old man interrupted before Ehler could come up with a reply. "Tell me Reverend, do you believe in God?"

"Yes, of course! I'm a minister promoting the Word every week."

"Yes," the aged one pressed on, "but how does the Word inform you about this young lady's association with the devil? How do you claim special knowledge about someone you have never met?"

"I, I—" He had to stop. A piercing pain shot through the base of his brain. The answer came to him in spite of that flash. "I don't. I don't have any special knowledge. But I know that her abilities are not human."

The old man's visage became indistinct. The wrinkled face took on an overlay that seemed as if he was looking at him through water or a soft filter.

"Am I human?"

"You look to me to be—" He stopped. When the face resolved into focus again, he was darker, coffee brown, and a maroon dot had appeared on his forehead.

The visage now prompted, "Still human?"

"Uhhmm." Ehler could not speak. His tongue had turned to hard leather.

Again, the face morphed, this time darker still. Its nose had broadened, lips thickened slightly, and the forehead seemed to shrink back a few degrees. To Ehler, the face looked to be that of a sun-beaten Australian Aboriginal in his prime.

"And now?" The old man persisted, his voice now firm, commanding. The face lightened several shades, taking on the characteristics of an amalgam of Asian races and finally resolved into the smiling face of the custodian of Ehler's church, a Vietnamese immigrant. "How about now? Remind you of any humans you've met?"

Still, Ehler could not make a sound other than a grunt. Before him, the face's skin tones changed again, more Mediterranean now. A long tightly curled black mane and flowing beard grew on a face with a pronounced nose and jet-black eyes. Wrinkles flattened and a youthful man in his twenties appeared in long flowing cotton. Another wrap of white cloth sheathed his head. Ehler looked around for the young girl who seemed to have disappeared.

The stranger asked in a voice that demanded his attention. "Would you recognize Jesus if you saw him?"

Ehler was confused. The image forming before him looked more like an Iranian terrorist. All the image needed was an automatic weapon. As he scanned quickly behind him, the girl sat cross-legged, Buddha style, hands on her knees, her middle fingers just curled enough to touch her thumbs. A perfect pose of meditation. Her eyes closed in concentration.

"Or maybe this?" Again, the shape before him shifted. The man's face lightened; his hair unfurled into softly curving amber. His eyes brightened to a steely blue. "Do you see? Can you see?" The image of a Christian bookstore's Methodist Jesus teased him.

"Oh! Oh Jegesss!" Ehler tried to speak, but his throat could not make the right sounds. With some effort he grunted an amazed, "Ungh!" and lost all further ability to speak.

"Now," the Methodist Jesus said, pointing to the meditating child, "what right do you have to speak of this child as being from or in league with the devil?" The Jesus figure before him placed a hand on the girl's shoulder.

Try as he might, Ehler's tongue refused to move. He found by experimenting that he could still make grunting sounds at the back of his throat. Nothing he could do would move lips or tongue in a concerted fashion.

"I can't understand you," the old man said. Again, the image sitting beside the girl was the stoop-shouldered, heavily wrinkled old man.

"Unghh, eh ghee." He had tried to say, "I'm trying, I see."

Silent while this confrontation was developing, the girl finally spoke again. "Reverend Ehler, we will see you again. Be careful of your message, delivering hate is inconsistent with everything your Bible tells you. Inventing lies and delivering them as truth revealed to you is blasphemy, a stain on your soul. My friend and I will come for you in a few days, but not in a way you would ever expect. I want you to be open to new knowledge – to a new message."

Nervously glancing between the old man and the young girl, he recognized her as the Hitchens kid. She opened her eyes and peered directly into the wreckage of his soul.

The old man straightened and fixed him with a hard stare. "Drake Ehler, I have a series of questions, or topics for you to consider over the next few days. An adequate period for personal reflection, if you will. As a messenger, you have been extremely successful. In your moments of pride, you've weighed that success on the wealth you've accumulated not the help you've brought. Instead of helping your flock, you have garnished their money, their spare change, their bank accounts, and their life support. You have taught them that giving you money will incur favor in the hereafter. You've cheated by the thousands those who are very much more in need of real solace."

"Ehgehg," was the only response Ehler could make in his defense.

"Consider too," the man said, "how many opportunities you've had to be truly noble. You've taken an easier road and decided to accumulate more to your person than to be more than a token contributor. You do not provide real succor. You tell your followers that to give, to you, is divine.

Tally up the times when your greed has taken primacy over generosity, when demeaning others was your message rather than lifting them up. This, Drake Ehler is your walk in the wilderness. When we meet again, and you've recovered mastery of your tongue, we can talk."

"Ughegh," was all he could manage. He found himself weeping. The old man's image had now resolved to a twentieth-century businessman in white crisply creased slacks and a white shirt. The girl took the man by the hand and stood. Ehler's legs would not move. His arms were leaden, seemingly glued to his chair arms. He looked down at the immovable limbs in confusion. He'd wanted to follow the pair, but when he looked up, they were gone.

When he blinked, he found himself staring at the seventy-inch television on his media wall. Before him the image of the Hitchens' yard flattened to the screen image he'd seen on the news, as supplied by Paige and his friends. Realization flooded in, *Thank God, that was only a dream*. He felt a sudden urge to get up and relieve himself. But his forearms and hands were strangely stiff. He struggled with the very simple button fly on his pajamas. He looked for some reassurance into the mirror and saw a worried, florid, overweight man with more than enough reasons to be happier. The dream edged back into his thoughts. Its realism had been truly frightening. He thought he said, *Glad that was only a dream*. What came out was, "Ghwuhhee, ghhe egeh heheem."

18

I Have Worry

"Connie, Lenka, we have a problem." Martin tried to keep his voice calm, but two of the planet's best interpreters of mental state were in the room with him.

Lenka put her bags down and stepped back out onto the porch. Somewhere, from downslope, she could hear the low muttering and surging of motorcycles. She'd only ever heard massed motorcycles in movies with Connie, but these sounded ominous, like beasts in the dark, like the growls of crant; the six-legged hunter-monsters of her home planet. For only the third or fourth time on Earth, she was afraid. *Martin, please come.* She called out to him in psi. She knew Martin had only been taking Selli fruit extract for a few months, but his skills were improving. The small grove growing deep in the wildlife refuge property and the small seed crop facility growing in a secreted USDA research lab were the only places the fruit could be harvested. Martin, because of his close contact with the Hitchens, had volunteered to be on the shortlist of experimental human users.

She turned as she felt Martin's footsteps over the faint rumbling below. *You heard!*

Yes, I'm getting better. "But I prefer still speech." He unconsciously moved his left hand to the back of his neck; close to the location of the 'hearing' center for psi.

"I think they come for me. That is the energy I feel. I have worry."

He hated to admit it, but said, "I think you may be right, Lenka." Silently, inwardly, he cursed a storm of self-recrimination for thinking his mountain cabin might be private. He tried to think back to where or when his plans to come here might have been leaked.

She heard the violent turmoil going on in his head. "Not your fault, Martin." She understood his sense of responsibility and she understood the hatred. "On Dzura too, many still afraid of humans." She remembered the days before the war. "Many in the High Pel Council were unhappy to have Brad take part in the plans to take down the city-ships. Many

111

conversations out of his hearing. Some thought he and Connie should be kept in a thing like zoo. Always, some simple minds afraid of something not known."

Martin had heard the stories so often he could probably write the book himself. But Connie had already written the book or books. Her diary had been converted into book form for mass publication. and covered Brad's early discovery of the small piece of space junk embedded in an ancient cypress tree The described their discovery of the 'voice in the woods' that turned out to be Jai. They had thought they were rescuing a trapped pilot but discovered the psi-capable sentient AI of a deceased Dzuran fighter pilot's gunship. Martin had been there, in the sixty mile-per-hour tailwinds of Hurricane Kate, as Brad and Connie successfully aided the ship in powering up and breaking loose from its limestone prison. His reverie was broken by a series of beeps coming from a console in the house. "Excuse me Lenka."

Lenka listened again, her senses growing more attuned as the noise from below gradually went quiet. Now, in the absence of mechanical noise, the unfamiliar night noises of the Bitterroot Mountains returned. Unknown insects resumed their chatter and hum. In the near distance, to her left and right, a pair of western screech owls cried out in call and response. The occasional fall of small bits of tree litter to the forest floor had her head on a swivel trying to identify movement in the dark. She knew Martin had night vision glasses, goggles he called them, in his equipment but they would not fit her head shape. This was some technology that could be useful on Dzura.

She mentally added the goggles to a list of technologies that humans possessed in abundance that Dzuran culture could benefit from. Her specific mission was to not only identify tech that could be useful on Dzura, but to understand the context in which the Terran technology could be translated in Elioi culture. She also looked for gaps in human technology in which the Elioi could trade. She thought, "It is not my job to sit and wonder in fear at the strange sounds of this forest."

"Lenka, please come in here." She turned to Connie's voice and returned to the cabin.

Martin and Connie were looking at an array of video panels lined up in an arc above one of his desks. The larger one in the center was split into sixteen squares. Each showed a view of the approaches to the cabin or the areas immediately surrounding the cabin itself. Two of them showed men moving in single file up the steep driveway. Some carried projectile weapons, others, unknown equipment.

Martin pointed to one of the screens. One of the men wearing night-vision goggles had stopped, raised his hand in military mode to stop the column of men behind him. He pointed directly at a camera that was sending out short wave infrared to illuminate an area so covered by trees that even if there had been a full moon, the ambient light would not have offered much. Martin said, "Well, they now know we can see them coming." They watched as the group gathered around the man. The image was in shades of pixilated green, but as Martin directed the camera's focus and zoom, individuals' features became clear. The man with the night vision gear had shifted his night vision lenses up and had turned to face the growing crowd.

"Son of a gun!" Martin growled in growing anger. "I know that guy." He pointed to one of the faces staring intently at the man in charge. "That guy was in Florida a few days back. He was arrested in the media assault on your house. This time the guy's going to jail."

"Martin, I hate to say this," Connie's concern was palpable even without psi, "but there's a dozen or more of those guys out there, and most of them have rifles. I'd be surprised if they were here just to take pictures."

Martin nodded in agreement. "You may be right about that, Connie." He looked away from the screens and up at her worried face. "I've called in reinforcements. If we can hold them off for a bit, help will be here presently."

"When did you do that?" Lenka was surprised and relieved.

Martin smiled through thin lips. His self-satisfaction was dampened by uncertainty. "When we left Florida."

1

Lights, Cameras, Action

The cabin's three occupants huddled over Martin's surveillance system and watched the array of green screen images for movement. First one, then another, and soon five of the sixteen infrared cameras indicated stealthy approaches from the downhill approaches to the cabin. Moments later, a sixth screen showed two men approaching from the cabin's rear. All were still more than forty or fifty yards out and were taking ever closer positions behind trees or boulders. A few held elaborate camera gear, others sported carbines and automatic rifles. Two huddled a dozen yards closer behind his woodpile. Martin muttered an oath.

"Connie, see that light switch by the door? Please turn on the last switch on the right."

As she did so. The monitor screens flashed bright white before going to black and white as the low-light sensors were briefly overpowered by the sudden burst of photons. Screams of surprise and pain could be heard as retinas straining to make out detail in night vision goggles were overpowered. The cameras automatically switched over to visible light as the cabin's perimeter was awash in the glow of high-powered floodlights. As the hardware recovered, the screens resolved showing most of the men shielding their eyes from the intense glare of multiple banks of floodlights.

Martin keyed the mike on his exterior audio system. "Gentlemen, I would not advise moving forward. I have a perimeter defense system in place, and this is a long way up the mountain for an EMS truck to come after your bodies. I'd hate to have your needless demise on my conscience, but I'd probably get over it."

As they watched, the small groups of men turned to each other. One man in plaid seemed to be talking on a radio set to another of the groups. The two that had been coming from the rear were not visible. One of the cameras showed two men walking away from the cabin with occasional nervous looks back. Another showed two men in heated argument. Martin's mouth formed a grim, thin-lipped smile of victory, he had at least delayed the assault.

Lenka asked. "Do you really have a perimeter defense system? Is it lethal?"

"No, I wish I did! I have cameras and lights because there are some dangerous predators out there at night and I like to go out on the porch at times to take phone calls." He gestured at his small cabin. "Phone signal inside isn't as good here as on the front porch. It faces down the mountain toward civilization."

Lenka's forehead wrinkled in worry. "There are predators?"

"Bears, mountain lions." Connie knew Lenka would not understand the reference. "Imagine very large cats and very much larger dogs that are more hungry than cautious."

"Oh!" Lenka seemed to shrink a little, thinking of the fast-moving predator crant from the lush Dzuran jungles.

"Dammit!" Martin swore at the monitors on his desk. Lenka and Connie turned to see that two of the rectangles had gone to gray static fuzz. He punched at his console in rapid finger strokes. The scenes backed up to show a human figure with a hood pulled tight around a face covered with oversized sunglasses running forward to spray paint on the cameras. Changes in the surrounding scenes indicated the loss of the floodlights in those locations as well. "Dammit, all to hell."

Another man vigorously shaking a spray can ran toward the camera facing the backyard and disarmed that lens and light set as well. Martin pulled a desk drawer open and took out a revolver and a box of ammo. In a quiet rage, he flicked open the revolver and began inserting rounds. He didn't even hint at a smile until he'd flicked the gun shut again and given the chambers a spin.

His satisfaction was short-lived. A crash and splinter of glass announced the arrival of a small fist-sized rock that rolled to a stop under his couch. While their attention was turned to the broken window and the spray of glittering shards on the floor, two more of the cameras covering the back of the house and side yards went blank.

"Everyone, get down!" Martin issued it in a harsh whisper that still carried command authority. Connie dropped to her knees between the couch and coffee table. She noticed for the first time that it was really a workbench for tying his fishing flies. She was eyeball to eyeball with a life-sized, beautifully crafted bumblebee sporting a barbed hook for a stinger.

Martin flicked off the interior lights and was in a crouch just inside the kitchen counter's ell. He paused, gun drawn, peering toward the broken window. Movement and light to his right caused him to pivot, increasing pressure on the trigger guard. Lenka was still standing, her white head and hands illuminated by the glowing screens of Martin's video surveillance equipment. "Lenka, would you please get down?" He thought to try to explain night vision scopes. "They have guns that can see in the dark."

He felt her objection in psi, then heard her soft voice. "Nine men still in trees, five men run back down mountain road." She tilted her head to her right, toward the front door. "Two more slowly come to front of house." He heard two voices cry out in surprise, then pain. "They go away now."

"Lenka, please. I am responsible for you – for all of Earth. To keep them from giving you harm. Please?"

He heard a scrape on the floor, tracked it, and saw that she was bringing a dinette chair over to his position. She sat beside him, nearly blocking his shot-angle toward the broken window. "Now, only five men outside looking here. Four lying on the ground."

He gained a fresh understanding of her abilities. "What are the men on the ground doing? Can you see if they are pointing weapons at the house?"

"No, they are curled in ball like small child."

Fetal position? Oh! "Lenka, are you projecting at them?"

"Yes, just want them stop being…what you say? Anal holes."

Connie started laughing. She could see Lenka's head, dim in the darkened house. Lenka was calmly seated in a dinette chair, hands in her lap.

Martin couldn't see Connie, but he could tell she was having a hard time stifling her giggles. "Yes, Lenka," he said, "they are being anal holes." Then, "What about the other five men, can you see them?" He wasn't sure if 'see' was the right term for whatever she was projecting/receiving.

"Not see, two behind a small stack of cut tree parts."

That would be my firewood stack, he thought. Two layers thick, five feet high. The only cover in the approaches to the house. *But they were covered in a tarp. How did she know it was 'parts of trees'?* He made a quick mental note to build the covered shelter next to the cabin's walls to deprive an ambusher of cover larger than a ponderosa pine.

Lenka tilted her head slightly, projecting out into the yard. "Now all men lying on the ground, curl in balls like small child."

He shifted his gaze from the jagged edges of the broken window back to Lenka. Shards of light from the remaining outside floodlight caromed off the freshly shattered edges. In contrast, she was serenely quiet two feet away sitting in his dining room chair, wreaking mental havoc on the remainder of the attack force.

Martin asked, "Lenka, is it safe for me to go outside now?"

"Yes, I go with you."

Martin thought the response was almost musical as it had psi overtones he could feel.

She said softly, "It no problem, they not move until I say."

Connie peered over the back of the couch toward them, "Be careful, Lenka. Do be careful." She stood and brushed off her knees, then came over to the door to stand watch as Lenka and Martin went to the door. The remaining floodlights facing the front yard clearly illuminated a handful of curled bodies lying a hundred feet down the driveway, still partially shielded by trees. Martin looked toward the woodpile. *What was that guy's name? Paine? Pace? Ah, Paige.* He called out toward the woodpile. "Paige, Victor Paige, that you out there?"

"NGnnhhgg."

"I thought so, do you want me to tell her to turn it off?"

"Yynggsss."

"Slowly, very slowly, all of you toss your firearms away from you. I want to see it happening before she turns down the volume." Out in the diminishing cone of light, he could see dark shapes tossed into the blanket of natural forest litter that was his yard. He looked to Lenka, "It's OK now. I think you can stop doing whatever you are doing."

"OK, all of you, listen up." He spoke loudly into the darkness. "I've already dialed up a contingent of US Marshalls as well as the sheriff. This will all be over soon as simple trespass. And, maybe the sheriff would want to toss in some kind of intent charge, but I'm not going to throw anything Federal at you unless you get stupid." A few grunts and whispers came out of the gloom. "Do we understand each other?" A grudging yes or two came from behind the trees, some of them began to stand. Two heads bobbed up behind the woodpile.

Bruce Ballister

He pointed a finger at them. "You two, come closer." Is one of you Victor Paige?"

"Yeah, that would be me." Paige emerged from cover massaging the back of his neck.

"Who's your friend? Speak up?" An unintelligible garble came from the guy, then a cough.

"Robert, er, Bob." The man was rubbing at his eye sockets as if to relieve a migraine.

"Bob who?"

"O'Lary. Bob O'Lary."

"Both of you step forward, come to about ten feet from the bottom of these steps." He raised his voice and shouted out into the darker areas further out. "The rest of you stay put for now. You can get up off the ground but stay put." He felt a pull at his psi receptors that said Lenka had just sent a message to not reach for weapons. He had to smile at that. He wasn't sure who they were afraid of most, but he figured it was Lenka.

Farther down his drive, he heard the throaty growl of motorcycles coming to life as some of the posse had given up the cause. "Not to worry," he thought. He could see flickers of blue and red flashes from across the canyon. There was no escape for the first wave of deserters.

The two from the woodpile shuffled toward them and stopped, more or less ten to twelve feet away from the steps. Lenka said softly. "I not someone to fear. I am an ambassador from my planet to yours. How is it you want to hurt me or my friends?"

The two looked at each other in astonishment. "Yes, I speak. I am good friend of Connie for long time. I help Connie with her baby at my home." She paused, probing. "You think me dangerous? Why me dangerous? Why you want to hurt me, or hurt my friend?" Connie had come out of the house and stood beside her. Lenka made an extremely uncharacteristic move for an Elioi and placed her hand on Connie's shoulder.

In a few minutes, Martin's comfortable-for-one mountain cabin was stuffed to capacity by the remaining former antagonists. Given the order to approach slowly from their places behind trees, three had come forward, two more had run at all possible speed away from the cabin before being brought down by a discouraging blast of psi from Lenka. A few others slowly approached with obvious apprehension. They were now

118

all arrayed on his couch, the two available chairs, with two more seated on the fireplace's raised stone hearth. Their attitudes seemed to radiate either stark fear, hatred, or some combination especially when their gazes focused on the white-furred alien. Connie and Lenka stood together facing Victor Paige and Bob O'Lary who were seated on the couch. Bob's expression, since he'd come down from the pain of Lenka's psi attack was of distrust and almost palpable malevolence. Martin had three others cuffed to each other and lined against a wall.

Martin looked at the collection, four of them wore motorcycle club colors. O'Lary's black tactical onesie was reminiscent of the assault on the Hitchens's home. He asked, "O'Lary, Bob. Were you with Paige there on the assault?

Paige spoke first. "It wasn't an assault; it was a fact-finding expedition. The world deserves to know what the hell is going on."

O'Lary added, "No, we just know each other through the network."

Connie asked, "Yeah? And what network would that be?"

Paige glanced quickly at O'Lary, shrugged, and said, "Pick one, there's ten or fifteen I know about that share information on what the government has been trying to hide."

"Well," Connie replied, "I admit that I've had a bit of a struggle trying to protect my private life, but we were just giving interviews last week! Trying to do our best to bring the world, as you call it, up to date."

"But that freak child of yours screwed the deal. Scared the crap out of that reporter chick." This outburst came from one of the motorcycle crew.

"Where is that kid anyway?" Another called out.

Lenka put her arm out to stop Connie from moving closer to the guy. "Connie has some skill at what she calls psi because food she ate in prison on my planet. It had chemicals that magnify the ability to mind talk/feel. My old enemy, the Dzurans, thought to find out more about these two humans if they could read their minds. Like your truth test machine, only vegetable induced truth drug. It not work. It make Connie and Brad good at talking with mind." Lenka held Connie's hand and clasped it with her other hand. Looking at Connie as she spoke, Lenka continued. "We not know for long time that Connie is pregnant. The food Elioi eat have this compound, Connie eat while pregnant and it affect little Myahh when inside Connie. We very sorry. If we know Connie pregnant, we not give this. We do not give this food to our own when they go to the…birthing creches to become mothers."

Connie collected her emotions. She took in a breath, then said, "Myahh is especially skilled at the telepathic abilities we call psi communication. But she is still a child. She's almost eight and has a lot of the impulses of someone who is seven or eight. It is true that she cannot always stop from hearing others, and she does not like people lying to her." She turned to the guy who'd just called Myahh a freak. "Myahh and her dad are, at this moment, learning some very important truths about those two new spacecraft in our solar system."

She sighed in exasperation. "Truth is, when we first learned of her abilities, how good she is, we were worried about her socialization. Three-year-olds are bluntly honest. By the time kids are five, they are learning from their parents to lie, to fudge. And they don't like being told that they are lying. We had to pull her from pre-K and begin home schooling. She's almost eight now, and she's still a long way from full control of her abilities."

Connie scanned the room, these people wanted to do physical harm to her, to her friend Lenka, and if she were here – to her daughter. A laugh of scorn, and derision bubbled and died in her throat. "You, you band of what? Brothers? I think not. You have no idea at all what you are involved in. You and your petty internet fantasies!" She did laugh now, a derisive grunt. "Huh! I've seen a city in the stars erupt in flame, watched from the safe firm soil of an alien planet while over two-hundred thousand souls in that city-ship fell through the lavender skies of that planet and perished. That crash site is now a holy place of remembrance for a civil war that did not have to happen."

She paused, remembering. "But I'm glad it happened." She grasped Lenka's hand and brought it to her chest. "This woman, this mother of nine, she saved my life as I lay struggling to birth my daughter. The occupants of that ship that fell to ground would have cut me open as a specimen. Indeed, they tossed us, Brad and me, into a prison to see if we were contagious." Her face hardened into a fire-borne glare as she passed her gaze across the would-be marauders. She pointed to one of the two on the hearth. "You, what do you do as a day job?"

The guy wore a shiny grenade-styled insulated jacket over jeans. "I'm an accountant. Mountain Bank & Trust." He looked down and away, as if shame had finally kicked in.

"And you?" She pointed at the man seated beside the accountant. He sported a leather vest, with loops filled with ammo brass over a thick leather collared plaid jacket.

"Ranch. Ehm, I'm a rancher, goats, mostly. We have a line of goat milk products. Yogurts, cheeses." He held her stare, defiant.

Connie nodded, pointed to one of the men wearing biker colors, in his late twenties to early thirties, she guessed. She asked, "You, what about you? Tough guy, biker's credo, a real independent? What do you do?"

The young man, blondish hair thick on top and trimmed tight to the skin on the sides, had signs of a hard physical youth. "I'm a cutter. I drop trees downslope so the draggers can chain the trees down to waiting trucks."

"You have a family?"

Reluctantly, "Yeah, wife and three kids. Why" The young biker's insolence rose above his fear.

"Because if you love them, you'll need to show them. Your macho schtick isn't good for anyone, especially your children who are learning from every move you make, and everything you say." She scanned the faces that were glued to hers. "This thing that happened tonight could have been a tragedy for humanity."

"How so?" O'Lary spoke from his shared spot with Paige on the couch.

"If Lenka had been injured or worse, you could have incurred the wrath of an entire race of spacefaring Elioi that could literally rain hell down upon this planet." Her mouth formed a brief razor-thin smile. "Their culture mines asteroids for metals. Just imagine how easy it would be to find a half-dozen asteroids and toss them at random into our oceans, our fragile volcanic regions, and our cities. Think about that! And think about those shotguns and rifles out there on the ground. Just think about your shotguns vs. mile-wide asteroids."

O'Lary looked down at his knees and rubbed his knuckles across a nose still running from the chill air outside. Connie looked at his couch-mate, "You were at my house a few days ago, right?"

Paige looked away, toward the few men lining the wall, then looked up to return her glare. "Yes, I was. We were trying to find out more. We deserve to know more."

"More than the book I wrote about how Brad and I found the spaceship? More than the account we co-wrote of our time on Dzura? I know they were written as adventures, but as God is my witness, they are true." Her timbre grew throaty with emotional content as she continued.

121

Bruce Ballister

"Lenka, my good dear friend Lenka, is an ambassador to Earth from her people on the twin system of Dzura and Erra fourteen light-years from here. Myahh is my treasure. She's also Earth's treasure. Myahh, my dear sweet precocious daughter, is an ambassador from Earth to a culture we do not even know much about yet. You can believe me or not, you can write about this evening in whatever slant your preconceptions will dictate, or you can write about this evening as it actually happened." She allowed a slight smile to pull a dimple in her left cheek. "Or you can transcribe verbatim what that recorder in your right shirt pocket is recording. Your choice."

Paige's eyebrows raised in surprise as his left hand reached over the pocket, felt for the small lump there.

"Go ahead," Connie urged, "go ahead and see if it's still on and recording." Paige pulled it out, glanced at it, and turned it to show Connie its bright indicator light shining red.

"Good," Connie continued. "At this moment, Myahh is somewhere between the Earth and the Sun, she's there with her father and someone I can't wait to meet. That...that individual is an ambassador to Earth from—" she waved a hand above her as if to encompass the night sky outside. "—from out there. Somewhere we can't imagine."

~ ~ ~

In the early hours of the following morning, Lenka and Connie were out on the porch enjoying a morning cup of tea. Martin Jenks brewed coffee and was serving the handcuffed men in his cabin. Most of the motorcycle club was being rounded up as they exited the mountain trail. Handing a cup of the steaming brew to Bob O'Lary, the would be commando glared up at him. Martin asked, "What exactly is your problem? Is it the 'I don't know what it is, so I don't like it?' or the 'It ain't from here so I need to kill it' argument?"

O'Lary sniffed at the cup, blew on the edge and took a cautious first sip, then looked up at Jenks. "Between the two, probably the first, but it's closer to trying to help Paige here get the truth out to the world."

Martin huffed, "Hmmpf, and which truth will that be?" He shifted attention to Victor Paige who was in mid-sip of his coffee. "You're the reporter, what would you be reporting on, if these idiots and their shotguns, long rifles, and pistols had actually killed one of the two resident alien guests on this planet. Perhaps the start of an interplanetary war that we would certainly lose?"

Paige's sidelong glance at O'Lary indicated he hadn't thought about that scenario. "I—uh—never really thought that it might go that far." He squinted up at Martin Jenks, "I wanted to shine a light inside the secrecy surrounding the Hitchens, the aliens, and whatever they're cooking up." He looked off, thinking. "Yeah, that's about it. I wanted to know what was really going on, tell that story."

O'Lary joined in. "Yeah, the public deserves to know, needs to know."

"Has it ever occurred to you to listen to the news? You got the three broadcast majors, then pick your flavor, MSNBC, Fox, BBC. And the papers; the Washington Post, New York Times, the Chicago Tribune, Houston Chronical..." His list slowed to a stop. "Ever think of looking at what is being reported everyday as opposed to trying to go underground, to scoop the world press with something you *think* is going on? Something that your suspicious mind has cooked up with these other yahoos and their conspiracy fringe theories?"

From the front porch he heard a small pop, like a sudden puff of air. Connie's voice called out, "Martin!"

He rushed to the door in time to watch a vanishing ball of swirling gold vapors dissipate into nothing but a memory. Connie and Lenka were gone. "Jesus H –!" His expletive stopped in mid-thought as he received a calming answer to their disappearance. *All is good, Martin. We are with the Visitor.* Recovering from the shock, he returned to the living room. He swallowed, looked at his watch, and addressed his guests. "FBI will be up here momentarily to pick you all up. I suggest you don't try to play dumb. Lying to the FBI is not your best move."

O'Lary asked from his perch on the hearth, "What happened on the porch?"

Martin sighed, "I'd have to call it a miracle, but ... I really don't have an explanation that I want to share. He thought back to the night of Hurricane Kate's landfall and the discovery of a dead alien in a space suit. Brad and Connie had just left in the alien's spaceship, apparently having been given instantaneous or miraculous access to its controls. It seemed everything about his assignment to the Hitchens was destined to bring moments of unanticipated wonder and amazement.

He thought, "Miracles never do cease to amaze!" Then, looking down at the two on the hearth and around at the others, who were still waiting for transport down to the command center at the Missoula airport, he sighed, hoping he could finally get back to finishing the bumble bee lure on his work bench.

2

Homecoming

Brad, and Shaand felt a subtle but rapid change in air pressure. Myahh let out a small, "Oh!" and almost fell against Brad's desk. Furniture shifted slightly, shifted subtly from the alien's construct to the physical reality of his home office. Brad looked through the picture window view opposite the desk and had the peculiar feeling of its reality. In answer to his question, a mockingbird swooped across his view out the picture window. Breathing deeply, the smells were right. He caught a glimpse of one of the security guards walking the perimeter, staring out across the grassy beds with some intensity. She continued on her perimeter walk and seemed to check in on her radio.

"I think we're back." Brad said, the view through his sliding glass doors overlooking Goose Creek Bay was obviously the real thing with wind rustling the marsh grass beds and sprinkling the bay's waters with flashes of the last of the setting sun's light. He turned to Shaand smiling in wonder at their instantaneous transport home, when he felt a psi disturbance. A series of subtle pops of air pressure announced other arrivals as Myahh, Lenka, Connie, and Martin joined them.

"How did it do that?" Shaand said. "It says it is not a god. But it might as well be..."

Myahh, went over to the window and stared out across the grassy flats. "He did that when he took me to where you were, Daddy. I was out there in the yard, I felt a little chill, I floated through a little tunnel, then I just went 'pop' and I was there with you."

Brad looked at Shaand. "Same for me too, I guess. I fell through a panel on the asteroid ship and fell into nothingness. A featureless void. Then it took the form of this office, then you appeared."

Shaand, adopting a learned human behavior, shook his head in wonder. "Yes, just a minor pop in the ears, and I was there too." His forehead wrinkled in a grin. "One minute I with the Colonel Kuznetsov, then 'pop' and I am not."

A gentle puff of air seemed to pass across the room, like the cool breath of an oscillating fan. They all heard/felt the next pop and turned to see the Visitor. Again, he materialized before them in the appearance of a barefoot elderly human in a crisp, white linen suit. "I see we are all here now, good!" He opened his arms expansively, taking them all in. "Now that we are all here," he nodded in turn to Connie, Bradley, Myahh, Shaand, and Lenka, "I must tell you that you are all good souls. You each possess a kind spirit, a sense of what is right, and from what I have observed, you can keep each other's trust." His arms lowered as he continued, "That is a most important component in any group that is working toward a common goal."

Myahh raised her hand, slowly. Although she had only attended a few weeks of public classes, she knew the convention for taking a turn. "Excuse me?"

The visitor smiled and bowed. "Yes, what would you like to say?"

"What is your name? What should we call you?"

His smile was magical, Brad thought. Welcoming, open, accepting. His eyes seemed to take in everything around him and yet focus specifically on who he was addressing. "If," Brad thought, "if the shape-shifting persona in front of him *was* a 'he.'

The visitor bent slightly toward Myahh, bending a listening ear toward her in a completely natural gesture for an elderly human. "And what do you hear, when you think of me?"

Myahh's eyes opened wide, on the receiving end of something private. "Sailor? No Sailora?"

"Almost. Try again."

Their mutual gaze lasted a few more moments as the room's sound vanished to allow only the soft hush of air conditioning to intrude. "Sayala." She nodded after she said it. "Yes, it sounds like 'Sayala.' Is that right?"

The visitor's smile broadened even wider as his shoulders shook lightly in silent laughter. "You are very good child. You may not remember but I introduced myself to you many weeks ago when you were outside. But I was very far away then." Sayala straightened and addressed the semi-circle facing him. He gave a very slight neck bow and said, "I am called Sayala, at least, that is as close as I can get using human vocal cords."

125

A loud bang interrupted the reverent mood when a wren impacted the bay view sliding glass door. All turned to the sound as its tiny body fell to the deck. A visceral wave of sorrowful emotion and psi energy passed through the group. The little bird, extended a week slowly, righted itself, and stood. It gave a quick glance inside the house, turned and flew away.

Brad muttered, "Clarke's third law."

Myahh turned her head in question. "What? Whose law?"

Brad rubbed his chin, thinking. "I don't remember the exact words, Myahh, but it goes something like, 'If somebody's technology is advanced enough, it will appear to be magic to a less developed culture.'"

Shaand nodded. "Yes, or God force."

The entity's enigmatic smile returned. "Ah, yes! The technology I assure you is not a God force." It folded its arms across its chest. "As I told you before on my ship. I am not a god. I am a traveler, but with my technology, I can travel in more dimensions than can you and I have a certain facility in reading thoughts in others." The visitor seemed to look off elsewhere for a moment, then – "and I have a purpose, a mission. If you will allow me another imposition, I need to bring another guest here." Brad felt Sayala's gaze reach into his psi space. Felt reassurance, comfort, and trust.

Sure, whoever, whatever. He felt himself respond.

Another gentle pop or puff of air shattered the following stillness and the Right Reverend Drake Ehler stumbled into their space then fell against a side chair. Shaand was nearest and knelt to help the obviously confused new guest. Brad knelt and intercepted him. "Better let me help here, my friend. I think he is going to be confused and you might just scare the bejeezus out of him."

Ehler straightened, took in Brad's face in instant recognition, then whirled around taking in the gathering, his gaze dropped to see Myahh's discomforting grin. Confusion distorted his face, then as he regained his composure, a weird calm. He stood more erect and took a deep breath.

Brad said, "Dr. Ehler? Welcome to my home." He gestured to the others in the room. "I believe you know, at least from video, Shaand and my daughter, Myahh, and Sayala."

Sayala approached Ehler, who shrank back. "Do you remember me?"

"Eh, no?"

Sayala transformed back to the form of Methodist Jesus.

Ehler took a step and a half back, "Oh, my God!" His face contorted in succession from recognition to awe, then fear. He bowed, then fell to his knees, prostrate, cheek to the floor. A contrite sinner in fear of judgment.

The Visitor smiled, back in the form of a white-haired, almond-skinned, ethnically indistinct man in a loose linen suit. "No, not your God." He reached a hand down, palm up, in perfect imitation of the beckoning Jesus and said, "Stand, come closer, no need to fear me."

Ehler looked to the side, left then right, he saw mostly shoes, the lower edges of furniture, then lifting slightly, he took in the immaculately clean bare feet extending from white linen. *Could it be? Could it be? Emmanuel? Come in human form again?*

"No, I am not your Emmanuel, preacher."

"But, but I've been sharing your word all these years."

"Silence!" The voice and psi impact pushed Ehler back a foot, making him almost fall into an easy chair.

The groveling preacher recovered and lowered himself closer to the floor. His back began to wrack with sobs.

"Stop that, get control of yourself. Heed this!"

The four standing figures, arrayed in a half circle, looked down at the wreckage of Drake Ehler's ego. They could not hear what messages were being sent to the preacher, but it was becoming hard to watch. Brad reached over the small table separating him from Myahh and took her hand. He led her around the table and gave her a reassuring hug. Shaand looked away, out at the grassy flats beyond. He had seen humiliation before, in Erran prisons. He knew shame when he saw it.

Ehler slowly stood, and taking a deep breath, held himself at something approaching military attention before Sayala. Brad thought Ehler's skin sickly pale, the man's eyes betrayed something between fear and awe. It was clear as he watched that Sayala was still communicating through whatever level of psi Sayala had been able to teach the televangelist. Ehler shuddered, faltered, and finally coughed up a quiet, "Yes, Sir."

Sayala smiled again, "Thank you, I'm sure you will. And truly, I think you have come a very long way in understanding today. Not many have that ability."

Bruce Ballister

Ehler reached to the back of his skull, rubbing it, absent of conscious thought. Brad recognized the back brain headache that came in the early stages of psi ability. The skills shared by all mammals that utilize pack hunting, from canines and felines to elephants and the aquatic mammals, was lost by most of humanity when speech happened. The skill, when reawakened, caused the rapid growth of the capillary network supplying blood to the region and produced some terrific headaches.

"Reverend Ehler," Brad said. "I see he's given you a crash course in telepathic communication. We refer to it as psi. But it can hurt at first. It will get easier, and if you'd like, I can give you some extract that will help you greatly."

The preacher looked at Brad, reassessing. "Thanks, Hutchins, er, Hitchens." Then feeling the communication from Brad, "Bradley."

Brad extended a hand in friendship and took the preacher's hand in a firm shake, prolonging the gesture with an open message of bonding trust. It took a moment, but the feeling came back from the slightly startled preacher. Brad smiled as Ehler stood before him and said, "Reverend, we're going to need you. We're going to need you and your kind, and rabbis, and mullahs, and gurus; the whoevers that are in clerical leadership positions across the globe."

The preacher raised his eyebrows in appreciation of the problem and sighed. "Yes, I think I can help in a small way."

~ ~ ~

In the absence of the principal parties, the security detail at the Hitchens's home was reduced to a detail of two. With all of its occupants gone, or missing in Myahh's case, the two on-duty officers sat in the relative comfort of their black Chevy Suburban and monitored the homesite's perimeter motion detectors. The sudden darkness that can overtake a dense forest at dusk left them in the soft green glow of the vehicle's dash lights before Officer Potts noticed lights on inside the home.

"Hey Paula, when you checked the house, did you mean to leave lights on? I think the checklist said to turn them all off."

Paula Pilcher craned her neck over the back of the seat and noted the yellow glow on the deck. "Sumbitch!" She made a sound that ranged somewhere between a grunt and a guard dog's growl. "Ok, I'll go turn 'em off." She got out grumbling about missing her daughter's soccer practice, hiked up her gear belt, and strode off down the driveway. It did

128

not help that she could hear Potts snickering in the car before she shut the door. Her irritation turned to caution as she approached. The glass patio door shone a rough rectangle of light out onto the palmetto fringe of the yard and that light revealed moving figures in the house.

She thumbed her shoulder mike. "Potts, come 'ere. On the double." Then, "We've got company."

Pott's complaint started out an octave too high. "How the hell? None of the perimeter monitors picked up any movement."

"Not my problem right now, partner." Pilcher demanded. "Get your butt up here so we can check this out."

She held her position thirty yards from the house and behind a stout pine until she heard Potts approaching. "Stay about ten feet back, but not much farther. I'm going to go up those deck stairs there to see who all is in that house."

"How do you know someone's there?"

She indicated the shadows moving in the illuminated vegetation to their right and began to approach the house. As she moved forward, she undid the flap of her holster, then reached up and dialed down the volume on her radio. She wanted to be the one in charge of any surprises.

She remembered from the two media episodes at the house the previous week that the third stair had a bad loose-nail squeak. As she carefully stepped over to the fourth step, she heard the voices. Several different individuals could be made out. Tilting her head toward the house in concentration, she could make out two local accents, one male and one female, with another foreign-sounding accent. She pivoted to make eye contact with Potts. She raised four fingers then pointed to the living room, then shrugged and mouthed 'maybe more.' Potts nodded in understanding and loosened the flap of his holster then rested his palm on the hilt of the automatic pistol.

With great care to be silent, she ascended several more steps until she could see over the top of the deck planking. She saw a fairly tall man, back to the door, dressed in loose light clothing. He was facing two others on the couch. "Hey, what the—"

The girl, Myahh, was handing out glasses of what looked like iced tea. Looking past the reflection of the salt flats behind her, she could clearly make out Mr. Hitchens and his alien friend. Sandy or something. She should know that. Someone else, sat in a corner chair, not as well lit, but almost recognizable. *Wasn't he a preacher? Or something?* Clearly, all was well. Pilcher backed down the staircase a few steps and turned toward the view of the salt flats fronting the Bay. She keyed her mike. "Stand down. I don't know how they did it, but the Master is in the Castle."

She heard a sound. A soft pop through the glass slider facing the bay. Another person had joined the owners in the living room. She wasn't sure how, but she'd seen it.

She blew out a breath of frustration. Not prying was part of the job. She turned against the railing to look out over the bay and caught the swirling colors of Jai's energy shield as it went through evening systems checks. Swatting a mosquito on the back of her hand, she casually wiped the blood off on the back of her britches. "Damn skeeters." Little did she know that the spaceship Jai was a Skeeter Class warship.

~ ~ ~

In the days following the visit with Reverend Ehler, the Emissary and one or both of the Hitchens traveled the world in virtual space. They also 'dropped in' personally, shocking their hosts by appearing suddenly in secure antechambers and inner sanctums. The subjects visited were persons of power and influence who, like Ehler had much to do with securing their position through animus toward others. Their visits were with leaders of militant orders, secular and clerical heads, leaders of industry, and political leaders of all stripes. Each had his or her own particular edge or advantage who counseled policies or actions that increased world disorder. Each was given their particular set of hard questions and the promise of a next meeting.

Little notice was taken that Reverend Ehler had canceled his Wednesday sermon due to laryngitis. In the evening news coverage, there was a furor in the Latin world when the Dean of the College of Cardinals circulated a memo indicating that the College would be debating the end of the prohibition of birth control. He acknowledged in his memo that a large portion of the flock could not afford to adequately feed additional children and that the church was suspending its official ban on birth control due to mounting over-population crises in predominantly Catholic areas.

The revision of his thinking was not unique; it was in line with Supreme Leader Ali Khamenei's announcement of peace with Saudi Arabia, an end to hostilities in Yemen, and his suggestion of a regional summit be hosted by the Caliphate to bring peace to the Muslim world. His announcement included an impassioned message for unanimity and an end to internecine bloodshed between Shia and Sunni, and an end to the bloodshed between Persian and Arab. The goal, he stated, was for the Arab and Persian worlds to regain their historical supremacy in economic and cultural attainment and to stop wasting limited resources on military spending. State departments and secret services across the world went into deep huddle mode as media outlets in all languages welcomed the news. Egypt remained suspicious of the announcement. Afghanistan continued its official censorship of outside news services.

In China, General Secretary Xi Jinping went into seclusion following a self-described bout of 'soulful introspection.' He sought solace from a Buddhist monk that he'd released from a hard labor camp in the western provinces. He later abolished two-thirds of the camps, reconnecting the inmates with families and temples across western China and Mongolia. Across the globe, other interventions brought less newsworthy results, but Emissary Sayala and the Hitchens felt that perhaps some small movement had begun. There was talk of 'The Girl and the Old Man' in some circumspect press releases.

There was a period of several weeks when news reports across the globe were full of good news for mankind. The New York Times declared; PEACE IS BUSTING OUT ALL OVER! The London Daily News's banner described the dismantling of the peace walls segregating Catholic and Protestant neighborhoods in Belfast, Portadown, and other cities in Northern Ireland. Pravda announced the release of over fourteen hundred political activists from 'retraining' camps spread across the northern steppes of Siberia. LeMonde celebrated a conference between French and ethnic Moroccan and Arab leaders who had long sought relaxation of unofficial real estate policies that discriminated against those groups in France's major metro markets. India and Pakistan exchanged cultural missions to defuse border tensions in Kashmir.

21

TV

Across the globe, other interventions brought less newsworthy results, but Sayala and the Hitchens felt that perhaps some small movement had begun. Brad thought things were looking hopeful before Turkey invaded the Kurdish homelands in Northern Iraq.

Despite headlines proclaiming that peace was busting out all over. The tide began to turn as their efforts seemed to have the opposite effect. As if in response to good news headlines, a pub and a community center erupted in flames in Belfast. Sunni and Shia militants clashed in impoverished neighborhoods in Baghdad. Rockets blasted over Palestine's 'security wall' raining indiscriminate death. Media coverage of Israeli reprisals nearly brought down the hardline Israeli government. Despite these notable setbacks, global violence did seem to be diminishing overall.

Conjecture over the causes of these historical changes in the level of hostility led to an unknown but theorized influence of the 'Visitors.' Continuing coverage of the new monitor in the asteroid belt and the second monitor station between the Earth and Sun ran below the usual lead political headlines. Despite the story's relegation to page three in print media and bottom-of-the-hour slots on news shows, slow recognition of this other-worldly presence began to rise above the daily political bickering and posturing on Capitol Hill, the State Duma, Parliament, and other world houses of power.

The public outcry for more information became inflamed as marchers in Brussels demanded more information. Parallel marches in Tokyo and Seoul were followed in short order in Washington, San Francisco, and New York and in major metropolitan centers across the globe. Finally, the media got it. Engaged news-consuming citizens of the world were more interested in who or what was invading the solar system. Neil deGrasse Tyson had Bill Nye on his show to discuss the latest information. Unsatisfied with the conclusions of these two science oracles, Tyson's producers made a call.

~ ~ ~

After months in the public spotlight, Brad was no longer fazed by cameras, sound booms, and black-clad attendees behind and around the production of the studio set du jour. He did notice one absence from the setup he'd expected. When the StarTalk host finished his opening comments, Brad responded, "I notice you don't have a designated comedian on the show with us."

Tyson's smile broadened. "I think you will agree that levity is perhaps not what we're going for tonight."

"For sure, it's no laughing matter," Brad's face reflected his disappointment. "Although in a grim sort of way, I see macabre humor in the response on the street."

Their host nodded, perhaps from a cue from the producer's control room. "You're referring to the demonstrations?" Instantly, a video box appeared with the previous night's news footage of rioters. He thought the scene being displayed might have been Berlin. "— and the riots." Brad glanced over at the Sayala, feeling a message of calming reassurance. "I think the thing is, there is a clear counter-message being delivered from the highest pulpits and the highest podiums that seek the public's attention, and they provide misinformation in minute detail. And this while the biggest opportunity the Human race has ever had is being suppressed by—well—by I don't know who."

"Suppression of speech, of news!" The camera had moved to Dr. Tyson. "That's a big claim." He shifted his attention and line of questioning to the Stranger, Brad's guest. "Sir, you were introduced by my producers as a visitor, 'The Visitor.' With all the fanfare that's been generated by the public in response to world events lately, how exactly are you directly involved in these events?" As soon as he said it, he had the urge to reach for the back of his neck. He simultaneously had a knife-like sharpness at the base of his skull and a flood of doubt and insecurity. His field of vision seemed to go gray. The pain quickly subsided, his vision restored, and Brad's co-guest met his gaze with quiet reserve. Tyson felt his need for information filled with impressions, senses, and calming peace. "Oh," was all he could manage.

The strange little man smiled and responded to Tyson, "I hope this is the right platform. I've taken the time to do appropriate research and I believe your show has the credibility needed."

Tyson's expressive eyebrows lifted in surprise or awe? Brad couldn't tell, but he'd seen the twinge in Tyson's eyes and thought perhaps Sayala was probing. When getting that first burst of psi, some people looked panicked, some pained, some worked through it, not

133

Bruce Ballister

comprehending at first that a second line of communication had been opened. The famous public face of astrophysics and perhaps quite a few more areas of hard science leaned back in his chair. "What?" He glanced quickly at the head-shot camera then leaned forward to peer intently into the Visitor's eyes. "How did you do that?"

Sayala smiled. "I was just trying to see if you were an adequate receptor."

"Receptor? That's just…well, awesome, and…a little rude."

Brad smiled; he had gone through the confusion of telepathic probing by his spaceship Jai. Now he was watching de Grasse Tyson's introduction to psi communication.

Sayala continued. "You are a man of science, a notable man of science. Yes?"

Tyson leaned back; his usual affable mannerisms took over. He smiled broadly at the complement. "Some people might say that. Sure, I'd admit to that with some humility."

"Humility is not to be overrated. It will become even more essential in the coming weeks, and months. Returning to your question of my purpose here? I am a messenger. Some of your commentators have proposed that the artifact sharing an orbit with your asteroid belt is a messenger. That is incorrect, it is merely a monitor."

"I've heard that proposal too." Tyson's eyes shifted back and forth between Brad and the Visitor, took a deep breath, and asked, "Brad, you've been with us once before. When you returned with your friend from Erra. When you had asked if you could "bring a friend," he hooked air quotes, I, we assumed you were returning with the Shaand, the Erran Ambassador. This," he gestured with a nod at Sayala, "is fascinating." His gaze shifted back and refocused on the Visitor again.

Brad replied. "He can have that effect." He paused, turned to his companion, and received an answer. "Our relationship, though short has been remarkable in so many ways. We've been doing some traveling, making some contacts. I've given a lot of thought to where I—uhm—we, should make a public statement." He waved both hands, palms up, weighing possibilities. "We thought about the Hague, but security there is ridiculous, I didn't want to introduce him at the White House, or any country's statehouse." He paused for a breath. This was important, important for the whole world, for both worlds! "When Connie and I traveled to Dzura several years ago, this choice would have been an interview with Carl Sagan."

134

Brad's eyes shaded in a brief flash of remembrance. "He died too early by far. Sayala has traveled a long way, and as he said, he's done his research. He knows that media is a big deal on this planet as it is becoming again on Erra and Dzura. So, the podium, as he's referenced it to me is important."

"Thank you, Brad. I'm humbled by the comparison with Carl Sagan." Tyson leaned forward again; a look of quiet awe had transformed his face. He looked radiant, joyful. "Brad, it's happening again. You're talking to me, and I'm getting the message two ways. Is that you? Or—"

Dr. Tyson looked again at the Visitor, collected his thoughts, and decided to get on with the interview. In his hand, his cue cards fanned out. He picked one from near the top of the pile. "My producers provided me with a little bit of a clue." He raised the card reading. "Mr. Hitchens will be accompanied by Ambassador Shaand of the Erran High Pel Council. But I see now that the line was crossed out and surprise guest is penciled in."

He reached across the small table, extending his hand. "Hello, I'm Neil de Grasse Tyson, and you are?"

What followed was a sing-song string of syllables sounding more like birdsong than speech. Then, "Most think of me as 'The Visitor.' My name is Sayala.'"

Tyson frowned at the obscure name. Then his eyes lifted in recognition and surprise. He said in a tone that suggested humor. "And you are, just supposing here, associated with the objects 'visiting' our solar system?"

"An astute deduction." Brad's companion smiled, and at his side, Brad could feel the warmth, the comfort emanating. He felt his chest expanding as he might at a crucially emotive point in a movie. As if the next thing he'd experience would be tears of happiness or love. Apparently, Tyson felt it too, as his eyes glinted wet. "Dr. Tyson, those are my ships. The one in your asteroid belt is a monitor, no crew, just technology. It is intended to replace the one stolen almost thirty years ago in error by a profiteering Dzuran. He's had his comeuppance. The other craft—"

Tyson interrupted. "The one parked impossibly between Earth and Sun? That's yours too?"

"That is my personal base for this mission."

Bruce Ballister

Brad found his attention bouncing between his new metaphysical mentor, Sayala, and the world-renowned scientist who had taken Carl Sagan's place as the voice of science since he left Earth back in the 1980s.

Tyson flicked open three fingers on his left hand and flicked them in turn. "So, there's one in the asteroid belt, one in what we will call an orbit between the Earth and Sun, and another you are using to move around? To get here? Like a shuttle?"

"No Sir, there are only the two."

Brad explained, "Sometimes we use my ship, Jai, to get around. I miss his companionship, and he's extremely efficient at getting around. And with his new transponder, we don't have to worry about being shot at anymore." He shot a glance at Sayala, "and sometimes Sayala uses his skillset to get us around."

The physicist's brow furrowed trying to make sense of the last phrase. "Then ..." deGrasse Tyson's attention was interrupted by motion off set, behind the cameras.

A crash and clatter somewhere in the darkness behind stage left interrupted the discussion and all eyes turned to the sound. Shouts and complaints grew closer. Out of the darkness a lone protestor leaped into the camera's field of view behind Tyson's chair. Tyson ducked away to his left. Brad stood to block the intruder from the Entity's personal space. Brad only had a brief few seconds to read the small sign the intruder held. 'Only God has the Answers! Repent before God!' Sounds of argument and a physical fight began to erupt in a hallway connecting the studio.

Then the world went gray.

~ ~ ~

Dr. Tyson flailed, weightless. "Ow! Whaaat?" Wide-eyed and grasping for a foothold, a handhold, anything in the gray void he was floating in. He managed a cat-like pivot and found that he was only a few feet from Brad Hitchens and his unexpected guest, Sayala. As he made eye contact with the Entity, the space around him resolved into a simulacrum of the set, complete with table, chairs, large lumps for cameras, and generalized light sources where the stage lights had been. Collecting his wits, he managed to ask, "Would gravity be an option?"

He settled into his chair. Then, feeling his weight return, stood. "What the hell was that?"

Settling into his own chair, Sayala said, "I sensed we were in some danger—there were more approaching from the other side of the set and

136

Just in case you skip ahead of all that front end stuff and get right to it...

The purpose of an Advance Reader Copy is two-fold. First, and importantly, I need reader reactions, and reviews, not newspaper length copy, but brief paragraphs. Something that could be posted on Goodreads, or excerpted for the front pages section to pique interest. (Amazon allows readers to see the first 20 pages, so it would help a fence sitter. Short blurbs might be used on the back cover copy.

Secondly, if it just doesn't work... If I've blundered in planning these characters and their actions- reactions, bungled the plot or message, (and there is one), I need to know that and go back to work. AND... if you find a missing closed quote, or an errant paragraph break, lost period, etc. Those things do happen, escaping my first, second, and bleary-eyed third review of the editor's notes. So, a simple page no, and paragraph note back to me will ensure a better market product.

And finally,
Thank you for being an Advanced Reader for PASS-Fail, its message is consistent with my previous Room for Tomorrow but its target is another audience and hopefully ads to the limited genre of cli-fi or climate fiction. I'll just stop and let you get on with the book.
Thanks.

others in the stairwells, still more in the elevators. I believe our session was about to come to an abrupt end."

"Ambassador Hitchens?"

"Please call me Brad."

"OK, Brad, you want to tell me what just happened."

The two guests exchanged a glance, Brad answered. "My best guess is that we were removed from a dangerous situation. And the situation is being resolved by the usual security forces."

"But—"

Sayala provided the answer. "I have some personal protective abilities that can include others in my immediate space if situations warrant. It appeared that the intruder and his friends intended personal harm to my being, to Brad, and to you."

Brad said, "Dr. Tyson, he's being modest. He managed to personally remove me from the object in the asteroid belt to the ship in synchronous solar orbit in a matter of seconds."

The Visitor's aspect smiled. "No, my young traveler, you happened upon the teleportation chamber quite by accident. That was a physical event."

DeGrasse-Tyson asked, "Getting us here wasn't—uhm—physical?"

The Visitor paused as if searching for the correct vocabulary. "I believe you would call it metaphysical, in that the effect is more of the mind than your understanding of the traditional four physical world's dimensions."

The scientist tilted his head, examining the word choices. "Interesting, the 'four physical world dimensions.'"

"Yes, the three that define your typical world space, and duration, or existence."

DeGrasse-Tyson chuckled a short puff, his grin widening. "Existence. Yes, existence works." His eyes glistened with excitement. "I have so many questions to ask you." He looked at his hands, began to put them in order as he unfolded fingers digit by digit, then, looking up, "First, where are we now? Or should I ask, 'When are we now?'"

"Can we not focus on the mechanics just now?" The Visitor sent Tyson a calming wave of contentment. Tyson's heart rate dropped, his amygdala-induced response of fight or flight calmed, he no longer felt an urge to leave this small gray capsule of unreality. He felt at peace.

"How did you do that?" He stretched his arms wide, flexed his fingers, and looking beyond them, realized he could not gauge the distance to the edge of this small gray 'place' into which he and his guest had been, been what? Teleported?

His usual mobile face broadened into a wide grin. "That was fantastic! I guess thank you is in order."

"You're welcome." The visitor, eyes closed as if in thought or deep concentration, bowed slightly, an extended nod actually. "I believe the disruption in your recording space has been cleared. We are safe to return. Shall we?"

"Brad?" Dr. Tyson asked. "Should we return?"

"Yes, Sir. I don't know why not if our guest feels it is safe. I'd hate for the network to toss up some old episode of Ancient Aliens in place of your show."

The scientist laughed. "Different network, but, OK. Let's go back."

22

Back in the Studio

Dr. Neil deGrasse-Tyson found himself standing behind his studio chair. No fumbling for gravity. Grasping the seat back, just in case, he saw Brad Hitchens and his surprise guest, Sayala, solidifying immediately behind their chairs. "Neat trick," he thought. He peered into the darkness behind the stage lights and saw that the crew was still around. He scanned the usually dark void where the four cameras stood, only one cameraman stood nearby. No red indicator lights shone on any of the cameras. He shouted into the void. "Can we get on the air?"

The answer came back into his ear. "Owww! Dammit Dr. Tyson, you're miked! You damn near burst my eardrums!" Then, "Yes. Let me get a camera on." Tyson grinned at his own foolishness; yes, he was still plugged into the wifi'd sound system. He took his chair and gestured for the two guests to do likewise. He looked down, tugged at his suit, and pulled at the open collars of his shirt. Everything was in order. Except that it wasn't. He and his guests had just popped into what? Parallel space? Parallel time? A complex of those; maybe a parallel universe?

Scanning the cameras, one of them winked red. He began. "It seems there was a minor incident. We apologize for the interruption." He turned to Brad's guest.

"I said before that I had a lot of questions. I gotta say, I now have a lot more. Whatever you just did, was mighty impressive." He nodded toward Sayala, affirming, "Very well done, Sir."

Sayala simply nodded, smiling. The visitor's appearance was that of an updated Gandhi. A better suit, more hair. In fact, an impressive head of bone-white hair, unruffled by the recent trip to somewhere and back. His guest said. "We did not travel far. I sensed that our personal safety was compromised."

"Yes, well." Leaning forward and toward Hitchens, he asked. "Brad, when you said you were teleported from the asteroid base to the one in solar orbit, I was skeptical, but now … was that anything similar to what just happened?" He held up his hand to hold back the reply and turned to the headshot camera. "I'm sorry. I don't know what you all just

Bruce Ballister

saw. But we three just left what I consider to be the physical universe and, sort of, stepped aside into a similar space." He found that he couldn't easily describe the sensation, the space he'd just been taken to. How could he? He could right now be easily talked out of it.

Drawing a finger across his throat, he spoke softly into the microphone. "Kill it. We're going to have to start this over."

In what passed for a prep lounge, the green room was pretty baren, Dr. Tyson cleared the room and asked his two guests to sit at a small four-seat table. "Listen, we're going to have to re-tape the show, but apparently, what just happened made it to the news feeds. And because I don't really understand it, I'd like to avoid looking like an idiot. Because, right now, I *do* feel like an idiot. I usually have a scripted set of questions, my guests know approximately what I'm going to ask them, nothing out of their wheelhouse, and things go as smoothly as they can without the comedian *du jour* upsetting the flow of the show." He shrugged, "Of course, that often happens." He took a breath, tried to slow his over-revving heart. He looked at the Visitor. "Apparently, you have a message for all of us—for Earth. Right?"

~ ~ ~

They had shifted from the green room back to the recording studio, all cameras were manned, the recent disruption cleared. Heightened security guarded the room, the elevator, and all entrances to the building. Except for the line of placard-bearing protestors gathering on the sidewalk outside, no one would suspect who was upstairs facing the cameras. The interview began again, on a more familiar note. After all, they'd been mugged, teleported to safety, and returned unharmed, but at least in his case, not unshaken. Whatever kind of being Sayala was, it was clear it had talents.

His right hand went to his neck, feeling to center a tie that wasn't there, a nervous tic, then moved to the clip-on microphone to ensure it was in position. Clearing his throat, he leaned forward. "Brad, I know the audience won't appreciate what just happened, so can you summarize it, in simple terms, for them?" He chuckled softly, "and for me?"

Hitchens's brow furrowed then relaxed. "What just happened. Well, it's happened before. Once in traffic while we were enroute to the Hague in Brussels. An accident appeared to be imminent, a truck was speeding toward our car from a side street. Before I knew it, the driver, my companion, and I were not in the car anymore. For a few seconds, it seemed, we were in a gray, unformed space. Seconds later we were on the sidewalk, looking at the wreckage."

140

"That's essentially what happened here. We were in danger, and we were removed from the scene. When the danger had passed, we returned."

"OK." Tyson felt a shiver prick the hairs on the back of his wrists. "I guess I'm glad we're back."

He looked at Hitchens's replacement guest. "I'm sorry, I don't think I got a title before. How may I address you? Is it just Sayala?" As the visitor considered the question, his image shimmered, not quite a substantial solid. For the first time, Tyson began to doubt the physical reality of the presence seated beside Hitchens.

I am as real as you are, just in more dimensions than you. The answer came through as thought but thought that felt like a direct transmission from the visitor to him alone.

"Tyson took it in, understanding, but said. "Could you repeat that so that the audience might hear you?"

The visitor said, "Certainly, I am as real as you all are here. I am just able to access more than four dimensions." Sayala let that hang in the air a moment before continuing. "My official title is Messenger but that is a minor role in your hierarchy. Believe me, in my professional duties, the obligations are much more important than that title might imply. But in answer, you can call me by my name, Sayala."

He had received the answer both telepathically and audibly. Out of habit more than anything, Tyson tapped his ear. "Sayala, did I get that correctly?"

"Yes. You are a good receptor." The face of the now thoroughly solid visitor broadened in a wide smile. "I believe we will be able to communicate very well."

Tyson felt a flood of emotional content beaming his way and tried to suppress a laugh and failed. "OK, Sayala, let's get on with our interview. Mr. Hitchens, your friend and escort these last weeks has taken you to see some of our planet's leaders and leading philosophers. Some of them have expressed great hope in your message, and some, well, not so much. Can you please, express in the simplest terms possible, the reason for your visit?"

Sayala noted that cameras shifted in the darkness behind the studio lights to get a full-face shot and was aware that the live monitor suspended behind it showed his manifested face almost filling the screen. It expressed a human-friendly smile, and he considered his opening. The

141

many discussions with leaders around this planet behind closed doors had opened some pathways, but this interview would be for the masses. In simple language, this interview would provide his message to the widest audience and perhaps prevent misunderstanding his presence. Sayala was aware that the local language wasn't the most widely used, but it was the most translated language. This was as good an opportunity as any to talk to the people of this new world.

Sayala began. "Dr. Tyson, thank you for this opportunity. My presence here represents a culture, no, a complex of cultures, which spans three-quarters of this galaxy and has inroads on the cluster nearest. Our members include over fourteen hundred civilized cultures that have achieved interstellar flight, many of these are expanding as you might expect onto nearby systems that offer vital resources if not life-affirming climates. In all, from my most recent inquiries, there are over forty-thousand occupied planets represented in and accepted into our alliance."

The host raised a hand, leaned forward for attention. Sayala transmitted a pause request and the man Tyson leaned back in his chair. He had already heard the question forming in the man's consciousness.

"These forty-thousand planets all prosper to varying degrees of peace. That is the one condition we require of all fourteen-hundred-thirty-six cultures, the several thousand trillion citizens of our collaboration. Peace. Peaceful coexistence is our hallmark, our standard. Warlike behavior, exclusivity, military or economic domination of one culture by another is simply not permitted. Trade agreements and cultural and technology exchanges are voluntary."

"That brings us to a question—one that has troubled us recently with the Elioi, and now again with humanity here on Earth. We had considered that there was some level of stability on the worlds the Elioi were expanding onto. Beyond the two worlds in their star system, there are a few other systems in their immediate sphere of influence. Other than minor contact with other species with less than planetary awareness, they have been left to prosper in their own ways, and there had been hope that they could be offered full access to our trade routes and technologies.

"Unfortunately, the recent reversal in leadership indicates that the Elioi culture is not stable. While it still seeks expansion to new worlds, it is not sufficiently advanced to permit full access to citizenship for all of its own species. They have much to learn but seem to be adopting a path that will permit universal use of the plant proteins that permit shared and open communication with all Elioi. There are other issues within their culture that are reasons for concern that I will not air here."

He looked to his left, to see Brad smiling in acknowledgment. "But I've digressed, I'm here to discuss humanity. Nothing is more effective in creating an atmosphere conducive to peaceful prosperity than full and open communication between all members of a species." Turning back to the host, he felt a barrage of questions forming.

"Mr. Tyson, you have questions."

"Hundreds, but you said there were several thousand trillion citizens in your, your what, confederation?"

"I said collaboration. You could call it a confederation, in your own context. You could call it a gestalt. In your language that is what you would call an assembly by many names, but an oversight body to which delegates or ambassadors are assigned. But the collective *all* is more aptly compared to a trade collective. Dr. Tyson, you are a trained astrophysicist so you must be aware that the raw materials available in one star system may not be readily available in others. So, to a large extent, trading materials is necessary. Trading of cultural assets is also important. The arts are not exclusive to any one culture."

Tyson, shining with enthusiasm, would not be stopped. He leaned forward, his face glowing with curiosity. "You've mentioned the Elioi and their progress; what about us—humans?" His arms opened expansively, "humanity?"

"I did want to get a frame of reference opened; I mention the Elioi for comparison. Humans have been considering travel within your star system for only a few of your decades. Your use of hydrocarbons as fuel is basic, if not wasteful. If left alone, your culture would be expected to have colonies on other planets and a collection of other minor satellites in another hundred years. And by that time, you will be adept at collecting fuels and reaction mass from the atmospheres of the gas giants."

Sayala noted the host, Tyson, nodding in understanding. "But, Dr. Tyson, you are not aware that in many star systems, those gas giants *are* the inhabited planets. Those are the dominant intelligent species of the star system who are members of our trade alliance. Meanwhile, if there is life on that system's rocky planets, it might be still crawling around grubbing for the next meal, completely unaware of life or existence beyond its line of sight."

Tyson rubbed his chin, peering inward, then looked up and asked, "Are you saying that our gas planets have intelligent life?" He chuckled. "Seriously? We've been looking in all the wrong places."

"No, to my knowledge, not on the gas planets in your system. But your lack of understanding that there are complex life forms based on the chemistry and pressure gradients and thermal transfer systems in a gas planet is, to me, astounding."

"Fascinating. Who would have thought?"

"Exactly, you didn't think. As I understand, from talking with my friend Bradley, you are hoping to find evidence of prior life on the fourth planet as well as on the frozen satellites of the greater planet, Jupiter."

"Yes," the physicist replied. "Jupiter's moons are…" He trailed off. "Don't get me wrong, Mr. Sayala, I think we are getting into a whole new thing here and I'd love to have hours and hours of time with you. But," he paused momentarily to reframe his thoughts, "why exactly are you here?" He cocked his head to the side, "I've heard reports that you have a certain agenda."

Sayala nodded in agreement. "You are correct, Doctor Tyson. You are aware that Bradley Hitchens and his daughter," he looked to his left to acknowledge Brad, "and the Ambassador for the Elioi have been accompanying me as I have been meeting with many of the leading philosophers and a few world leaders as a courtesy. I have answered many questions and have learned a lot from these discussions. Your broadcast program, in contrast, offers an opportunity to speak to your world."

The physicist smiled and bowed, humbled, Sayala thought. It said, "Humans are a mixed bag of traits. I find that there are many qualities that you share across numerous cultures and languages that are fine and honorable. You are creative, resourceful, and in small groups; caring, nurturing, and supportive. But, in large numbers, you are still struggling with behaviors suited to an emerging species. Humanity in the larger collective, and I mean this as a generality because there are gradations in all things, are competitive, suspicious of other cultures, and aggressive— aggressive to a fault."

He noted that Bradley Hitchens was nodding, felt his agreement in psi. He turned to his traveling companion. "Bradley, have you ever known a period in your life that someone on this planet was not at war with a neighbor?"

"No, I really don't think I can. Of course, I was missing from Earth's timeline for about twenty-seven years. The conflicts in play when I left were resolved, but there were new ones when I returned. And our major powers, Russia, China, and the US are still at odds, either in trade wars or cold wars. And the age-old conflicts between Islam, Christianity, and Judaism are still with us. So, no. I'd say that it's normal for us to be hostile in subtext, even while our better agents are seeking peace."

The Visitor, Sayala, looked pointedly back to the show's host. "And you, Dr. Tyson, can you think of a time in your lifetime when there was peace?"

"The astrophysicist looked thoughtful for only a few seconds, before answering. "I think just before I was born, at the end of World War Two, there was hope for peace. A major global conflict had just come to an end. There was hope then. But tensions that had been ignored for the sake of forming a united front against aggression during that war erupted again. A new war of intrigue and competition started. We called it a cold war because there were very few dying, at least, well, no." He paused, and restarted, "One of the powers, Russia, brutally exterminated any internal opposition and actually annexed entire countries before its expansion was stopped." He furrowed his brow, remembering. "And in China, there was a terrible civil war that cost millions of lives."

"So," Sayala continued, "you can't remember or think of a time when human cultures on this planet were content. No political or military conflict?"

"No." Tyson's face betrayed his unhappiness with the answer.

"This then brings me to the central part of my mission. That was my assessment as well. I and others like me have been observing your rise from a tribal pre-agricultural culture and the record of humans living in peaceful coexistence is thin. Toleration of other cultures seems to have been best suited if the others were distant and trade was profitable. As you got better at transportation, some five or six centuries ago, aggression grew from regional conflicts to global. The strong overtook and subjugated the weak or obliterated them. Those behaviors persist in modified forms in modern times."

"It cannot be tolerated. Humanity has come to an important threshold too early. Your new contact across the stars, the Elioi, arrived here hundreds of your years ago. To their credit, their culture placed *your* world off-limits as a backward, planet-bound barbarous place, and deemed it dangerous to any who would visit. In summary, both Humans and Elioi have much to offer, and, much to learn."

"Therefore, it is with many deep regrets that I have the following judgment: Humans and Elioi alike are in the same situation. Your races, your cultures, will not be permitted to expand your existing areas of influence beyond the systems you and they currently have dominion over. The Elioi have access to one other developable planetary system with no

145

emerging sentient species. We will encourage the Elioi to share its abundant resources with you as long as we detect mutual respect and cooperation." He raised his hand to halt Tyson's apparent interruption. "My specific mission, which is what you asked, is to ensure that neither Humanity nor the Elioi expand beyond your present spheres of influence."

Hands flat on the small set table, Tyson leaned forward. Head cocked to one side, he asked. "Is that some sort of ultimatum? We are just now sharing technology with the Elioi that would permit our traveling throughout our solar system and to many of the nearest stars that appear to have planets. What would stop us from visiting them, from colonizing them? If the Elioi provide access to the technetium isotope that makes the Elioi navy interstellar capable."

"I would stop you, or, we would. Others like myself." The Visitor's face displayed no emotion and transmitted none in psi. "My associate is right now bringing this same message to the Elioi system. Both cultures, Human and Elioi, are prone to forcible exploitation and seemingly incapable of peaceful co-existence.

Tyson leaned back into his chair. "You must understand that there has been considerable excitement among our scientists and some political leaders about expansion, and exploration, opening up new worlds." He gestured to Hitchens who had been silent for most of the interview. "Bradley, you must have known about this." His eyes looked for hope in the young star traveler.

"No, Sir. I did not." He sighed in apparent exasperation. "But I can see the point."

Tyson turned back to Sayala. Eyebrows raised in wide-eyed question. "You do realize that there will be many of us who will not accept this condition. Right?"

Sayala's response was calming in psi and assertive vocally. "I understand. This is a likelihood which I am prepared to address." He leaned back against the seat's padding. Settling his weight, he'd learned was one of the human cues for asserting a position of intransigence. "I *do* have non-destructive means, non-lethal means of asserting our position. And as you may have learned, we are patient watchers."

~ ~ ~

Drake Ehler erupted out of his chair as he comprehended the rolling scroll at the bottom of his news feed. The scroll slowly revealed its message. The talking head continued to run on about the latest trivia from

Capitol Hill, but the scroll held news that Neil de Grasse Tyson, Brad Hitchens, and an unknown guest had disappeared from the production set, in front of a live feed had his attention. Eyes still glued to the ultra-widescreen on his office wall, he stood and walked toward the screen, pleading for the reporter to be given the update. "Dammit! I don't give a flip about the Attorney General's latest stupidity. *What the hell!"*

His expletive, one of his favorites, was cut off as a window appeared showing Tyson, Hitchens, and a dark-skinned elderly man seated opposite Tyson. *That's the guy from the dreams!* It was so fantastic; it couldn't have been real. And yet... The memory of the dream came back as he watched. The changes to Jesus Christ himself and seated beside him the little Hitchens girl. He realized his mouth was agape and closed it. That was him on TV, he pinched the web of his thumb to ensure he was awake. *What the Hell!*

The old man appeared to be in animated conversation explaining something to Tyson when an intruder broke through set security and ran toward the seated trio. As the intruder approached carrying a hand-drawn sign, security ran in from both sides. Another intruder coming in from behind the cameras barely missed hitting Tyson with his sign, but he'd tripped on one of the many cables strung along the floor. The camera angle jolted as the cameraman's back filled the screen and then fell out of view presumably on the sign-wielding intruder.

The panel was on its feet. Brad stood over the elderly guest, who seemed to shrink a half size, letting Brad put protective arms around him. Dr. Tyson moved in, putting his bulk between his guests and the attacker closing in from backstage. A gray-uniformed guard had already tackled another intruder and wrestled him to the ground amid a tangle of cables.

Security officers had both of the intruders on the floor when, abruptly, Tyson and his guests disappeared in a light gold shimmer. The camera feed went back to the moment immediately prior to the inexplicable event and it would be clear to anyone watching that a guard who had been trying to protect Tyson, and another reaching to provide cover for the elderly guest both found nothing to grab. Both he and Tyson's would-be protector fell across empty chairs.

Mouth open in disbelief, Ehler slowly backed until he felt the pressure of his easy chair on his calves, and he slowly dropped into it. The increasing bedlam in the scene continued before one of the engineers threw up a commercial. Three commercials later, the camera was on Tyson, two boxes to his right displayed the two faces of Brad Hitchens and the 'personage' he knew as Sayala. After an uncomfortable moment, another barrage of commercials ran on, blending in with station promos. He clicked the sound off and stared at the blank black screen.

"Shit! That's the guy! He wasn't a dream, or...a ghost." He sat back against the rear cushion, letting his weight settle in. He thought back to the 'visitation' as he'd come to think of it. The little brown man, Persian maybe? Indian? Then the second 'summoning' to the Hitchens' home in Florida, and his subsequent teleportation back to his office. That guy had rocked his world—left his basic belief system in shambles. He knew in his heart that he was not a good Christian. He could talk the talk, but had lost the ... the drive? The zeal? He'd spent the last two weeks in isolation claiming he wasn't feeling well.

He'd shooed everyone close to him away except for his executive secretary, the sweet gal who kept the empire running. He hadn't had to say much to his wife except to stay home in Palm Beach and try not to shop herself into a hole. She wasn't an actual caricature of a rich white bitch, but she was working on it. Any love in the relationship had vanished a long time ago. He couldn't remember when they'd had sex, or if either of them had enjoyed it.

"Shit," he said again, "the visitor is real!" He'd been off and on in his mind for the past two weeks, no, mostly on, he figured. "Sum bitch!" He listened to the sinews pop in his knees as he pushed himself up, grumbled about getting old, and moved to his home studio. *Time to pay the piper*, he thought.

He settled into his slightly larger-than-a-closet broadcast booth. A sound-insulated four-by-seven partition off his otherwise overblown office. He cleared his throat, forced a smile at the camera's tiny eye, and hit the mic. The broadcast started as a ramble, tending toward suspicions of change. He stopped, backed the file up, and watched. He saw an older version of himself. One several years older than he thought of himself. His recorded image came off as cranky and irritable, and not clearly expressing himself. *Well. Good thing I stopped!*

He took a short break and came back with a shave, his hair slicked down in its signature front-to-back comb-over. A clean shirt and bolo tie completed his image from his Wednesday night shows. For a Sunday show, he'd need one of his fourteen three-piece suits. He smiled into the camera and began.

"Folks, this is a special broadcast tonight. But I have some news for you, and I think it's good news."

Reverend Ehler's broadcast had some positive reviews, despite his audience's usual hard-focused adherence to what they considered their faith. Elsewhere, the reactions to Sayala's message across the globe were far less enthusiastic.

23

Backlash

The news feed avalanche was slow at first, but quickly filled the screens of the world's televisions. A multi-feed monitor at CNN noticed the disturbance on the set of Tyson's StarTalk on its home channel, National Geographic. The adroit feed monitor interrupted the host of the show in progress with news that something strange was going on at Nat Geo. The bungled attack scene and the vanishing of the host and guests had been carried live before being hastily replaced by commercials.

Since all news channels follow each other's feeds, in a few minutes, MSNBC, CBS, BBC, Das Erste, Télévision 1, Al Jazeera, Fox, and all of the world's news outlets were carrying or discussing the mayhem, and the apparent disappearance of Star Talk's host and his two guests. Within a few more minutes, the three were back in their seats only slightly ruffled, but media syndicates across the planet were now broadcasting or monitoring the exchange. China's state news channels didn't carry any of the coverage initially but had to relent when it seeped into the usually suppressed internet via sales channels. Russian feeds of TikTok coverage made the state-sponsored light night news.

The much-talked-about new 'Visitor' had finally been on a live feed and reactions were decidedly mixed. His face had already begun to appear on T-shirts and internet memes, dressed as Jesus. In other circles, he'd been shown riding as one of the four horsemen of the Apocalypse. He was revered and hated, loved and feared. He was, finally, very much in the mainstream and popular news.

For the world's military powers, his message wasn't welcome. Why should anyone restrict humanity's right to expansion? In a rare moment of collegial cooperation, Russian and American war machines, still brittle from the Ukraine War, were on the phone within hours discussing who could first send up a nuclear strike against the Visitor's solar-stationed vessel, and who could provide mission support and back-up. Should they attempt a simple EMP strike or go for destructive demolition? As the logistical and technical demands of the strike became apparent, Brazil and China were brought into the discussion. The EU's European Space Agency declined to participate.

As the preparations for a united military stand took shape, Brad and Sayala were in demand by talk shows across the globe. Some interviews were granted, most were not. Increased levels of protest at or near the Hitchens' homestead caused another relocation for Connie and Myahh. Shaand and Lenka, after confirmation by grav-wave dispatch, returned to Dzura to take up a mission of cooperation and trade with Humans. Splinter groups of Earth-Firsters and newly formed pro-Federation groups rallied in protests and appeals depending on the local political regime. But the majority of citizens in both planetary systems carried on with life as usual. The brief blossoming of humanitarian goodwill faded on the vine.

Sunnis murdered Shia. Irish Anglicans shunned Irish Catholics. Europe's Spanish descendants in South America casually obliterated native villages while harvesting their life-giving forests. Arabs and Persians eyed each other's oil and mineral wealth while gauging each other's military strength. American, Russian, and Chinese techno-geeks continued to harass each other's ability to maintain viable commerce on the web. In short, life continued as usual, while the military leaders of the world powers plotted. The all-to-brief period of peace busting out all over, was over.

Despite the array of troubles around the globe that usually filled local, national, and international news coverage, all stations were now discussing the dark spot on the sun. The thing, the spaceship, the alien invader, the ambassador's or visitor's craft. It was growing and it was growing in a way that could cool the earth. It seemed no one had ever seen this eventuality and couldn't even come up with a commonly known scenario in science fiction.

Some of the more creative news channels had panels of scientists discussing how, at its location, the alien craft was properly positioned to maximize casting a diffuse shadow on the earth that could in time cool the earth by several degrees, and eventually bring on a freeze. It wouldn't take long if the thing kept growing, and due to the glare, most wouldn't even notice the spot unless they risked looking directly at the sun.

Reports were coming in from virtually everywhere of people who had looked for evidence themselves with everything from unaided eyes, or sunglasses to worst-case scenarios, binoculars. Responsible reporters were broadcasting the advice usually given to areas due for an eclipse. "PLEASE DO NOT LOOK DIRECTLY AT THE SUN!"

Stock markets were in turmoil, trending downward before leveling out at about seventy percent of previous levels. No one had seen the Visitor, Mr. Sayala, the Ambassador of Doom, and many much worse labels in two weeks. Brad Hitchens had not been seen at his home in

Florida; his wife and child were under US Federal protection—somewhere!

~ ~ ~

Brad manipulated the joystick control on the ship's receiver to try to get a clear signal from one of the hundreds of broadcast signals emanating from the side of the planet currently facing the sun. Sayala had explained that his best results would be from near the east and west terminators. That made sense to Brad since most transmitters sent their signals out horizontally, and consequentially toward him. Near the edge of the planet that was experiencing morning, a signal resolved itself. He locked on and tweaked the instrument's gain to boost the faint signal. The station was German language, but he could clearly see from the graphic behind the speaker that the newscaster was demonstrating how a large enough object could cast shade on a significant portion of the planet.

"Sayala," he said without turning away from the monitor, "I think we have their attention."

"Yes, yes. We spoke to so many people. Nothing but doubters."

"Well, the scientists seemed to understand." Brad countered.

"Scientists deal in realities, not politics." Sayala laughed the peculiar laugh that he'd picked up in social situations with humans. "The politicians are the skeptics, and they seem to have the biggest microphones."

"Yeah, true." Brad scratched his beard stubble. He'd packed a few days-worth of clothes that Sayala's replicators were able to use for a pattern. Clean clothing hadn't been an issue, but he really missed a clean shave. "But the politicians are paid to be skeptical." He didn't express what he really thought of politicians.

Sayala picked up on the psi undertones anyway. "True, and it's true that they have many paymasters. But they are the leaders of public opinion, regardless."

"When do think we should go back?" Brad was anxious to return to Connie, too. He missed her counsel, her support and he missed Myahh. In psi, he wondered what the Visitor called his ship. A craft? Certainly not a ship. A spaceship?"

"Translated as closely as I can in your English," Sayala had been scanning his thoughts again, "I would call it an umbra ship. Or a shadow ship. A shade ship?" There was a little bit of a questioning tone in the last try.

Brad considered the options. "Shadow ship has negative undertones, like something trying to hide in the shadows. In reality, you remained hidden from everyone but astronomers in the glare of our sun." He scratched absently at his stubble again, looking around him at the spare detail in the control room. Seats had been created for his comfort alone. A monitoring station had been manifested so he could keep track of the unfolding of the sails. He thought of them as sails anyway. They could be called fans, blades, spokes, or masts. Yes, masts. The masts that were extending or extruding—he wasn't sure which—from the inner sphere had already exceeded thirty kilometers and were still growing. They were extending sails or webbing—again he wasn't sure what name to use—that would close on their neighbors.

"Sayala, how large will the sail be when it's fully deployed?"

"Sail? Yes you could call it that. It does catch the solar wind. I have to monitor pressure on the sail to maintain our position." He seemed thoughtful. "Yes, sail. I like that. Per my latest command set, the masts will deploy to eighty-eight diameters."

"Eighty-eight, what?"

"They stow inside the ship, each mast extends eighty-eight diameters." He saw confusion on Brad's face. "The cross-section diameter of this ship is approximately four of your kilometers."

Brad did the math quickly, even though the dimensions seemed unimaginably large. "So, four kilometers for the ship and two times eighty-eight for the sail. Eighty-eight kilometers! Then he rethought the math, "No, not eighty-eight kilometers, it's eighty-eight diameters times two, plus one for the ship."

He did a quick calculation mentally. Eight-eight, four, uhm, thirty two, carry the, … a hundred and seventy-seven plus one kilometers. A hundred seventy-seven kilometers. Oh wow!" He leaned back against his chair astounded.

Sayala smiled, shaking his head in the negative. Then Brad realized his mistake. That was ship diameters not kilometers, each diameter was about four kilometers.

Brad leaned into the back of his chair; mouth agape as he mentally ran the numbers again. "Whoa! These sails will create a sunspot seven hundred and eight kilometers across!" He blew out through puckered lips.

"That's over four hundred-something miles across. That's going to throw a lot of shade on the Earth. Is that dangerous?" He was beginning to wonder about the strategy.

Bruce Ballister

"Not as much as you might think. It will amount to a very small reduction in the amount of sunlight falling on the equatorial zones of your planet. Fully extended, it is a little more than one percent of the total radiation falling on the surface. It won't even form a complete shadow. The sun will appear to dim for several minutes as those under its shadow pass beneath." He turned from the tablet in his hand and pointed up with his stylus. Our records show that your planet has been warming for the past two hundred years, and dangerously so, for the past seventy years. This installation will reverse that trend."

"So, this ship is here to help?"

"It should slow the warming that is going to kill your civilization."

"From what I'm picking up on broadcast signals, my leaders see that as a threat."

"Yes, my friend. But they also know that they are powerless to do anything about it. They really don't have a bargaining chit."

"It's a bargaining chip." Brad smiled at the mistaken idiom. Sayala, or one of his kind, had been studying earth's cultures for hundreds of years. Most recently from the remote outpost in the asteroid belt. They had absorbed some of the older knowledge of the cataloging visiting alien species the human's called the tall whites, and the more invasive and inquisitive grays. Brad had been surprised that these races had until very recently, been more than myth and sub-culture. They were real and they had been warned off. There would be no more visitations by their research teams while under the watchful presence of Sayala.

Brad looked over at Sayala, he was in one of his more fluid forms. At least, Brad thought of it as fluid. Sayala was in one of his working modes. Its shifting multi-armed glowing entity faced a battery of workstations as its appendages flicked over panels and screens. Four of the screens were a deep blue-black to Brad's eye, their displays were ultraviolet emitters, usable only by Sayala. Two others glowed a deep-red that occasionally emitted information in wavelengths that Brad could discern, but in a language that was impossible to penetrate. "Sayala?" He remembered a question from a few moments before.

The multi-armed visage slowed, coalesced into the form of the aged Persian, and turned. "Yes, my friend?"

"When do you believe we should go back?" He glanced at one of the screens that showed the Earth's blue, brown, and white globe." The view was a full circle with no shadowed edge because the sun was at their

154

backs. The only shadow visible on the fully lit disc was a small smudge at the equator. Their umbra, their shadow.

"Soon, but I'm not sure if I'm the right messenger." Sayala rose from his workstation and took a step toward his human companion.

"No? Who then?"

Sayala continued, "and, it's not the right time. There are some on your world that are about to demonstrate their obstinance and their futile resistance." There was a psi overtone of humor in the last. "When that episode has played out, I believe there might be a more receptive response."

Brad didn't know what that implied, Sayala hadn't mentioned before any effort to take action against the visitor. But his question hadn't been answered. "If not you, who would be the messenger. Surely, you don't think *I* should be the messenger. Maybe a panel of our leading scientists?"

Sayala smiled. "No. There are several messages we need to deliver, but the important one, the message that will have the greatest impact should come from another. I think it should be a child, a representative of those who will inherit your earth and face the damages that are accumulating. That messenger should be your daughter, Myahh."

24

War Room

There were more generals in the room than aides, and the aides were all majors or above. The assembly had been called to bear witness to the results of a month of hasty work. In a model of intergovernmental cooperation, multiple warheads were married to lift and acceleration vehicles, testing, and retesting equipment, and new systems not previously integrated. The techs had been running simulations twenty-four seven. Agency heads considered and approved delays of a few supply missions to the ISS. This was an all out attempt to show that good old planet earth could exercise its muscles.

Rocket science is still not a perfect science, but the planetary emergency was being dealt with. The payloads were on the way. Space-X provided four additional lift vehicles in a gesture of cooperation. Bezos offered help, but his vehicles were more for fun and games than real work. Then there was the long wait. Solid rocket boosters from military stockpiles had been lifted into orbit for the delivery vehicle that would 'address the threat.' Even with the use of these boosters that had been lifted into orbit for an accelerated ride down the gravity well to the sun's newest satellite, there had to be this lag, the waiting.

The American Space Force Major General Pat Stanford presided over the meeting, primarily because it was on her turf, the fourth floor of the Pentagon. Since the inception of the Space Force, she had taken ribbing from her peers, many of whom were also former astronauts, and had been given the behind-the-back moniker of Captain America. She simply had the cachet of being a NASA astronaut and as a younger woman, had thought leadership was a perk of the job. As she looked around the table, none of those seated had ever been higher than forty-thousand feet. Most were fit, keeping themselves trim well into their fifties, but a few were grossly inadequate for any strenuous activity.

Stanford briefly wondered what the repercussions of this mission might be. But she knew in her soul that humanity needed to show that it was not without resources and was destined to be a player in the several systems being identified as expansion areas. There were simply too many promising planets discovered every year to forever write them off. No one was going to screw with that destiny and tell her humans were not worthy. Damn the ultimatums and pass the ammunition!

General Stanford looked around at her guests. To a man, and the one other woman, all were raptly glued to the countdown screen. Seconds to go now. if the scientists were even close to the range—

even if it was true that the concussion effects of pressure waves would be ineffective in space. If they did not directly hit their target, she was assured that the electromagnetic pulse would knock out their visitor's control systems. Although she had doubts, there *was* that silvered outer coating on everything.

Stanford had her bets on the simple targeting system, find the black dot in the middle of the sun's view, and hit it. Someone near the back of the room loudly whispered, "forty-five seconds." At thirty, the room took up the count in unison at five-second intervals. At ten, she couldn't help herself. She began softly at first, and as the room's voices took up the chant, they all counted down from ten. The clock was set to account for the delay in signals from the warhead. Zero would be impact.

At three, two, one, she was breathless. Out of air, she held on, waiting. "What the..." The room's countdown clock had begun counting up from the predicted time of impact. "Damn rocket scientists got the distance wrong." She muttered under her breath to the Brazilian Lieutenant General at her side. The warhead was still sending back its simple signal; the non-threatening Temptations tune, *My Girl*. Its maddening lyric, "*I got sunshine on a cloudy day,*" had been driving her too close to the edge.

The clock continued its upward count. One, then two, then five minutes. At fifteen she was pacing. She jabbed at a phone. "Yes! I imagine he is busy! Get me Schindberg now! This is General Stanford." A pause as everyone's attention focused on the General. She turned her back on the table and shouted into the phone. "Yes, I know the distance and timing were approximate." A shorter pause. "What? You're telling me it missed?" Then lower, a sense of awe in her voice, "What? It moved?" Her eyes darted around a blank spot on the wall. "It just moved out of the way? Um-hmm."

The General started pacing across the short side of the room in front of the huge display that covered a wall. She suddenly stopped and pointed at the image of the sun, darkened so that it wasn't a white disk. "Yes, I see the dark spot. Uh-hmm, uh-huh." It was impossible now for anyone in the room not to fix Stanford with their undivided attention. "It's what? Bigger?" She turned to look at the black spot again, leaning into the

Bruce Ballister

display until its image was pixelated. "Yeah, I see them. So what? It's been there for months." She stared absently at the ceiling, listening. Her trademark trimmed eyebrows knit together as she received the bad news, her eyelids shrank to a squint as her lips screwed into something between a pout and a frown. She turned to the digital display forwarded from the space telescope. As she and the rest watched, the scene changed, zooming in to the object silhouetted black by the sun's glare. Stanford muttered, "Oh shit," under her breath, but those in the nearest seats picked up on it. "How long?" Another short pause, then, "Jesus H. Keerist! OK, I'll tell 'em."

Stanford stepped to the side without taking her eyes off the screen. The small black dot that had been the focus of the world's attention for two months was growing appendages. It had been estimated, despite the glare and the total reflectivity of its edges that the original sphere was a little over four kilometers in diameter. The best estimates of the appendages made the diameter of the ship's structure with its arms extended was almost ninety kilometers across. Palomar had just confirmed that the diameter was now growing. The observatories conclusion was that the shadowed zone would grow larger.

"General Stanford, please?" Vasily Tsibliyev, head of all Russian military was standing, illuminated now by the sun-bleached background on the screen. The reflected glare on Tsibliyev's small, round glasses over his Stalinesque mustache gave Stanford the impression of headlamps on a Jeep. Stanford acknowledged him with a nod, and turned back to the screen, transfixed. Either the telescope was still zooming in, or the things that looked like spokes were really growing again.

Tsibliyev in a more demanding tone, "General Stanford. Would you please share what you have just learned? What is it you have just agreed to tell us?"

What she said in reply put a chill through the spine of everyone in the room. "It appears that the net effect of our mission was a minor blip. The thing just moved out of the way, or wobbled, JPL was a little vague on that. It was there, it wasn't there, then it was back." She pointed at the screen, "Those things—the things growing out of it started before the explosion, but not before it could have noticed our payload approaching." She scanned the worried faces around the table in the makeshift war room. "We might as well have aimed a BB gun at it. In response to the best we could throw at it on three months' notice is that it seems to be growing something that may be a weapon or a defensive shield. And those appendages are still growing." Her sigh fully deflated the general's

158

usually erect posture, betraying her frustration and their combined impotence in the face of an unknown. "We just don't know."

25

Myahh

Myahh felt the tug behind her left ear. The visitor she knew as Sayala was asking her to be ready to come to him. It would be another visit to his ship she knew, and this fourth visit would not be as worrisome as the first. Instead of a grey copy of her dad's office, it might be anywhere Sayala had visited himself. She, her mother and Lenka had been secreted away in a ranger's cabin on the eastern slopes of the Rockies. She looked out across the parkland near the continental divide west of Boulder, Colorado, and smiled at the simple beauty of it all. This was a beautiful planet, but she knew as her dad had explained, that it was in danger. Long ago, when people first started to cut down forests for firewood and crops, when coal began to be burned for heat, processes had started that began to change the air and the way it stored heat.

Now the ocean was warming and that was the big problem because it was the planet's thermostat. The Earth was getting too warm for a lot of the life on the planet. Below her to the east, far beyond the grey smudge that was the polluted air above Denver, checkerboard fields of gold and green faded to grey near the far horizon. She remembered a speech at the UN by a young girl not much older than her, Greta something, and wondered how many people there would do anything differently.

Gradually the mountain views around her softened, became a little less tangible, then there were the few moments that at first felt like falling. Sayala had shown her how to posture herself and now it was a lot more like flying. He said he couldn't help the darkness. It was just the way it was. When she felt pressure under her legs again, she put her arms back to steady herself and opened her eyes. The new view was an entirely different planet.

She turned right, then left, and saw Sayala sitting cross-legged beside her. Behind him was a low hedge in deep purple hues. Behind the hedge, thick creamy-yellow tree trunks rose to a crimson and purple canopy high overhead. Beyond the trees, reflecting red-tinted sunlight, lay a monstrously huge pile of crumpled metal. Beyond that irregular black outline, a too-large ruddy sun was dropping below the horizon. She sat beside him, caught his eyes. He smiled, nodded, and psi'd for her to look around, to enjoy the view.

She did. In front of them and to her right, a broad sandy beach with normal-looking sand. A normal-looking ocean with modest surf rolled in toward their feet. Above the horizon though, the sky was very not normal. Lavender is not a color she would expect for a sky. She found her cheeks swelling in a grin as she recognized the view from images Uncle Shaand had shared of his home planet, Dzura. Far across the water, a low line of hills ran across the horizon. She remembered the globe Shaand had shown her. She thought they must be near the Isthmus, the narrow band of ocean that separated the northern and southern continents.

Yes, you are right.

She turned back to Sayala. "I didn't know you could take me this far. Your spaceship is nice too, but this is so very far away."

Right again, child. Then. Are you OK? Is your stomach settled?

She had become a little nauseated on two of the earlier trips to his ship. "Yes, my stomach is fine, I feel OK." She took a mental inventory and checked again. *Yes, I'm fine. Behind the trees, is that a part of the city-ship?*

His eyes became more serious. "Yes, that was the first of the Erran city ships to crash."

She looked back up behind the tree line. The wreckage, the piece of it she could see was immense. "Were very many people hurt?"

He gave a weak smile. "Yes, do you know what a thousand is?"

She felt a little insulted. "Yes, it's ten times a hundred."

"OK." He sent a psi note of apology. "When this ship crashed, over two hundred thousand of the Elioi died. Either in the explosions in space, or when it broke apart in vacuum, or when it came down here." He paused; sadness filled his next thought. *Very few of them escaped. And many of those died later from injuries.*

"Is this the city-ship that my dad killed?" Her eyebrows wrinkled in worried anticipation of the answer.

"Yes," a calming subtext was transmitted through psi, "but I want you to understand a few things about your father."

She sat still, a small, seated statue on the beach, cross-legged and as calm as Buddha, waiting to hear something terrible. She knew that her dad had been a hero of the Dzuran civil war but had only a dim understanding of the terrible toll it took.

Sayala continued in speech, wanting to make sure she understood. "The Errans in this ship and in two others had kept Shaand and his friends on Dzura in slavery. Do you understand what slavery is?"

"Yes, I think so." She thought of a definition from what she understood. "It's where people are kept almost like prisoners and made to work at things they don't want to do. And they can get hurt or killed if they try to leave."

"Yes, and much worse."

"I don't think I want to know worse."

That's fine my girl, you are young and don't need to know more yet. He reverted back to speech. "Your father helped Uncle Shaand to free the Elioi who lived here on Dzura from being slaves of the Errans who lived in space. It was not right for the Errans to keep them as prisoners and do slave work."

"And so they had a war?"

"Yes, and now the Elioi on Dzura and the Elioi on Erra work together."

"That's a good thing, right?" She looked down at her fingers, clasping them together a little too tightly. Looking back up at Sayala she said, "but it's too bad all those people had to die."

"Yes, you're right. It *is* too bad. But this is a good example of what I want to show you, so you understand. The Elioi and humans like you, both have a long history of hurting each other. I need you, ... I would like you to help me bring a message to the people here and on your home planet that the warring behavior must stop." He pointed to the far horizon where a glow from over the edge was backlighting clouds. "Even now, there are some on the Erran planet who want revenge for the killing of the city-ships and those thousands who died during the revolt."

"Revolt?"

"Yes, in a war, there are two realities. Two different reasons for each to be at war."

She thought about that, the two different sides. Two kinds of thinking about the war. "Revolt is what happens to you, against you; and revolution is what you did."

"Yes, exactly!"

"I think I understand. The Errans thought it was their right to keep the Dzurans in slavery?"

She got a reassuring psi wave.

"And the Dzurans here were hurt if they didn't do as they were told?"

"Yes, and often much worse."

"That's terrible." Then she looked up at the wreckage behind the trees. *But destroying the city ships was terrible too.* She looked back down at her fingers while trying to imagine being on a ship that was crashing into a planet with no hope of anything." She wiped a tear track from each cheek and felt her lip start to tremble. She took in a very deep breath to try to control the wave of emotion engulfing her. For the briefest of moments, she appreciated the terrors of falling through an atmosphere toward death. Her breathing sped up—she had to bite her lower lip to stop its shuddering.

Do not blame your father for this. "In a war, there are often only quite simple choices. He was in a situation where he made good choices that helped stop the slavery, and it had costs. Many of the Errans died on that last day of the war. But all of the Dzurans were freed from that slavery. Brad, your father, is often upset about the many he killed. I've had long discussions with him as I am having with you."

Myahh snorked up some mucus oozing onto her lip and rubbed her nose on her upper sleeve to wipe it clean. "I think I understand." Beyond them, a glimmer of light on the horizon had been brightening a thin row of distant clouds. A silver disc began to rise above the horizon line, as she watched and thought about what he'd said, weighing the cost of slavery against the cost of killing to be free.

Sayala pointed at the rising disc. "That's Erra, the twin planet of Dzura."

"Is that like a moon? For Dzura?"

"A little bit except that it's very much larger than a moon, almost as big as Dzura." She waited for more. She'd felt a hesitation as if Sayala had more explanation. "The people of Dzura saw that planet rise overhead for their entire history of looking up toward the Light. And they wondered how to reach out and touch it, to go to it. Like your people have gone to your moon."

In a moment, he continued. "And they went there, and some of the Dzurans stayed, but on that lighter planet, and from living in space, they became different, and thought of themselves as different. They became Errans from Erra and forgot their bonds with the Dzurans they came from. There was, a long, long time ago, another war and the Errans tossed very large rocks, asteroids, at this planet, and when the dying ended, and the dust clouds went away, those Errans became the masters of the Dzurans that survived and kept them in slavery to grow food that was harder to grow in space."

As he spoke and they watched, the entire silver disc of Erra lost its grip on the horizon and lifted higher, partially hidden by the band of distant clouds. Something he'd said intruded on her quiet reverie. "What is the light that Shaand talks about?" Now she pointed at the sister planet. "Is that it?"

He said simply, "Look up."

She did. The heavens overhead were thinning as Dzura's sun dropped behind them. Overhead, bands of lavender, grey, and some yellows were beginning to shine through the atmosphere. A sprinkling of yellow, red, and white suns shone through and illuminated the gas cloud. "Oh! It's beautiful!"

"That color is from a vast cloud of gasses from a dead star, and it's being lit up by those other stars around it. It's called a nebula." He waited as she let her eyes take in the beauty. "Now," he said, reflecting a serious note, "imagine if the people of Earth wanted to come here to see this sky, to come this far just to see the inside of this nebular cloud. Do you think there would be tourists that would want to come here?"

"Yes." She nodded absently, looking up and straining her neck a little as the lavender sky faded and the overhead view of the nebula became clearer. "It's amazing!"

"And the trees and forests here, they are very different from those on Earth, right? Do you think humans would come to look at these sights?"

"Yes. And I think a lot of Dzurans would want to see some of the wonderful sights on Earth too. Don't you think?" She turned to see that his physical expression had changed. He was no longer in the form of a small dark-skinned Persian. He was now in the form of a Dzuran female. White fur covered most of her face except for its tan nose and forehead. He looked a lot like Aunt Lenka. "Why did you change?"

"You know it's still me, correct?"

"Yes." The identity of the psi signal was unmistakably Sayala's voice, it just seemed to have a distinct clipped tone, like Aunt Lenka's accent.

"As you can see," and there was a psi undertone of a chuckle; "the view is remarkable through the eyes of an Elioi. They've grown up under this lavender sky and inside this gas cloud. Their eyes can appreciate more of the colors. There are blues out there that... just a second."

She felt something shift, like a blink she didn't do herself. When she looked up again, there was much more depth to the lavenders. They had shifted into purples, new stars seemed to glow in brilliant pinpricks through a fog.

"Wow!"

You're welcome. The psi undertones now had that distinct Elioi flavor as if they had come from Uncle Shaand or Aunt Lenka.

And yes, thank you!

"I wanted to make a point." He said it softly, in the accent of an Elioi speaking English.

"It's still beautiful."

"Yes, but do you see the difference. You might have described the same experience differently than an Elioi if I hadn't shared that vision with you."

"Um-hmm." She felt like that was obvious, like what was the point.

"My point is that what you see, what you experience depends on your point of view. We each experience the world and our place in it from our own point of view."

Her vision had lost its blue undertones and was, she thought, human normal again. "I see."

"But do you understand?"

"Oh, you mean it's more than what kind of light we can see." The ideas came from her, but with his suggestions. The understanding came, in loose concepts at first, then in words she could put together for herself. "So, it's more who we are, who we have been." She struggled to remember a word that fit best. "It's more an issue of perception than vision."

"You're getting very close." He felt assured that he was making the right decision to select this precocious child to be his chosen speaker.

When the time came, she could deliver it with full understanding, rather than just a recitation.

She continued. "Sometimes what we think we see, is not what is there to be seen. We see what we think we do because of who we are, who we were, who we already agree with, how we were taught to think." She turned away from the darkened sky, now in its full starlit glory, and looked at Sayala's outline beside her. The white fur was now a deep shade of lavender in the darkness. The one-piece traditional clothing of the Elioi was nearly black with only a few buckles and snaps reflecting light off the rising sister planet.

"I see great promise in you, my child. It is hard to believe that you are only eight years of age. Many may have a hard time understanding you."

"Why?"

There was a laugh, half psi, half aspirated in the darkness.

"Because so many are going to view you only through all the misconceptions and preconceptions of what they already think about you, and about who you are, and about what can an eight-year-old know."

She looked back to Sayala to see if she understood what had been given to her. The lavender illumined white fur of an Elioi female was gone. A simple shape beside her glowed in yellow to gold tones. The deep Light of the nebular canopy gave it a shimmering edge, but she understood that there really was no edge. There was only a suggestion of a something, a being beside her. Its shape was undefinable.

It gave her comfort, and reassurance in psi. *Still me.* A bit of humor to soften the blow.

"Are you God?"

No, I am what I am

But

I am only a messenger.

But

And you are what you are. We come from different origins but are on the same path.

Where does the path go?

To understanding. You understand a lot more than you believe you do. You were well-named. I do not think it was an accident.

She thought her name, then said it out loud. "Myahh."

"Do you know what it means?" Sayala's spoken voice was soft, encouraging.

"There were people in Mexico a long time ago. They had huge cities built of stone."

"That is true, but across the world, there were other people who thought of the word Maya much differently."

She turned toward his shining form in the darkness. Erra's nebular light provided a soft deep grey to the sand and seemed to refract and shimmer through Sayala's neutral resting form.

Sayala added, "To the Hindu people in India and elsewhere, Myahh is magic, or illusion, or sometimes, a treasure." An image of a gilded temple formed in her mind with several people kneeling in front of a woman wrapped in red and gold brocade. Her arms were extended out in welcome as she smiled upon the kneeling people at her feet.

"What does this illusion maya do?"

"Excellent question. It allows people to see the real world, the physical world. But it can also mask the essence of the person, the thing that makes people different from animals that simply are."

She stumbled over the thought. *Simply are?*

Sayala considered his response. "No other creatures on Earth, think of anything beyond their life. Only a few species understand that they will die, they merely have more or less sophisticated survival instincts. Some may share consciousness with others, even communicate and share a hunt for food, but none think about or wonder about what lies beyond their planet, or question where they came from, where will they go after death, or if there is anything at all after death. It is another dimension of understanding that sets humans apart from other earthly creatures. Globally, the billions of humans create an additional layer of presence to the many layers of living things. The global sphere of mental activity is active and tends toward peace as a survival tool, but it is countered and too often disrupted by selfish individual actions. The Elioi are similar."

They sat together in silence for several minutes. Sayala continued in psi. *And you are not alone. There are thousands of others out beyond this beautiful nebula who share this quest for understanding of that other dimension.*

She felt a shudder pass along her spine. Gooseflesh bloomed on her forearms. The hair at the back of her head tickled. Her next question was full of sudden awareness. *What do you want from me?*

"Ah, the understanding deepens." Then, "I want you to help deliver a message... and later, in another setting, much more."

They sat quietly, in shared meditation, contemplation. Erra rose above them, bathing the isthmus in shimmering silver. The northern continent beyond was a dark smudge on the far shore. A few lights from the distant port city told of the new life coming to the Elioi homeworld.

~ ~ ~

They sat together for some time, she thought about what had been said, how she felt about the fallen city behind her, the other planet rising higher in the sky, and the many deeper questions and answers they had shared. Sayala's next question came much later, "Where would you like to go?" When she turned to look, Sayala was again in the form of a white-haired human in white linen.

Sayala had let Myahh be for a long while she sat quietly, legs crossed, eyes closed absorbing what had been said and expressed. She had been given far more than an eight-year-old's common understanding of very complex relationships between life, and existence, and the subtle differences among commonalities. The silver disc of Dzura's sister planet Erra had risen a third of its way higher in the night sky. The sea breeze had become cool, even chilly. Still, she sat quietly, putting together the words and images Sayala had shown her with what she had already known.

"I think," she said, almost too quietly above the increasing breakers of the rising tide, "back to the mountain house."

"Mr. Martin's house?"

"No, the one in Colorado where mom is staying safe. I want to be with her. That's where dad will want to go when he comes back."

26

The Announcement

Cameras packed the floor and gallery of the General Assembly Hall of the United Nations in New York. The world media was ready for the event. They had been anxious and strident as tension mounted after the failed military strike. Translators were on hand in a hundred countries to provide expert, and too often politically filtered, versions of whatever had been promised to be revealed. Rumors had been circling and recycling through the pro and con talking-head networks for a week. Normally, only the static feeds from the in-house press facilities at the assembly hall were used, but in the interest of free and open communication, the world press had been invited. This last was at the insistence of Brad Hitchens with the backup of Colonel Doherty and Martin Jenks, and finally brokered by General Stanford with the UN's Security Council. As many wanted to religiously follow the 'visitor' Sayala as wanted to assassinate him as an infidel.

In the intervening weeks since the failed strike, no cameras had been permitted at any of the visitor's interviews with the planet's political, philosophical, and religious leaders. Some had reacted in outrage, most in humble appreciation of the visit, and some reported a usually unbelieved experience with out-of-body travel and temporal dislocations. These were few and the few were unable to produce any evidence of those experiences. The world was primed for the event. The Announcement.

Since the now famous DeGrasse-Tyson interview, it was common knowledge across the globe that the visitor's name was Sayala. Although vaguely suggestive of eastern naming norms, it had no definite roots in any of planet Earth's languages, its pronunciation was reminiscent of the name of a small desert camp in Egypt, and a slightly larger village nestled among the arid fields of Rajasthan, India but with no connection to either locale.

His appearance had been described as that of a roughly Greek or Persian elder, an angelic child, or something many described in vague uncertain terms as 'variable.' A few had actually reported that while expecting a visit from Brad Hitchens and Ambassador Shaand, they had instead received Hitchens and his daughter. Only changing that

169

Bruce Ballister

assessment when the press compared images of his daughter Myahh. This 'variable' aspect of his visits seemed to have raised as much skeptical suspicion as it did excitement.

Early on, Sayala was normally accompanied by either Brad Hitchens or Ambassador Shaand. Later he was accompanied only by the space child, Myahh. As media attention grew, many were surprised to learn that Ambassador Shaand had been called back to Dzura taking with him a small contingent of Terrans representative of Earth's major cultures.

Myahh peered around the corner of the entrance to the General Assembly Hall, taking in the sounds of several hundred different conversations in almost as many languages. She shut the door quickly, dampening the audible roar but only a little of the din of mental images flooding in. She had been warned. She reached for her mother's hand and looked up for reassurance.

"You are going to be great!" Connie leaned over to plant a kiss on Myahh's forehead.

Ambassador Leink-Knaa , Aunt Lenka to Myahh, said, "I think you best messenger for this. Visitor Sayala is right in selecting you." The remaining Dzuran representative was impressive in full official ambassador's uniform behind Connie. Brad was due to arrive soon but getting clearance for Jai to land on the UN's central drive court had been holding things up.

"Mom, they're getting noisy. I hear too many people thinking this meeting is a waste of time." Myahh, was beginning to be impatient. She'd spoken to small groups before, but the assembly hall was now full. One hundred and ninety-three delegations of up to six with other service organizations such as the World Health Organization, UNESCO, and the World Bank. The tour guide, the day before, had said to expect about nineteen hundred seated guests and two or three hundred more in the press corps. Enhanced security would be in and around the building as well. The mental noise of those hundreds and their heightened anxiety were giving her a headache.

Myahh looked up and found Lenka smiling down at her. She asked. "Did you get that, too?"

"Yes, your father and Sayala come very soon."

Connie released Myahh's hand and turned to talk quietly with Martin Jenks. He had his hand over his radio's earpiece and waved for her attention. He turned immediately and trotted over to the head of security

170

for the detail behind the assembly hall's main stage. A few of the guards posted near the doors slipped out purposefully. Martin came back, smiling. "Brad and Sayala have just landed out on the lawn."

Myahh had been eavesdropping through psi on a nearby, grew puzzled, and looked up at Jenks. "Hammers cold? What does that mean?"

A frown flashed across Martin's face before he smiled in understanding. "Hammarskjöld, my dear. Dag Hammarskjöld used to be a big boss around here quite a while ago. One of the UN office buildings is named after him. Your dad just landed Jai in that building's front yard. They'll be here in a moment."

Bradley Hitchens and Sayala walked into the ready room behind the stage flanked by security forces. Brad leaned down to receive Myahh's hug, then stood for a peck on the cheek from Connie. "Are we all ready in here?" Then down to Myahh, "Kiddo, you going to be OK with all those people out there?"

"I can do this, Daddy. I'll just try to turn off all those voices in my head. Sayala said he could help with that."

Brad chucked her under the chin. "You can do this!"

They walked onto the stage area to the right of the rostrum and its bank of microphones. Hitchens led the small group, followed by Connie, Myahh, and Sayala. The normally sedate group erupted in shouts and calls for attention. At the audio control panel behind the front wall of the assembly hall, the light board lit up as more than half of the seated delegates wished to have a time slot.

It was a show of hubris. Each of the two hundred plus delegates had representation back home who they needed to impress. None of them had any idea of what was to come, but all wanted to know the extent of the threat of the ever-expanding black disk that was painting a growing gray dot of shadow on its path across the equatorial zones. In the first month since the umbra ship had deployed its sails, only a few noticed the slight dimming of the sun near noon. But as the word spread down to the man-on-the-street level, the world's citizenry had been either temporarily blinding themselves or inventing the little tubes and artifices that helped during a solar eclipse. Now, everyone knew of the small black dot on the sun, and almost everyone was angry about it.

Brad took his place behind the rostrum and made sure his daughter's stool was ample to let her see out across the full house. He looked over her head to Sayala and nodded an affirmative. Turning back out to the sea of faces, he put two hands out, palms down— requesting quiet. The din diminished, from angry mob to unruly crowd. Sayala repeated the gesture and sent out a calming signal. At this, most of the remaining members quieted down. Now, the few noisy members of the audience that remained, became aware of their isolation and began to follow suit. Many still stood, seeking attention from the floor. Their several voices could not be distinguished over each other's interference and the vast distances across the assembly hall.

"Thank you!" Brad started, still holding his palms out for order. "Thank you, could I please ask you to calm down. I'm sure if you would allow us to address the assembled dignitaries here today, and their representatives, and the press, much can be learned. Many of your questions can and will be answered."

He felt at peace, an ease he hadn't felt in weeks. He'd been nervous about the address, and now all that was gone. He realized that the calm was emanating from Sayala. His friend, an interstellar messenger, was transmitting a message of calm and submission.

All attention was on the rostrum and the guest speakers. Brad cleared his throat and began, "On behalf of my family—Connie is with me today in the wings." He turned to his left to see her pulling the stage door closed. "And my daughter who I am very proud to have with me here. We two are very proud and honored to bring you another ambassador.

"Most of you, I am sure, know of my good friend Shaand, the Eloi ambassador to Earth. He's been called back to his homeworld to serve as the head of their Parliament on Dzura. The other Eloi Ambassador, Leeink-Knaa will be returning as well in a few months, taking with her a dozen ambassadors from many of your countries to seek trade and cultural exchanges. You can apply here at the UN Secretariat's office for permission. Acceptance will be based on your home country's acceptance of non-proliferation policies.

Technology exchanges, as you must know, are being worked out over the somewhat faster grav-wave transmitters the Dzurans have provided, but your chosen ambassadors can learn so much more by visiting Dzura themselves. Remember though, the round trip is over twenty seven years not counting time spent on the other world. So, be patient; we have much to share today." He took a deep breath, paused, and began.

"Today, I look out at a multitude of different cultures, different belief systems, and the different political systems that provide for the needs of this world's burgeoning population. But, I have one message for you all. Before my friend Sayala and daughter Myahh speak, I want to remind you that we all—all of us—share one commonality. We share this planet. We are collectively, humanity. We have risen from a single tribe in eastern Africa almost two million years ago. We spread across this planet in its virgin state and barely survived as we found new ways to live. Under conditions of almost unbelievable adversity, our ancestors learned to survive in the bitter cold and learned to thrive in tropical heat. Through trial and error, we survived the diseases of those tropics, and the tongue-strangling aridity of the world's deserts.

"In meeting these demands we diverged into different racial lines and adopted different religions. We emerged from territorial tribalism to clan-based groups of roving hunter-scavengers, to small agrarian kingdoms, to region-wide civilizations that have left us all their histories carved in stone. No matter our varying histories. No matter our current religious beliefs or political systems, all of us, human. All of you, all of us together on this small blue planet, exist within a thin layer of atmosphere. We've filled that thin layer of life-giving air with caustic acids, carbon dioxide, and other more exotic poisons as we in our different industrial efforts created the energy that lights our globe from space at night."

"So," he paused to catch his breath, "all of you are here today to listen to my friend Sayala. I say my friend in all honestly because I have learned that he has our future in mind and has an important message for all of you here, and to the millions who are tuning in across this one single blue planet." Brad looked over to Sayala, nodded, and stepped back half a step from the front of the rostrum. Listen carefully my friends, to his message, and then to his chosen messenger, my daughter, Myahh. You will undoubtedly be shocked by her grasp of vocabulary for one so young. Her words are her own. Consider both of their messages carefully.

Sayala stood erect, seeming to Brad to be a little taller. *Is that my imagination?* Sayala sent out another psi call for quiet as rumblings of a hundred almost whispered side conversations erupted across the gallery. As the hush grew total, Brad became aware of the soft whir of air conditioning. No one was talking. It seemed as if no one was breathing.

"My name, in a phonetic form that you can understand is Sayala. I have roots in this galaxy in a star system that your scientists have named only by a number. I am a member of a few hundred of my kind who come to worlds like yours that are on the brink of expanding outward to other star systems. From some distance, I and others like me have been monitoring your world for the last few of your centuries. It has only been

173

the last few years, that we have considered it necessary for my current mission to be critical.

"As you know, one of our monitors that had been in your system's asteroid belt was taken, quite unexpectedly, by an Elioi prospector. That act, on its own, would have precipitated our current presence in the Elioi star system." He paused as heads nodded toward their partners or the delegates at adjacent desks. "That act of piracy was a trigger for us to take action with the Dzuran system, just as other signals we have been getting from your planet have precipitated my presence here. Now, there are two monitors, one in your asteroid belt tracking humanity, and the other in orbit around Alal, the Elioi's central star. "And yes, another messenger like myself is in their system preparing to have a talk much like I am giving here today."

His attention swiveled to a delegate a few rows back from the front. "Yes, I can read many of your thoughts. But please, try not to be so hostile; it will be bad for your heart muscle." Open-mouthed the delegate from Brazil stood, started to complain, and sat dumbfounded. Another thought stream from the assembly caught his attention and Sayala looked to the far right of the floor near one of the several aisles. "I agree. At first, your mullahs will take issue with what I have to say." He had made direct eye and psi contact with the delegate from Iran. The delegate shared a glance at the neighboring desk occupied by Iraq, stood, and stormed out of the hall with his immediate entourage following quickly behind.

Palms out again, he silently called for quiet. "Many of you, are more interested in your thoughts than in what I have to say. Please calm your minds. Close your eyes for one-half minute and please listen to my thoughts. Brad felt a sudden chill as if he'd paused in front of an air conditioner after a long walk. The mental energy in the giant hall dropped immediately. He wondered anew at Sayala's ability to think, to speak, and to listen to the thousand mental images broadcasting from the delegates and their support staff. The Iraqi delegation stopped at the top of the ramp, just inside the doorway and turned to listen.

Sayala lowered his arms and started again. "I am Sayala, and I represent a governing assembly much like this one. But its delegates are from the governing councils of a myriad of different star systems that thrive in this and the neighboring spiral arms of this galaxy. We are largely a peaceful assembly. There have been skirmishes as we encountered new cultures, but we find that at the scale where inter-system skirmishes require expenditures of resources and the resulting losses of life, these petty arguments over resources cannot be tolerated. Neither the aggressor nor the defender has ever benefited from these conflicts in, as you say, the long run.

"I am here today, to offer a provisional seat at that council for this planet—for humanity." He let the thought and the message linger. "Again, I have come here with the message of welcome and an offer of a seat at our high council. As a new member of our council, this star system will be welcome as a witness only, without voting rights. But a path exists for Earth toward full accreditation. That accreditation and future voting rights do come with conditions." Again, Sayala waited for the translators to confirm what he was broadcasting in psi in fifty different languages and dialects.

"Upon my departure, one of your first orders of business should be the consideration of a pair of delegates, one male and one female. If they are a natural couple, they will be permitted to bring along family members because the transit time can take upwards of one of your years, and the opportunities for communication with this council require as long for messages." He smiled, as a single common question arose from a majority before him. "No, this seat of government is not within one light-year of this star.

How can this be, you ask?" His chuckle of amusement was neither condescending nor ridiculing. Your science has brought you tremendous gains in understanding the physical laws of the universe. But you have many more things to learn. Your study of the very smallest particles brings you closer to understanding the very small, but it does not inform you of the mysteries you have yet to learn of the vast reaches between the stars. Imagine what you will know when you understand fully, the implications of the fifth and sixth dimensions.

"Did you not question in amazement that my friend Hitchens traveled from the distant home of the Elioi in only fourteen years? Their use of another parallel dimension defined by gravity waves is itself an area of discovery and development that is only a beginning. We will make available for the use of a delegate that you select a craft to make that transit. In addition, I will make available for the use of this august Council a communication device that will serve to maintain communication with your delegate."

Amid the myriad questions arising from this announcement, a new strain was rising. "Ah yes. My ship. Many of you are wondering at the craft I have positioned between Earth and your star, Sol. It is a specialized craft we can deploy in desperate situations when we find a culture like yours that is on the brink of collapse." Sayala found the new rush of questions jelling around this issue, and it began to overtake the earlier issue of delegate selectio. "If you will consider the effect it is having. At its current deployment size, it casts a tiny shadow on your equatorial zones. At its present size, it will have little effect. But it is growing now to its next stage of development, which in nine of your days will almost double in diameter.

"When this stage is fully developed, there will be full born on those hottest zones on your surface, a shadow. Briefly felt each day, as those areas pass into that shadow, there will be a minor cooling effect. Relieved of about fifteen percent of its mid-day heat for a period of about an hour, the cooling effect will begin to have a minor effect on your overall weather systems."

Several of the delegates were now on their feet. Fully half were shouting toward the rostrum. Some were seeking cooperative engagement from their neighbors. Against a rising tide of anger, a blast of psi from Sayala spread calm and quiet across the hall like a wave on a beach. Only one agitator, the delegate from China was so engaged in arguing for resistance of some kind, that he failed to notice the quiet. He turned, and with a face screwed in anger sat sullenly to listen. He could do little else under Sayala's mental command.

27

The Agenda

When the grand hall was silent again, Sayala took up his message. "I do have an agenda here. I did not come to this remote and endangered planet on an idle journey. I came first to learn, to study, to interpret the messages that are being broadcast in so many languages. From billions of minute information bits you have provided me and my kind an understanding of your history, and by projection, your immediate future.

"I will grant you this, many of your professional class understand full well the precipice humanity faces as this world becomes even warmer. Your use of carbon fuels over the last several hundred years, and especially over the last one hundred years, is dangerous. THIS MUST STOP." This exhortation was both profound in its vocal delivery and the accompanying psi blast. "You would kill yourselves, stifle your human condition with unbelievable suffering if each small principality and nation considers only its own parochial needs.

"Some are doing remarkably well—especially those of you in western Europe. This may be because you are naturally deficient in these fuels yourselves. You are learning to harness the wind, the sun, the tides, the currents of the oceans, and the latent heat in the rock layers deep beneath the crust. Unfortunately, and I cannot overestimate the potential foe misfortune, many more of you are performing miserably. You are creating new energy plants that will push your atmosphere beyond a point at which it will not recover for several lifetimes. Such a terrible waste. These fossil fuels will be much more useful to you if converted into recyclable materials. To send their waste up a smokestack or out one of your vehicles tailpipes will be seen by a future generation as misguided and misused. So stop building these power plants. Stop building fuel driven vehicles. Adapt before irreparable harm has been done. I recognize that it will take some time and that it will be difficult. But you must begin now!

"To this challenge, I bring you the immediate relief of my shadow maker, my umbra ship. It will provide a small grace period for the people of this world to take corrective action. To develop alternatives to the

177

burning of wood fires, coal fires, and petroleum fires, and waste those resources on electric lights and propellants for your vehicles.

"When the final stage of my ship's deployment is reached, the increase in temperatures you are now experiencing should level off. It may take a little more than one of your years for this equilibrium to be established. It will take even longer for you to develop the needed fusion energy plants. This still-secret source, the gift of the universe, fusion of elementals into water will be your future power source. I have arranged for its technologies to be made available to you all."

"But you must not build more of these carbon-fired energy plants."

He paused to consider his options and the negative reactions in his audience. After a moment's reflection, Sayala added. "You will find that you cannot pursue these projects. I will see to that as your benefactor." He released a calming message and let the rush of rising emotions tamp down. "Some of your cultures have a saying about a carrot and a stick. The stick will be your inability to bring new carbon-burning energy systems into being. The carrot will be the gift of fusion energy."

A burst of psychic energy from several of the delegates coalesced into a single stream.

"No!" Sayala seemed to become radiant. "No! I am not a god. I am not the god of so many of your religions that promise a savior. Those promises have been made in many emergent cultures on hundreds of emerging planets. I am not a god, and do not make of me a god; you will do so at your own peril."

"I need you all to understand that my agenda here is to be helpful, to bring humanity back from its precipice. You must do this to avoid the environmental disaster that will surely set your course back many hundred years." He stopped; letting the message be absorbed and understood by the millions of viewers watching the worldwide broadcast. "Beyond that precipice is … a worldwide calamity which will create widespread suffering and loss.

His message in psi was delivered to the gathered delegates in every language present on the floor *My agenda is to move instead toward eventual recovery. That recovery could take a few of your centuries to come about even if you do not use nuclear weapons to settle your competing differences.*

He paused, letting the message take hold and continued aloud in a somber tone, "If you settle your differences with nuclear weapons, recovery will take centuries or more seriously, might render you and most of the species on this planet impotent and incapable of any future. Then, perhaps in another ten million years, another species might dominate a re-emergent ecosystem."

"Do you really want to pursue your own narrow-minded pathways, competing as rivals for the last ton of coal, for the last barrel of petroleum? Is the future of your world worth the quarterly profits derived from this quest for calamity? For your stock portfolios?" Sayala paused, the assembly hall was quiet except for the occasional cough. He reached down and took Myahh's hand. He helped her up to her stool and stood back to allow her to face the microphones. He turned one final time to the microphones. "Please listen carefully to this gifted child. In her generation, there lies hope."

~ ~ ~

Myahh leaned forward so she could see over the edge of the rostrum to take in the front row. Arrayed from right to left were the delegates from Afghanistan to Armenia. She sensed genuine hostility from the turbaned Afghani and only a little more acceptance from the Armenian. She took in the faces arrayed behind them, not quite believing that Sayala had asked her to be here, to be one of the messengers. She looked back to her dad's smiling face, flashed a grin that was reminiscent of her mother's trademark lop-sided smile, and looked back out across the world's delegates.

She leaned forward and pulled one of the microphones down to her level. "My father introduced Sayala as his friend. Sayala is also my friend. I have had many hours of discussion with him sharing what he knows and what I know of people. A lot of people are afraid of me because I can hear them when they think. It is unusual but I am not the only human who can do this; most of them are turned away, put in instutu, uhm, institutions." She struggled through the word. "I am lucky, I am not a freak. It is true that my mind sometimes hears what others are thinking. But, I am learning to control the noise, so I am not always listening. I am this way because when my mother was on Dzura, and I was growing inside her, the Dzurans gave my mom and dad a special fruit from the Dzuran selli plant that helps with the listening of thoughts. It helped them to learn how to understand and speak the Elioi language a little bit. The same fruit also helps many of those Elioi citizens to communicate and solve problems by understanding."

"It did not stop them from having a war. But that was mostly because the Errans rarely mixed with the Dzurans. Like us, they had their war like we have wars because they did not communicate. The Dzurans

179

are now free. They won their rebellion and are free from slavery under the Erran city ships. Now, the Errans and Dzurans, all the same Elioi, are working to rebuild their broken planet and repair their broken trust."

She saw some nodding heads in the audience and continued. "In talking with Sayala, I have learned that his ambassador friend in that star system has many things to do to help Elioi understand that all of them need to be able to get school, and to share in the fruit so that slavery on that planet might finally come to an end." She shut her eyes listening to the hundreds of thought streams in the audience, trying to filter them—to sort them.

"And yes, the selli fruit. There is a plot of it growing on earth, and it will help bring new understanding to us. I hope at first it can be used to help people communicate. I hope we will start with diplomats and politicians. I hope they and all of us can speak what is truly in our hearts. That this new form of communication

is good and open and will express what should be felt when we talk and try to solve the many problems Sayala was talking to you about."

"You are now wondering why a child is talking to you. I am not the first. An Afghan girl was here recently talking about injustice in her land. Adela was almost killed because she simply wanted to learn; to go to school." A pained look crossed her face as she looked for sincerity to put behind her next words. "Why? Why is it harmful for a girl to learn to read, to do math, to understand her world? A girl's mind is no different from a boy's mind. We are all curious and want to learn." Across the great hall, grumblings could be heard. It's vehemence shocked Myahh into momentary silence and was quelled only by a psi blast from Sayala.

When the vocal and mental outburst subsided, she began again. "Another young girl was in this same UN General Assembly Hall recently talking about the climate. She was wonderful! Greta helped some of you understand how dangerous our climate crisis is. I want to let you know this. This is not *your* world to mess up! It's MY world. I AM EIGHT YEARS OLD!" She paused to calm her emotions. "If an accident does not happen, I might live to be eighty years old or more. I would live to see most of the great cities on the Chinese coast go underwater, and the same for India, and many in Africa, Northern Europe, and here in my country. Miami, New Orleans, and Houston. Tampa and heck, most of the cities of my home state Florida, here in the US. These cities cannot survive if the ocean rises even two or three feet in the next eighty years. Miami Beach might be able to build a dike like they have in the Netherlands, but what about Mumbai, or Bangkok, or Singapore? Where will you house the billions of people that will be displaced across the globe from the west coast of Florida to the island nations of the Pacific?"

She hit her stride, barely looking at the small note cards in hand, and continued. "And the rising oceans is just one problem!"

Her small voice carried a charismatic overtone that grabbed the attention of the hundreds in the assembly hall. "What happens when there are no more glaciers? What happens when there are no more surplus winter snowpacks that desert cities depend on for drinking water? What happens to cities like Denver, Las Vegas, Kolkata, and New Delhi, and a hundred cities in western China. I forget all those names. What will happen when the Sahara Desert moves five hundred miles south? Where will all those people go? Can all the people in Sudan move to Uganda without bloodshed? No, simply put to you—no, they can not."

"And no, this is not YOUR planet, you have wasted your time in command and control. This is MY planet. Most of YOU will be dead in twenty or thirty years. YOU are using up MY precious resources in preparing for petty wars, concentrating wealth among a tiny few!" She paused to catch her breath and tone down her anger. "I and other children who are now eight years old, or eighteen years, or eighteen months old will be the ones trying to fix this mess. YOUR MESS!" She did not realize it, but her unbidden psi powers were projecting her anger and frustration as overtones to her oration. The assembled delegates and attendees were quiet in astonished awe without fully understanding how they had become entranced.

"What will happen when your greed and lack of planning cuts down the rain forests, or the great forests of Siberia? Will you notice the lower levels of oxygen immediately? Will you be smart enough to allow them to recover?" She was on her toes, leaning forward into the microphone. She'd dropped her cards and was pushing forward on adrenaline and emotion.

"For all the children in the world—YOUR CHILDREN—I ASK YOU TO LISTEN TO SAYALA." She shut her eyes and put her hands to her ears. "Yes, I hear you, you are angry. You think who am I to come here and tell YOU how to behave? You are all acting like children in a playground. You want your turn with the ball, you want your team to win. Let me tell you what I want. I want you all to do everything you can possibly do to make sure that your grandchildren and their grandchildren have a—."

~ ~ ~

Myahh's speech was broken as the stuttering sounds of automatic gunfire coming from outside the building grew louder. A muffled boom followed by a small crash sounded outside the hall. Then the pop-pop-pop of automatic rifles grew louder. A repeated buzzing sounded, known by the delegates as an immediate evacuation notice, permeated the great hall. The signal directed all parties to immediately descend into a secure bunker below. Black-clad uniforms led by Martin Jenks came running out from behind the front wall to secure Sayala, Brad, and Myahh Hitchens. In the planned evacuation of the delegates, the lower tier of countries at the head of the alphabet began to head toward the lower exits. Several of these headed for the same doors behind the desk of the General Affairs officers that Martin Jenks and his charges controlled. Brad met Connie at that doorway and took two more steps into the back room where Martin corralled all of them into a circle.

"Wait here." He looked directly into Sayala's eyes. His question held hope amid his uncertainty of Sayala's real abilities. "Do you have a way to get them to safety?" He'd been briefed on the earlier trips to Sayala's 'safe rooms.' He wasn't sure if it was on the umbra ship or in some kind of parallel universe only Sayala could create. He just wanted to go there now.

Sayala nodded, then bowed. He called to the few dozen people in the immediate area behind the doors to the GA hall into a small cluster. Brad called out to Jai to be on standby, to power up if needed. A reassuring, *yes Brad, bringing all systems online,* was returned immediately.

The chatter of gunfire still sporadic as they left the hall had ceased. Brad looked to Martin. "I think we should stay put for now."

"I do too. If our friend here pulls us away now," Martin agreed, "I think that would cause more confusion."

Sayala said quietly, "There is no problem now." He looked down at Myahh. "I wish you could have finished your talk. You were doing very well."

Myahh beamed, "Thank you, I was almost finished!"

"It was a message they needed to understand."

Brad asked, "Do you think they did."

Sayala's smile was smug. "Those in the hall did. I cannot project out to all of the people watching on their TVs, tablets, and computers."

Myahh added, "and phones."

Martin asked him, "How do you know there is no problem now?"

"Because I told them to put down their weapons and lie down," he gave a very human shrug, "and they did."

28

Last Call

The studio at the American Museum of Natural History had unaccustomed security outside. Police in full riot gear and long guns could be found at the lobby elevator bank, rooftop, and major hallway intersections. Even the bathrooms and maintenance areas had been scanned prior to their arrival. In a guarded ready room, not the actual television ready room, makeup artists were applying flesh-colored makeup to Brad's already tanned face. Myahh was pulling on a popsicle and trying not to fidget. She wasn't going to be on air for this session. Sayala had respectfully declined any makeup at all. "Please, no, my chemistry will not be compatible with your chemistry. Over the objections of the makeup artist, he quietly gave her a strong enough psi hint that he was probably right.

Taps at the door, three light ones, a pause, and two more preceded DeGrasse-Tyson's entrance. "Hello all." His broad smile, betrayed only by a twinge near the corners of his eyes, that there was worry over the previous day's scene uptown at the UN building. "Is everyone OK in here?" He stooped to shake Myahh's hand and surprised himself by thinking hello back to her silent greeting. From her off-center smile, he had the real impression that she had received the thought. Then he told her, "Yes, thanks. I did receive the sample of your fruit." He smiled, remembering. "It tastes pretty good, kind of a cross between kiwi and avocado, but not as bad as that might sound."

Brad stood to greet him and took two steps to shake their host's hand. "Thanks for letting us come over here to finish the announcement." He sighed with relief and exasperation. "I suppose there are a whole lot of people out there who don't really want to hear it. The announcement that is."

Tyson's smile now came with a twinkle of good humor. "Young man, I learned a long time ago that science, and that's SCIENCE in all caps, still has enemies leftover from the early days of the reformation and new ones that crop up all over with clerical and political backing. It boggles my mind that vaccinations are still seen as a government plot or some other ploy of the forces of evil, or simply a political tool to get tracking devices injected in the unwilling."

"Yeah," Brad acknowledged, "stupidity can't be entirely bred out of the human race."

Tyson grinned. "There's an old saying I learned a long time ago in grad school statistics: the problem with IQ is that half of all people are below average. When you take the concept further, for all the very smart people out there, there are just as many stupid. Then you add politics and religion to the mix..." He let out a sigh of frustration. Tyson stepped out of the way of the makeup tech as she tried to slip out. "Thanks, Sheila, they all look great." Then looking at Sayala, "And you, Sir, how are you this afternoon? I'm very sorry about yesterday's incident at the UN."

Sayala had already stood from his chair and came forward to greet Tyson formerly. "Would you believe that I've experienced a lot worse?"

"Yes, I suppose I would. Can you share with me, how many worlds have you been involved with? I mean, at this stage?"

Sayala returned a knowing smile. "I think the unassisted count for me is approaching fifty. Some of those heeded my call and are now fully engaged in our collective. Some of them, as you would expect, reacted in hostility."

"As did we, did the attempt to disable your craft in solar orbit do any significant damage?

"No. That will be part of my address here today. There is only so much I can do. Your society has had the unfortunate development of the entertainment industry's ability to make all manner of imaginary happenings appear to be reality. Anything I might do on camera, while impressive in person, will be wholly unimpressive compared to your media's special effects. I can talk, and we can wait. I can only wait so long before I must move along. Many of the audience will believe this all to be science fiction—maybe a hoax as many thought your landing on the moon to be."

"I understand." The physicist shared a long moment with Sayala, receiving, Brad thought, and more insights. Brad looked at his watch. The time was approaching the top of the hour and it would be a good time to break into the ongoing news channel feeds. The major national and international networks in the Metro New York area had been alerted. Most would pick up the feed as soon as either Sayala or DeGrasse Tyson came on the set.

Bruce Ballister

Tyson's gaze met each, in turn, he shrugged, smiled. "I think there are a few million people waiting on us. The incident at the UN only magnified the crowd. Let's go."

This time, Sayala had the chair closest to the host with Brad and Myahh sitting across a small table set with water glasses for each. Tyson did not have his usual small stack of comment cards ready. A floor producer made the countdown to zero and pointed at Tyson. He made a few opening remarks to cover the hasty exit from the UN and thanked the museum for readying the StarTalk set so quickly. He turned to Myahh, "I believe you were saying something to us all at the UN before you were so rudely interrupted."

Myahh's lips pressed into a thin line as her eyes narrowed to slightly more than slits. She had not expected to be asked to talk today. She seemed to fight for the right words. "I'm sorry to hear about the four people who died yesterday at the UN. I know the security forces were following their orders, but..." She faltered, recovered. "Sayala and I could have stopped them." She looked over to Sayala. "And Ambassador Sayala *did* easily stop them." She shook her head in an obvious display of distress. "There is so much we can all learn from Sayala, from the Elioi, and from our inner selves. The more humans who can learn to communicate with their minds and true selves and not their words, the better chances we all have to come together in peace and cooperation. If you remember, this *is* the Ambassador's message. We must learn to communicate and cooperate."

She stopped, blew out her frustration from puffed cheeks. "When we were interrupted earlier at the United Nations, I was trying to say that grownups are acting like jealous children. The men who came to end that meeting with guns had hatred in their hearts. Now some of those hearts are gone. They will never grow old, learn to love grandchildren. Never learn to appreciate the beauty of this planet. Never gain the wisdom of another person's point of view." She paused to collect her thoughts and her breath.

"Sayala's spaceship between us and the sun is a shadow maker ship. Its small shadow, although hundreds of miles across, only slightly reduces the daytime heat as the world's oceans, deserts, and tropics rotate beneath it. It will reduce the amount of heat on any day by just enough that it can slow and eventually stop the temperature rise that is killing off coral reefs, changing the balance in jungles, and spreading deserts. And again, because they did not understand, the adults in charge of our

186

countries tried to blow Sayala's ship up! Ask the generals, the politicians might not know of it. But the generals do"

"I have just turned eight years old, but I hope my voice can reach the thousands of you who can hear a message of peace." She stopped, blinked, looked up at her dad, and said, "I think that's it." She started to lean back in her chair but abruptly straightened and leaned forward. "There's one more thing. I did learn recently that there is one thing in common among all of our world's religions and that we share with the wisdom of the Elioi. It is simple—you already know it. 'Treat others as you would have them treat you.'"

Brad was beaming with pride. She'd gone off script as a result of the attempted violent disruption and added to the message she'd come to give. He met Sayala's glance and nodded for the Ambassador to pick up the conversation.

Sayala turned to the center camera. It had just swiveled toward him, and its red light blinked on. "When we were interrupted at the United Nations, my friend Myahh was telling of her hopes for the children of this world. Normally, the young adapt to their surroundings, the conditions they are born into, and accept their place in life. The same is true on almost all of the worlds I've monitored. It is also true that the conditions they are born into are not at all even. Some have more advantage over the multitudes that are born into families with little in the way of resources. I've learned that your culture divides itself into a first world with great wealth and opportunities, a second-world that is emerging into a condition with greater opportunities, and the third-world. This last contains the largest numbers of your population and they seek, as all sentient creatures do, to overcome their formidable obstacles and do better to create more opportunities for the next generation."

"Leaders of industry and commerce in the first world, think only of growth and profit for their select peers, thinking little of the cost they impose on the ecosystems that support that growth." He looked hard into the lens of the camera. "That second world, struggles to keep up, expends enormous energy and resources to catch up. Even as they think to raise the standard of living for their millions, the wreak even more damage because they have almost no limits on environmental damage."

"And the last—in that third tier. The parents of children in these conditions often work hard and travel to new countries to find better work and opportunities. But you know all this. You are aware of the extreme hardships faced by immigrants, by refugees the world over. Much of this

Bruce Ballister

suffering is the result of your petty struggles over religious doctrine, material resources, and historical conflicts rooted in past generations.

"I find that humanity has one major flaw. You do not behave well in large numbers. This stems from smaller flaws. You do not trust those who look different, who speak different languages, or perhaps the greatest obstacle, those who have a different understanding of God."

He stopped, seemed to shimmer, and recollected his present manifestation as the gentle Persian in a linen suit. "Let me be clear. I AM NOT A GOD! I am a visitor to your world, and I exist in more than four dimensions. Many of my kind understand how to harness a higher plane of consciousness, another dimension. This is the explanation to those of you who have witnessed my altering manifestations. But returning to why I am here? Why am I bothering to address you today? My ship will remain to provide you with more time to solve your very real problems, but I will be leaving soon.

I am here to assist your world, your lovely planet earth, in joining a collective of civilized planets that can bring you all unparalleled opportunities to learn advanced technologies in energy production, communication, and travel. Creating these mechanisms will provide badly needed employment. Trading opportunities will exist with other worlds that are extremely short of materials your system has in abundance. Saturn is lifeless, so is Venus, you can reap their technologies to expand into these inner planets and harvest readily accessible quantities of raw materials badly needed elsewhere.

But for the children Myahh was addressing, another path lies ahead for them. For two of your centuries, your disparate nations have expanded into a global culture with the United Nations now serving as a centralized oversight body. You have also brought your ocean and atmosphere to the brink of planetary oblivion. Those children, Myahh and her generation, and the next generations to come will have to come to grips with ever-expanding lifeless deserts on land and at sea. You will not be able to create soil rapidly enough in the areas where ice used to be to grow foods needed for a population explosion that has no end.

"I can help you with that end but only in the smallest way. My ship is at this moment slowing the trend of a warming ocean and a warming atmosphere. What is the atmosphere anyway but the reflection of that powerful heat engine that is your ocean? The rise of its temperature by only a small fraction will have devastating effects on your climate: More storms, bigger storms, dryer and hotter summers, and ironically, wetter snowier winters. But not necessarily where you need them. If we manage to lower your ocean's temperatures by only a few degrees, your glaciers

188

will still take a thousand years to recover. Millions depend on a reduction in the accumulated mountain snowcaps for drinking and irrigation waters. The accelerating rush into privation and starvation has already begun. And what do you do about it?"

His next was an angry outburst Brad had never seen. "WAR! And war for all the wrong reasons. Not a war on starvation, or a massive effort to restore lost forests! Not a coordinated response to convert your power plants! No! You fight over your gods and their disciples. You fight over territorial squabbles that go back a thousand years!"

He looked almost pitying, Brad thought, but Sayala's intense glare into the camera's eye never wavered. "As a global population, you have every opportunity to reverse this cycle, and yet, many of your governments spend a majority of their capital wealth on war or the building up of defenses against a future war."

"I will tell you this! This same message has been given to countless other cultures that, like your own, were on the doorstep of interplanetary explorations and expansion to other star systems. Some cultures have accepted the challenge, some still languish in self-delusion of their own grandeur, others still have failed and face centuries or millennia of rebuilding." He paused for effect. "Not a few have perished, using nuclear or biological weapons that took those systems to their finality!"

"My simple message is this: you will not be permitted to go beyond the realm of your sun, Sol With the consent the Elioi, perhaps to their sun, Alal. Quite simply, this is a test. If you manage to pass this test, you can reap untold new opportunities. Opportunities so broad and amazing that most of you would not understand the implications, the benefits."

"Some of you have a saying: Failure is not an option." He paused, waited for the murmuring to die down. "What happens if you fail? What does failure look like? Failing this test is simply carrying on as you are. Mistrusting each other, competing with each other without consideration of your impact on your fellow humans or the limited resources you have on your world. IF YOU FAIL!" Sayala paused, dropped a level in his psi-enabled impact. "Well then, I would estimate you have only a few hundred years to enjoy life as you remember it. For each of your children who can survive malnutrition, they will dig and scrape and fight and wage wars because you cannot limit your need to grow your population." His messaging was calmer now; his tone less strident. "And failure will limit your expansion into the nearby star systems that you are just now discovering have planets in the habitable zone."

Bruce Ballister

Sayala relaxed a little, settled into the back of his chair. "If you fail, humanity will not be permitted to leave the orbits of this star and its satellites if you do not learn to act as one body. There is much good I have seen about your species. As individuals, families, and some communities, I have seen cooperation, intelligent problem solving, sacrifice, and sharing." He paused as if getting ready to deliver the power punch. "You need to learn to do this as a global collective." He raised a pointed finger, making the salient point, "as you have in your conquest of space. Your research station is a model of cooperation, but on the ground, you are a shambles of greed and corruption, and competition. This must change! If not, if you falter in this challenge. If your short-sighted selfishness, intolerance and greed fail you; you will not be permitted to pass beyond your waring, dying world."

Tyson, aware suddenly that he was on camera and that his mouth was open, closed it. He placed his palms down on the table thinking, '*Outstanding*!' He said, "Sayala, I agree absolutely with almost everything you have just said. But there is a fundamental trait among humans that does not like ultimatums. We don't like being threatened."

Sayala nodded, understanding. "My friend, there is no threat here. The statement is simple. The fundamental trait that you speak of was necessary when small bands of primitive men were ranging for resources in a pre-agricultural world. But that trait persists into the present-day's hyper-industrial culture, as my young friend Myahh said moments before. Even as you have grown your industrial empires, your corporation's and countries' actions are exemplified by greed and competition. I know that there have been philosophers who have spoken and sung about a unified world. Some of you have even looked to them for inspiration, but to date, all of the social experiments that have tried it have failed."

Tyson took in a breath, turned his head slightly to the right as he carefully formed his next question. "Do you have an immediate suggestion? How do we move along a path that might get humanity a pass, and entry into your galactic, em, what do you call it?"

"Whatever you'd like. A confederation, a federation, a collective, a trading union. We are not a government. But we do have entry requirements, and we do enforce our own simple rules within our group of trading partners. But in answer to your question, empower your world government. Arm it, if you must, to police the unruly and seal off the unrulable. If there are those that will not submit to world authority, they should not be able to participate in the world economy. When we see that these mechanism are taking shape, we will begin to aid where we can.

"So, do you have some sort of Navy? Ships that can enforce order on planetary systems would be pretty powerful." Tyson's eyes narrowed slightly as he imagined death stars or massive dreadnaughts in Earth orbit.

"We prefer much simpler mechanisms. Expulsion from the union or non-destructive coercion."

"Non-destructive?"

"Yes, but only as a means of saving innocent lives."

"What kind of non-destructive means might you employ, as punishment."

"For instance, … take my ship. It's in a holding orbit that maintains a small shadow on your equatorial zones. Its purpose is simply to gain your culture some time in combatting the greatest of your current challenges; your out-of-control climate crisis."

"That's hardly a threat. How—"

"Imagine if I asked for six more umbra ships to join this one. The resulting shadowing would begin to significantly cool down your planet. Deploying such an array always gets the attention of any wayward union member."

"Do those ships, your ship have offensive weapons? Are they dangerous?"

"See? See where your questioning is going? Humans have always assessed something that they don't understand as a threat. It's a dangerous trait and it tends to cause harm before it is quenched by information and understanding."

Tyson stopped, rubbed his chin thoughtfully. "I do see! Good object lesson." His head tilted back slightly as he pursued another thought. "I'd like to say, you have an extremely good sense of English and its idioms. How long have you been studying us?"

Sayala now smiled. "Several of your decades, *o varias de tus décadas, o molti dei tuoi decenni*. I've been studying much more than English."

Tyson's eyes opened wide. "I got Spanish, maybe some Italian, or — Portuguese?"

"I could go on."

"No need, but I believe you could." Tyson shifted back to his earlier unresolved line of questioning. "So, your ship has obvious self-defensive measures, but it has no direct offensive capabilities?"

191

"I can protect it. And it could grow substantially larger if your scientist community requests for the umbra field to be enlarged for more rapid cooling."

"So, as you said before, more of those ships could be used offensively."

"Yes, if you insist on characterizing that use as an offense. We don't intend to inflict loss of life and damage to supportive infrastructure to make a point. You humans do that when you don't like the behavior of a rogue government. I believe there were some incidents just last week in the former union of soviets that demonstrate that point."

"Mr. Sayala," Tyson tapped at his earpiece, "I have received a message that we have to interrupt this interview for a break. We are closing in on the top of the hour when most of the stations carrying this have to satisfy their broadcasting requirements. Before we go, do you have a succinct message for the viewers?"

Sayala turned from Tyson and directed his gaze at the head-shot camera facing him. "Humanity has an amazing and wonderful history of love, friendship, co-operation, invention, industry, and … I could go on. But you have, as you say, darker angels that work to destroy all the good that you could do. You exhibit a competitive drive to dominate—to subdue. And often to cheat, swindle, or steal are also a part of your nature. Cure these, and there are no limits to what your culture might aspire." His gaze into the camera bored into millions of homes across the planet. "Learn to communicate, to cooperate." The red light on his camera blinked off.

~ ~ ~

The responses created by the broadcast varied from angry crowds in the streets of the world's population centers to equally large peace marches. Occasional clashes occurred, many were mysteriously resolved as the opposing chanting crowds met and melded. A few did erupt in violence, but many reported a strange feeling of quiet acceptance that what was being asked was not unreasonable. News reports began to appear that laboratories across the globe working on nuclear research programs had begun to have breakthroughs on the magnetic containment apparatus that would channel and harness the significant energies produced when ionic hydrogen and oxygen formed simple water. Fusion power was finally on the threshold.

Even though a large majority of those who actually had access to and did listen to the news, were alarmed by the proclamations given in the

UN, there was a rising tide of commentators who began to come forward admitting to prior conversations with Sayala in one form or another. The visitations had been information gathering for Sayala but had been near-religious reckonings for those visited. Among the most influential of the new media influencers was a thinner, mellower Reverend Drake Ehler. Ehler was a strong supporter of Sayala's message of hope and reconciliation of old hostilities. He encouraged his Christian flock to follow the teachings of Christ in loving one another, following the golden rule, and asked that donations be made to support regional investments in alternative on and off-grid energy production.

Across the globe, a young woman of eighteen, recently released from imprisonment for teaching at a secret school for girls in Iraq, was invited by Mullah Raaji el-Rahaman to speak to the Iraqi minister of education on how to accommodate education for girls without threatening Shariah Law. In Mosul, a delegation of nationalist Kurds met with the Iraqi foreign minister on creating a self-administering Kurdish parliament subject to Iraqi hegemony. In western China, Muslims were being released from prison and allowed to return home on the promise that they would no longer preach strict adherence to the old laws.

Not every region immediately felt the glow of pan-globalism. Central Africa in particular and the several failing nation-states of Central and South America were finding that maintaining old hostilities toward former colonial powers could not sustain their status quo. Peaceful demonstrations demanded new elections. Local militias did what local militias have always done, and innocents were arrested, beaten, and killed. But overall, the message was growing across the globe. Things should be, could be, better. Conditions and mindsets were beginning to change in some unexpected places.

2

Outbound

The Hitchens family, their friend Martin Jenks, and Sayala sat in a simulated modern living room in a spread of comfortable padded leather chairs. Beyond a faux glass wall, scenes of Earth varied and alternated between garden spots, cliff-side vistas of oceans, tropical greenery, desert landscapes, forested tundras, and frozen mountains. They were in a space Sayala had created aboard his cubic control ship. The control ship could just as easily attach itself to the square opening of the umbra ship stationed between earth and sun providing the shade needed to slow and eventually stall the Terran climate crisis.

Martin had been speaking of home. "So yes, I guess I'll miss fishing. I'll probably miss tying flies the most. And there's a trail I love that runs from my cabin to a nearby stream. It rises to a cleft cut ages ago by the falling stream, and below it there's a pool that always seems to have a trout or two in it. Sometimes I just like to sit in the sun and watch them catch flies and mosquitoes off the surface." He turned to Connie. "What about you? What will you miss?"

Connie's face creased in worry. "I've been thinking. I think I'm going to miss the coast, our stretch of the Gulf of Mexico. And I'm not sure if it's our old place on Wakulla Beach or my folks' home in Apalachicola I'll miss most. I just love the region! It made me, molded us." She shot a quick glance toward Brad who sat in the adjacent chair. "And I'll miss Leeink-Knaa." Her lips pursed, quivered. Her eyes rimmed as she thought of the family and friendships left behind. "And momma. She got so old the last time we left for a joy ride and came back twenty-seven years later. This time..." She caught Sayala's eye. "Is there any way to take a few years off this trip?"

She received a psychic equivalent of a hug, via psi from their host. "Dear Connie, even if we took out some of the less important stops that you should experience, everyone you know will have passed on."

"I know," she sniffed. "I know." Sniff. "It's just that mom was left alone for so long when we ended up spending almost two decades on our first excursion out of the system. This last one was a hard goodbye. At least we will have Jai with us. I'm glad he can hitchhike in your equipment hangar. He's the one friend we didn't have to leave behind. He means a lot to us," she held Brad's gaze, "he was always there when we were in trouble."

Brad nodded. "You had all those hours in the woods when I was in Arizona. You taught him to read and expanded his vocabulary incredibly. You were friends."

She nodded, smiling at so many memories. "At least Jai will be able to serve as a shuttle to some of these new worlds we're going to visit."

Sayala asked, "And Brad, what will you miss?" He already had an inkling from reading the Terran's thoughts, but the exercise was for the group.

"I already miss Shaand, he was a great friend. From our time as cellmates, through that cosmically scary escape from the Jheln City jail." He grinned at Connie. She returned it with her characteristic one-sided grin; a huge dimple growing in her left cheek. "And like Connie, I'll miss our home. I understand that the old homestead up by the highway is going to be turned into a museum of sorts by the State Department."

Sayala focused on Myahh. Her legs did not quite touch the floor from her seat, and her legs had been slowly rocking in and out. First left, then right, and repeat for most of the time they'd been seated. "And you, my young friend. You are the first human I contacted when I reached out to your world in search of a telepath with any real power. What will you miss?"

Her legs stopped swinging. She brought a finger to her chin and looked up, scanning the blank white ceiling for some answer. Then her face brightened, and she looked back to Sayala, and then aside to her mother. "I think the woods. Back home. Even when there were too many mosquitoes in the summers, I really liked walking in our woods. I liked watching the water bugs dance on the springs and how the crickets made such a racket at sundown. I like tending my garden, and watching the sun come up over the bay in the mornings."

Sayala stood. "Quite understandable. Everyone with a long, pleasant history in one place will find sadness when leaving. But do understand, you will be coming back. Our voyage to Cinaloon will be relatively short, only a few months of our time, and I can maintain projections of your favorite places on these wall panels to lessen the heartsickness."

195

"But won't it be more than fifty years before we are back?" Connie looked genuinely pained.

"Yes, and I know that you will miss the passing of almost all of your friends and acquaintances. but when we return with other ambassadors from Cinaloon, they will bring with them many of the secrets of energy synthesis that your people and your planet will need. And you will come back with knowledge too. And young Myahh, yours will be the deepest knowledge because you will be able to converse with many of the cultures we meet."

At eight years old with the mental abilities of a sixteen-year-old or older, her enthusiasm for knowledge seemed unlimited. "I can't wait to talk to them. But what do they look like? Are they scary?"

"No, no." Sayala sent reassuring waves of comfort with understanding as overtones. "Two of the races you will meet have been visiting your world for almost a century. Another was the first to document your world but hasn't been back for over eight centuries. But they put your system on the maps. And no, I do not think you will find them scary. They may have DNA or at least RNA codes similar to your own. As I've told you, the Precursors spread genetic seeds far and wide on every world and moon they visited. So, these races walk on two legs, and like you, they have two arms, and two eyes. No, not very scary. One of them you will find very interesting because they talk very little and communicate mostly with their minds. I think this is one of the reasons their earlier visits scared so many humans they visited."

Brad asked, "So you are not one of the precursors? The Elioi scientists thought that the monitor ships had been sent by the Precursors."

"Yes, I know. It is a shame that so many of the early visitations across the galaxy have been so misunderstood by so many."

Martin had been listening carefully. Of the four, he had the most background in the study of visiting aliens. "Sayala, if you aren't one of the Precursors, then where do you come from?"

"Ah, I can show you." The room darkened as the white ceiling lost its illumination and faded to charcoal black. The view screens faded also. Connie cried out softly, "Oh," as the seat backs reclined. Above them, Sayala displayed the Milky Way as seen from Earth. "Does this look familiar?"

"Yes," from Martin, "Wow," from Brad, and "Oh, wonderful," from Connie.

Myahh clapped in delight. "Yes! The Milky Way."

"This is my home and yours, but where do I come from?" The view shifted slowly to a view that Brad thought must have been millions of light years perpendicular to the plane of the galaxy. As the view backed further, the spiral arms were distinct, and the white core moved to a corner of the ceiling. "Now," he continued, "I will remove all of the stars that are not home to sentient beings."

The white galactic center disappeared, and a majority of the stars did as well. The general configuration of their spiral arm remained as did most of a neighbor on one side and a small portion of another on the other side. Myahh exclaimed, "Wow, there are that many planets with thinking beings?"

"Only the ones we know about," Sayala explained, "but life exists on planets in these systems in some form more complex than simple organisms."

Connie looked puzzled. "I thought sentient meant thinking, or self-aware."

"No, it only means sensate, or sensing. Usually construed to be more than a single-celled organism with a whip or hairs, or a simple eyespot." He raised his hands expansively toward the ceiling display, taking in as much of it as he could. "But that's a lot of planets that will develop thinking, self-aware cultures. Many of those are buried under kilometrs of cloud and will never ponder life outside of their small orb unless they develop flying techniques or technologies capable of brushing the outer limits of their confining clouds."

He looked up at the ceiling again, giving some command to the visualization above. Brad thought that more than two thirds of the lights dimmed out. The remainder brightened, still maintaining the essential form of the incomplete spiral arms. "These several thousand worlds do have thinking, self-aware species. Dominant, more or less, on their own planets—masters of their own fates."

Brad asked, "Those are all in the trade union? The confederation?"

"No, not all of them have yet achieved space flight, or could even consider it based on their technological advancement."

Myahh had moved to the floor and was lying on her back looking up at the display. "That's a lot of different kinds of people."

Sayala smiled down at her. "Yes, and many of them will find it difficult to talk—even with you. Some communications are subsonic, musical, tonal. They speak in notes that have warmth or chill, with chords and disharmonies. "English is one of the most difficult of the western languages on your planet. These musical dialects are much more difficult." He glanced back up at the ceiling. Another two thirds of them faded out as the remainder brightened still and differentiated into clumps of different colors.

Martin said, "Still, that's a lot of planets ... what several hundred? Is this the trade union?"

"Yes, these are the current members." His glance fell back to Martin. "There are forty-one thousand, three-hundred and twelve members at present, based on my last query."

Myahh put her hands behind her head as a cushion and continued to scan the star systems overhead. "Sayala, why are there different clumps of colors?"

"An observant child, a questioning child; I like that. Before the creation of our union, there were several centers of power developing." He thought back through the data banks. "Seve

ral of your millennia ago, these different colored areas were small but growing empires. When on occasion, their outward explorations encountered each other, there were terrible wars. Peace and cooperation did not invent themselves out of some force of goodwill inherent in all living things. Indeed, the path to species dominance on a planet is often strewn with the debris of extinction and environmental calamity. You are not alone on that path. It was from the lesson of these horrid wars, the tremendous waste of resources and life, that the union was formed."

From the floor, she swiveled her head to find Sayala standing below her feet. She raised onto her ebows to see him better. "So, there were wars, thousands of years ago? Like Star Wars?"

"Unfortunately, yes. But I'm afraid Luke and Leia were not there. That was a prescient fantasy, and perhaps a good object lesson."

Martin was the military mind; he understood best the dangers of power and the attraction of maintaining power. He'd seen and participated in the long quest to keep the secret of alien visitations and the extent to which the military powers across the globe had suppressed truth. "Sayala, can you please explain what changed?" He reformulated the question. "What was the key to stopping these interplanetary, or inter-system wars?"

"Ah, the salient point! Communication."

"Talking is cheap, what about that inherent drive to expand, to dominate?"

"If you know that the representative you are communicating with *is* telling the truth, would that make a difference? Would treaty negotiations initiated in good faith come to a better result?"

"Of course. It would have to. But each side will negotiate to increase its own gain, to get the better deal."

Sayala asked, "Martin, are you a student of history?"

"I was, but it's been a while, I admit I've probably forgotten most of what I studied as a young man."

"Think back to only a few decades past in your planet's history. When the victors of your second global war were negotiating. Truman, Churchill, and Stalin were trying to impress their own philosophies on the redevelopment of the ruins of Europe and the far east. Truman wanted to bring his troops home to rebuild his economy on a peace platform, and he wanted to establish the United Nations. Churchill wanted more than anything to retain England's colonial system and ensure a his promise of a free Poland. Meanwhile, Stalin wanted to maintain control of the land he had conquered, especially the land called Poland because twice in twenty years, his country had been attacked by Germany through Poland."

"That sounds about right." Martin's thumb and forefinger stroked his chin, as he remembered his Air Force Academy military history.

"The thing to remember is that in none of these negotiations were any of them faithful negotiators. Although Stalin promised otherwise, he never intended to allow locally elected governments to become reestablished in the countries his troops now occupied. He played both Truman's and Churchill's desires against each other, especially beguiling Truman to acquiesce, knowing that he was sowing the seeds of revolution in most of Churchill's empire."

Martin nodded, remembering.

"Now imagine if each of these three negotiators had been able to share the thoughts of the others. Imagine if these negotiations had been made in good faith."

"It's hard to imagine Stalin being anything other than the ruthless murderer that he was."

"True, and this historical example may get strained, but try to see my point." He waved his hand at the ceiling. The various colors of the stellar empires shifted, waxing and waning as powers shifted. "As those nascent empires bumped into one another, and countless lives were lost at huge expense, the seeds of the trade union were born on the understanding that each negotiator must bring to the other side, all of the issues, in a full-faith negotiation. It was gradual. But when the two largest empires successfully joined and began to reap the rewards of honest brokering, the union was born. Hundreds of languages and cultures were involved, but mind-to-mind communication proved the key. Myahh here, is one of the first humans to be endowed with this talent. More will come."

Sayala walked over to Martin and placed one hand on his shoulder and the other to the side of his head. "Listen. Watch."

Martin closed his eyes and listened. Myahh sat up to see what Sayala was doing. Presently, a tear streaked down Martin's cheek, his chest heaved with emotion. Sayala removed his hands and stepped back. The other three had moderate to advanced psi abilities and received the message. Humanity's tendency for dominant expansion was not uncommon at all. Most of the species now in the Union had come through the trial by fire and passed. A few had failed and were exiled. But the dominant experience Martin had felt was unconditional trust.

Martin opened his eyes, wiped them dry with the back of his hand. "Are you sure you are not a god?"

"Yes, that is, I am *not* a god. That mistake has been made far too often."

"So then, the secret is in the fruit?" Martin thought back to the groves of fruit that were being tended for seed and experimentation across the globe.

"Yes, for humans as it is for the Elioi, it is a pathway to understanding. And in this regard, the Elioi are far closer to achieving access to the Union than Humans. They have adopted customs utilizing the fruit for hundreds of years. They simply need to start sharing it with the worker class and reorganize their system of labor and production. Far simpler to do with an existing central planetary government already in place. It's their system of slavery, or lower caste, upper caste that is unacceptable."

Connie sat up. "So our garden plot of selli fruit is the key for humans? If we all started to eat the selli fruit our communications would open up the necessary, trust bonds?"

"You were eating selli fruit on Dzura. What happened when your friend Leeink-Knaa understood that you were pregnant?"

"They stopped feeding me the fruit. Oh! Because they don't give it to pregnant mothers, and they don't give it to their very young in the creche schools. They start taking it as they approach the dividing ceremony." She watched as Myahh, nodded her understanding. "Myahh has always known. That's why she tended and weeded that little half-acre of selli fruit so well."

"Yes," Sayala's face glowed as she understood. "The innocent young do not need the fruit's gift of psi. Their early bonds of trust and love are natural. Later, when they need to openly share their feelings, the gift of psi communication opens up new channels of communication. It is impossible to lie if your thoughts are shared."

"And so much of my communication with Leeink-Knaa , with Jai, with Shaand were unspoken." She leaned back against her chair, grinning ear to ear. "So humanity has the key."

"Yes, and true to your heart, as well."

Brad sent a psi wave of understanding and support to Connie. She returned it with a look and a smile.

Martin sat forward on the edge of his chair. "Is this fruit available on all planets then?"

"No, some species possess the natural ability and do not need it. Others with entirely different chemistry have other plants that can enhance the ability. And fruits or compounds of this nature are valuable components in the trading between systems. Learning that psi will open those additional trust channels is why the trade union works, why it has worked for so many uncounted millennia."

Brad said, "I feel better now about humanity's ability to change. I had been worried that our darker angels would keep us entangled in wars and worse."

Martin added, "Me too, this has been an amazing conversation. I wish we'd been able to share it."

"We can," Myahh said, sitting up. She turned to Sayala, "Can't we?"

"It can and it is. I am sending the recording to the monitor ship by grav-wave, even as we are are speeding away from your sun. From there it will be condensed and sent to your media, and a few of your new allies."

Connie's eyes knit in question. "Who?"

"Reverend Ehler for one. I couldn't waste the enthusiasm of a talented proselytizer now could I? A preacher is a preacher. I'm sure he will help. After all, he's one of the few who made the trip here to my control ship."

Connie rubbed her chin, nodding, then, "Who else? You said a *few* of our allies."

Sayala shifted his attention to Martin. "You will remember the persistent reporter, Victor Paige?"

Martin's mouth opened slightly, then closed, about to question.

Sayala continued. "I think Connie will remember Victor Paige. He was reluctant at first, but I do have some gifts of persuasion. Brad, do you remember the Under Secretary to Chairman Xi?"

"Yes, Li Zedong. Him?"

Sayala's nod was slight, but the wink signed a yes. "We developed a certain affinity on back-channel as the proceedings were underway. He is an adept listener and will be an open-minded leader when that time comes. "China will lead Russia in adopting the use of psi, if the rest of the world does not follow suit, it will be at a distinct disadvantage for some time."

Myahh looked back up at the colored clumps of stars in the ceiling display. "Sayala, which one of those stars are we going to visit? Which one has the Union headquarters?"

Sayala followed her glance up at the ceiling. It expanded, zoomed in on a cluster of bright blue stars. The view zoomed in to one in particular and then down to a green and blue planet covered in swirls of cloud. "This one is Cinaloon, but it certainly isn't the closest. There are many more we could visit on the way." The stellar display on the ceiling shifted and flattened. Cinaloon fell behind another hundred stars as the viewpoint shifted to their current position. He moved to the control station, set his three-fingered hand on his nav panel.

Sayala looked back to Brad and Connie, then with a hint of mischief in his smile, looked down to Myahh. "My young friend, where would *you* like to go?"

The End

Author's Note

I hope you've enjoyed the conclusion of the Dreamland Diaries series. If you've read the entire series or just this book, I encourage you to go to Amazon books and leave a review. It doesn't need to be a lengthy discussion. A simple, "I loved this book" will do. It will help raise the book in the standings and make it more likely for other sci-fi readers to find it. If you happen to be a member of Goodreads, a review there can help your friends find it. And of course, your own social media platforms are possibly the easiest way for you to express your thoughts on the book and the series. I hope it provided the escape that good fiction should and that it made you think, just a little, about what is possible.

My other books can also be found at Amazon.com in paperback and Kindle formats. If you would like to gift or receive signed personalized copies I can mail them directly to you for list price via my website;

www.ballisterbooks.com

Thank you,

Bruce Ballister

Ballister Books
1111 Wisteria Drive
Tallahassee, FL 32312

Made in the USA
Columbia, SC
06 June 2023

17523282R00117